VALLEY OF DAY-GLO

VALLEY OF DAY-GLO
by
Nick DiChario

Introduction by
Nancy Kress

Robert J.
SAWYER
BOOKS

Robert J. Sawyer Books
Published by Red Deer Press
A Fitzhenry & Whiteside Company
1512, 1800–4 Street S.W.
Calgary, Alberta, Canada t2s 2s5
www.reddeerpress.com

Edited for the Press by Robert J. Sawyer
Cover and text design by Karen Thomas, Intuitive Design International Ltd.
Cover image courtesy NASA/JPL-Caltech
Printed and bound in Canada by Friesens for Red Deer Press

Financial support provided by the Canada Council, and the Government of Canada
through the Book Publishing Industry Development Program (BPIDP).

Canada Council   Conseil des Arts
for the Arts   du Canada

Library and Archives Canada Cataloguing in Publication
DiChario, Nick
     Valley of Day-Glo / Nick DiChario.
ISBN 978-0-88995-410-6 (bound).--ISBN 978-0-88995-415-1 (pbk.)
     I. Title.
PS3604.I25V34 2008   813'.6   C2008-900364-0

United States Cataloguing-in-Publication Data
(Library of Congress)
DiChario, Nick.
     Valley of day-glo / Nick DiChario.
Robert J. Sawyer Books.
[240] p. : cm.
ISBN 9780889954106   ISBN 9780889954151 (pbk.)
I. Title.
813.54 dc22   PR9199.D53437Va 2008

For the Absurdists: Franz Kafka, Mikhail Bulgakov, Samuel Beckett, Kurt Vonnegut, and the many fine authors who helped me see the world in a different way.

ACKNOWLEDGMENTS

Sincere thanks to my closest friends who have supported me and my writing life for so many years, including Jimmy Goff, Karen vanMeenen, Pat and Rich Ryan, Tim Wright, Rigel Klingman, Norm Davis, Anne Coon, Dan Plumeau, Kathryn Larrabee, and Rick Wilber. Thanks to my family for their love and support, especially my wonderful parents, my sister Roseann and brother-in-law Frank, and my beautiful nieces Julia and Angela who bring so much joy to my life. A special acknowledgement to Nancy Kress for writing such a fine introduction to this novel, and to Mike Resnick, who read it in novella form and would not let me give up on it. A heartfelt thanks to my good friend and editor Rob Sawyer for so enthusiastically pursuing this story for Robert J. Sawyer Books, and to all the people at Fitzhenry & Whiteside who worked so hard to see this project through. Thank you, Bev Geddes, for anointing me an honorary Canadian, a distinction that I shall forever cherish and work a lifetime to uphold. And thank you, finally, to the kind indulgences of my readers, who have made it possible for me to be twice charmed as a novelist.

N I C K   A T   T H E   L O O M

Introduction by Nancy Kress

Twenty pages into reading *Valley of Day-Glo*, I sent Nick DiChario an email: "Am reading your novel. You have a very warped mind." Nick forwarded the message to his publisher with a copy to me, saying, "Look! A cover blurb!"

Does Nick really have a warped mind? Not to look at him or talk to him at a party. He's courteous, affable, a good listener. He has always displayed these qualities, and I've known him since he was twenty-one.

We met in 1982 when I was, for the first time ever, teaching a summer writing workshop. I had not yet published very much myself—one novel and a handful of short stories—and felt uncertain of myself as a teacher of writing. It was pretty much the blind leading the blind. I can still see Nick, a few other students, and me sitting on the broad shallow steps of the Fine Arts building on the campus where the workshop was held. We're eating potato salad off soggy paper plates and earnestly discussing the state of publishing—as if any of us actually knew much about it.

Nick knows a lot about it now. He's owned a bookstore, published wonderful stories, collaborated extensively with the very knowledgeable and talented Mike Resnick, been nominated for both a Hugo and World Fantasy award for his lovely story "The Winterberry," and for the John W. Campbell Memorial Award for his previous novel, *A Small and Remarkable Life*. There is no doubt in my mind that eventually Nick will win one, or all, of these awards. Meanwhile, we have *Valley of Day-Glo.*

What to make of this book? In the first paragraph we have Indians named Broadway Danny Rose, The Outlaw Josey Wales, and Who's Afraid of Virginia Woolf?. Later on, we have a sacred Jug Dance involving "an original Igloo water cooler" and a sacred text titled *Network Marketing in the New Millennium.* We have a corpse that steadily rots for one hundred pages, but occasionally sits up to chime in with comments on the action. We have a very unorthodox cure for sexual dysfunction. Is all that warped, or what?

Yes, in that the world of *Day-Glo* is a distorted one that is highly unlikely as a direct descendant of our own. BUT—that all-important but!—in another sense, this world is very much our own. One meaning of "warp," after all, is "a system of spun threads extended lengthwise on a loom." The warp is then woven with the cross-threads, the "woof."

In *Day-Glo,* Nick is weaving a very intricate tapestry indeed. His warp may be fanciful and wildly inventive, but his cross-threads are deadly serious. They are love and the price that love exacts, violence and the grief it causes, striving and the ways that striving can be twisted by the larger world. Nick's tapestry is a life-like design of brilliant, heartbreaking colors, including that imaginative warp. You will be the richer for having viewed it, read it, pondered it. You will be the richer for having spent time with Broadway Danny Rose and shared his search for the Valley of Day-Glo.

Even if you never in your life witness a sacred Jug Dance.

The day Mother Who's Afraid of Virginia Woolf? killed Father The Outlaw
Josey Wales, they were arguing again about the Pre-Reddening game of
Major League Baseball. Mother's position was, as usual, supported by the
Tribal Bible. Dizzy Dean, not his brother Daffy, had suffered a broken toe
during the 1937 All-Star game. Although Father accurately identified Dizzy's
real name as Jay Hanna Dean, and Daffy's real name as Paul Dean, and both
baseball players did, in fact, pitch in the same game in which said injury
occurred, Father refused to attribute the broken toe to Dizzy.

Mother, incensed (as Father knew she would be, for it was his common
practice to infuriate her on the finer points of the game), grabbed him by
the neck and began to shake him mercilessly, until plumes of dust gathered
around them in the hazy, reddish, morning sunlight. Behind them loomed
barren hills and mountains, rocky plateaus and rutted basins, and endless
stretches of sand and gravel.

I yawned and decided I could make do with a short nap, for soon Mother,
Father, and I would inspect the dead bodies of our tribes-people for insects
and red worms suitable for eating, and it was good for the eyes to be well rested for the intricacies of such an endeavor. As soon as I returned to the hut
and began to doze, I heard Mother's O'gi'we, the Tribal Death Shriek:

"AIYEEEEEEEEEEE-YICK-YICK-EEEEEEEEEEEEEEoh—!"

It was a shriek I had heard often enough. The horrible sandstorm that
had decimated our tribe from forty-seven to three—the now nearly extinct

Gushedon'dada tribe, named after the Jug-shaking dance of our Iroquois Indian ancestors—had kept Mother shrieking (ad nauseam) for quite some time. I dashed out of the hut to see Mother, on her knees in the dirt, cradling my limp father in her arms.

"Ohhhhhh, Danny," she moaned. "He is dead! He is dead!"

"Are you sure?" I knelt beside Father and investigated for his pulse. Nothing. Father displayed a rather relieved, purple expression on his face; he was most certainly dead.

"I have killed him. I have killed my beautiful husband." Mother looked suddenly ill. She fell prostrate under the sun, choked on a mouthful of swirling dust, and bleated the unmistakable Honio'o slur—"Shit."

⌐ Father The Outlaw Josey Wales believed in the value of oral history, partly, I think, because he pretended he could not read whenever Mother cited an irrefutable fact from the Tribal Bible. In any case, he often told the tale of the Great Reddening, which went something like this:

Hed'iohe, the Creator, gave the Earth to the North American Iroquois Indians at the dawn of time. He then decided to take a long nap. When Hed'iohe awoke, he discovered that the white- and black- and yellow-skinned tribes had taken over the Earth and were badly abusing it. So Hed'iohe decided to turn the crafty inventions of the whites and blacks and yellows against them. Hed'iohe conjured up the carbon dioxide and methane and other anthropogenic gases from their fossil-fueled industries and began to slowly bake the oddly colored Earth people under the ozone layer. Icecaps melted. Droughts occurred. Horrible fires decimated great cities. Billions of Earth people died agonizing deaths. Eventually, the great oven Hed'iohe created became so hot that the sky and the earth burned red, and he boiled the water into vapor, and all of the white- and black- and yellow-skinned tribes perished (not possessing the secret ability of internal sweat), leaving only the red people to tread upon the overheated planet.

"History," Father always liked to say whenever he told the story of the Great Reddening, "repeats itself."

⌐ Here is another tale Father The Outlaw Josey Wales used to tell before Mother Who's Afraid of Virginia Woolf? strangled him to death:

There is a valley that glows brightly called the Valley of Day-Glo, where all the colors of the Pre-Reddening Earth can be found. Flowers are in constant bloom there. Trees reach up so far into the sky that it is impossible to know where the branches end and the clouds begin. Water flows freely. Fruits and vegetables flourish. In the Valley of Day-Glo, Father used to say, "death becomes life."

But this valley is hidden under a great transparent dome buried somewhere in Seneca Indian territory, where no man nor woman dares travel.

To be perfectly honest, none of us Gushedon'dada ever believed a word Father uttered. Mother had too often undermined his authority on matters of baseball trivia, and although he was much admired for his ability to separate a dune rat's head from its body with nothing more than his powerful teeth and jaws, this practice earned Father considerably more fear than respect, which, I dare say, might have been his intent all along.

⌐ "We must take your father to the Valley of Day-Glo." Mother sounded gravely determined.

"What?"

She slapped me across the face. "You heard me, idiot. We must take your father to the place where death becomes life. We must bring the eldest male Gushedon'dada back to the Land of the Living. Without him our tribal line shall perish forever."

Mother had a knack for making me feel physically and emotionally minuscule. "But Mother," I began, "there is no such place as—"

"Don't say another word! Would you call your father a liar, insult his spirit before his body has become cold? Honestly, I don't know whether to think of you as a sniveling coward or an absolute failure. Which do you prefer? It doesn't matter. I am the eldest Gushedon'dada now, and you must obey me."

I contemplated the consequences of breaking Gushedon'dada tribal law while there remained but two of us in the tribe. If I let Mother go without me, eventually she would die alone, and so, I imagined, would I. But what chance would we have of making it alive through Seneca territory to the mythical valley beyond, even if there was such a valley to be found?

"For the sake of argument," I said, "if the Valley of Day-Glo exists, how would we transport Father there with any dignity or grace? He is dead. Don't you think he deserves a proper burial?"

"I shall drag him," Mother stated.

"Nonsense. I cannot allow it."

"Try and stop me, eunuch-boy."

"Mother!"

"I killed him. He is my burden. If we bury him, he'll never see the Valley of Day-Glo. Fetch me some sticks."

So I did.

➣ True to her word, Mother Who's Afraid of Virginia Woolf? fashioned a harness and makeshift sled out of sticks and twine and rat skins from our hut. She spread Father The Outlaw Josey Wales across it, treating him with more tenderness and, dare I say, respect, than she ever had during his lifetime. Mother and I sat down together and ate some sweetroot and our final rodent in silence. The eunuch-boy remark was uncalled for, I thought, and I was angry at circumstance. Out of all the Gushedon'dada in the world, Mother was my least favorite, as I was her least favorite. The irony that we two should be the only surviving Gushedon'dada must have come as an equally crushing blow to Mother as it had to me. Perhaps this was why Mother was so intent upon bringing back from the dead a man she was never all that crazy about to begin with. As much as she might have disliked Father, he was clearly, in her view, the lesser of two fools.

When we finished our meal, Mother pulled on her Wrangler stone-washed jeans, threadbare now from years of use, her Puma sneakers with the Velcro straps, and her favorite T-shirt with the strange inscription *Esprit* emblazoned across the chest. She wrapped the Tribal Bible and the Tribal Jug in a gunnysack and slung them over her shoulder, stuck her gold hatpin in her Chicago Cubs baseball cap, strapped herself into her harness with Father attached behind her, and began walking in the direction of the setting sun, without so much as a glance toward me.

I sighed heavily and followed, carrying only the clothes upon my back: a magenta button-down oxford shirt, a pair of navy blue Levi's Dockers, and my favorite penny loafers. These articles of clothing amounted to all my earthly possessions, after losing everything in the great sandstorm.

I glanced back at the hut and the rocky ridge and the mounds of sandy graves cocooning the dead bodies of our fallen tribes-people, all of which I was sure I would never see again, and I mourned only that which I had mourned for as long as I could remember: the days ahead.

⟲ The landscape shone strikingly barren, littered with dirt and rocks and gigantic swirling dust motes, broken by an occasional fissure in the pitted earth. The scent of minerals seasoned the air—salt and lime and borax. I entertained but one hope for the journey ahead, the hope that Mother and I would indeed discover the Valley of Day-Glo, thus proving Father right about the valley at long last. I suppose if I had little to live for other than the remote possibility of knocking Mother down a peg or two, this was better than nothing.

Eventually, unable to remain silent, I said, "I am accompanying you on this journey, Mother, specifically so that I may see the Seneca Indians skin you alive and leave you skewered on a stake to dry in the sun like the curd you are, even if it means that I must lie skewered beside you in bitter agony."

I was not trying to be cruel, mind you. Father had been dead almost two hours, and I thought Mother might be missing him.

Mother stopped and looked at me with her small, hard eyes, with her unwavering, nasty expression, a look that could have uncoiled a snake, I'm quite certain, and then she leaned in and quickly kissed my cheek. The resounding *smack* surprised us both. We stared at one another for several seconds before Mother turned around and we resumed our funeral march.

⮌ Father began to rot. He was deoxygenating, his purple discoloration now spreading throughout his blood vessels. Muscular contraction had hardened his extremities. His skin had become translucent, his lips pale, his fingertips blue. Although I found it difficult to mourn a man who stank so ... well ... so terribly much like death, I found comfort in the fond remembrance of his ceaseless determination. The tenacity with which Father The Outlaw Josey Wales set about annoying Mother Who's Afraid of Virginia Woolf? was, in my opinion, the secret to his longevity, up until the moment Mother strangled him to death.

"You win some, you lose some," Father used to say. *Oh, how right he was!*

Now, gazing down upon his lifeless body, I decided Father's final record was something close to 5,649 to one in his favor, for although Mother vis-à-vis the Tribal Bible had always managed to prove him wrong, he had never lost his life, until now.

⮌ During our journey it would be my responsibility to trail ten paces behind Mother Who's Afraid of Virginia Woolf?—now the eldest Gushedon'dada—as she carried the Tribal Bible and the Tribal Jug and, of course, Father, her death burden, leaving me to snatch flies for dinner as the insects landed upon Father's decomposing body.

I had become quite an accomplished fly snatcher. So many of our tribe having perished in the sandstorm, it became necessary for me to cull as much sustenance as possible from our dearly departed. Flies were the first insects attracted to the dead, followed by the dust beetles that fed upon the flies, followed by the giant ants and the winged cockroaches that fed upon the beetles. When a body is at the height of its foul odor, it will attract dune rats and scavenger birds and desert dogs. We, the Gushedon'dada, are given to eat upon all these things. Death becomes life.

Father, I miss you.

꿈 We traveled along the ridge of a low, crusty canyon and followed a path that led us across a narrow ravine. This course eventually bent around a roughly chiseled, lonely mountain and pointed us in the direction of Seneca territory. It was a well-worn path, wide open to the north, south, and west, and easily traveled. It did not take us long to run into a disheveled tribe of Independent Indians. They numbered fewer than a dozen, bleary-eyed, slim, and scantily clad in tattered clothing from which all color had long since been sandblasted. They stared at us through sunken eyes, their legs rickety in the wind, their skin gray and burnt-looking.

Mother removed her harness and pulled the Tribal Jug from her gunnysack, warning me with a fierce glance not to interfere. She placed the Jug in the dirt and began to step slowly around it, left arm extended, right hand at her chest. One-two-three-four she stepped, back straight, neck stiff, chin pointed sharply in the direction of her extended arm, legs crisscrossing. One-two-three-four, turn, step, step, step. Around and around the Tribal Jug she danced.

I had never seen the Jug-shaking dance performed by one person; it was never meant for one. Father had always performed it with Mother. It was a sad sight to see Mother jugging alone, and I was hurt she had not asked me to accompany her, for I knew the steps well enough.

When Mother finished her dance, she introduced us, our tribe, the now nearly extinct Gushedon'dada. She explained how the great sandstorm had decimated our tribe from forty-seven to two (failing to point out that she had killed Father). Then she picked up the Tribal Jug and began the ritual shaking of it, a complicated arrangement that involved a thorough jostling above the head, behind the back, and between the legs.

When Mother completed the shaking, one of the men from the other tribe, the chief, no doubt, stepped forward. It was customary among all tribes for the chief to speak first. "May we inspect the Jug?"

This was indeed a good sign, an indication that they might accept Mother's offer of rapprochement. In other more volatile times, Mother and I alone, traveling the dust plains, might have been dead meat, killed for our treasures. But the Seneca were conquering all of the Independent tribes these days, and as of late it seemed an unspoken bond had developed among the remaining Independents not to kill each other unless there happened to be a really good reason for it.

Mother placed the Tribal Jug in the dirt, stepped aside, and said with an intonation of pride in her voice, "This is an original Igloo water cooler."

The chief approached the Jug, considered it briefly, and knelt in the dirt for closer inspection. Mother removed a pamphlet from her gunnysack and handed it to the chief. He unfolded it and began to read, glancing from Jug to pamphlet, pamphlet to Jug. "Pressure-fit lid with molded-in, easy-grip ball handles. Seamless, easy-to-clean plastic liner. Drip-proof, recessed spigot. Polyurethane insulation keeps drinks icy cold. Great for camping and picnics."

"Yes," Mother said. "Model number 4-3-1, with extra UV inhibitors to resist cracking, peeling, and fading caused by the sun. As you can see, it is still a very pretty blue color. We have kept our Tribal Jug extremely well preserved."

"The Gushedon'dada are known to be a very meticulous tribe." He stood and handed the pamphlet back to Mother. He looked at Father The Outlaw Josey Wales for a long moment, but did not say anything about him. Instead, he decided to say something about me: "Is this the infamous asexual boy named Broadway Danny Rose we have heard so much about?"

Mother nodded. "Yes, yes, I'm afraid so."

"My sympathies. We are the Gadages'kao, the Tribe of the Fetid Banks."

"Ah, the Gadages'kao," Mother said. "I have heard of you. Descendants of the Mohawks, correct?"

"Correct."

The chief motioned his people to sit. They responded like zombies, not exactly snapping to it, as they should have. Their lips, so dry and leathery, blended into their faces, as if hiding from the sun. They spaced themselves out in a semicircle and, once nestled into the stony sand, sat cross-legged behind their chief. They looked filthy and irritable, and sat as rigid as ancient bones, their clothing old and torn and barely clinging to their bodies. Our meeting had not yet become informal. Mother and I and the chief remained standing, while Father, attached to the makeshift sled, lay dead and disinterested (the only one of us, as far as I could tell, who had any reason to be happy).

Mother said, "It was my understanding that long ago the Gadages'kao had made the journey to Seneca territory to become part of the Seneca League of Nations."

The chief nodded. "That is also correct. But we are now officially, technically renegade."

He did not elaborate. It would have been rude to question him further, but I was extremely curious to know the details of their separation, as it was surely a death sentence for this haggard tribe of ghostly Independents to have separated themselves from the mighty Seneca.

The Gadages'kao chief eyed my rotting father. "You carry the dead one to attract food?" he said, his eyes brightening a bit.

"We carry the dead one upon a sacred quest," Mother said, "to the Valley of Day-Glo."

There came a murmuring from the semicircle of Gadages'kao. The twinkle of hunger I'd seen in the chief's eyes flashed into disbelief and, if I may say so, something of horror. He breathed deeply. "Have you any idea what is happening in Seneca territory? Have you not heard of the preposterous mega-city the Seneca have built? The overpopulation, the starvation, the disease, the impending revolution?"

Mother nodded. The rumors had, in fact, reached our tribe. "None of this matters to us. Our journey is not politically motivated."

"When it comes to politics, the motivations of those who claim neutrality make little difference."

"This is true," Mother agreed. How could she not? "But we are devoted to a higher purpose."

The Gadages'kao chief shrugged. "May we inspect the dead one?"

Mother hesitated. "He is my husband."

"*Was* your husband," said the chief, a comment that could easily have been interpreted as a challenge. "I have a wife who is quite accomplished at forensics. She might be able to help you better preserve his body for your difficult journey ahead."

Mother nodded and stepped away from Father, taking me by the arm and pulling me back with her. Whether she reached out to me for support, or whether she simply wished to show the Gadages'kao that the only two remaining Gushedon'dada stood all for one and one for all, I did not know. For whatever reason, it felt good to stand arm-in-arm with Mother. As much as I hated her, I had always hoped the stubborn old bat and I could one day become friends. She leaned close to me and whispered in my ear, "Don't do or say anything stupid and maybe they won't kill us."

The gaunt woman who was the chief's wife knelt beside Father. She much resembled Father, I thought, this wife of the Gadages'kao chief, with her tightly drawn skin and flat chest and skeletal chassis.

"Recently dead," muttered the woman. She unwrapped Father's bundled body and wrinkled her nose at his frightful stench. I noticed that some of Father's skin had paled, while some had turned a dull reddish-purple. "Hypostasis," the woman said. She pressed her fingers over a large purple spot near Father's lumbar region, and the purple slowly turned white. "Not dead yet." She continued to inspect Father with her fingers. Mother tensed beside me.

"Brace yourself," Mother whispered. "She's trying to challenge me for his body."

"Don't overreact," I said.

"We'll lose the old fool if we're not careful."

"I detect congestion of the basal and posterior areas of the lungs," said the wife of the Gadages'kao chief. "We still have some muscular rigidity, although many of the joints and bones have been broken due to the woman dragging him so inefficiently." Then she put her hand directly upon Father's crotch.

Mother clenched her fists. I grabbed her wrist. *Easy*, I said to myself, hoping she would hear.

"The old man's death appears to be violent and of a suspicious nature. I don't see any breaches of the skin, but noting the irregular patterns of lividity around the neck, I'd say strangulation would be the most likely cause of death." She stared directly at Mother. "How would you speak to that, old woman? Would you agree?"

Mother yanked her wrist out of my grip and said, "Let me go, eunuch-boy!" And then she lowered her head and bull-rushed the wife of the Gadages'kao chief. I cursed myself for letting her go, but there was nothing to be done about it.

In two giant leaps Mother was upon the woman. They tumbled to the ground in a puff of dust, Mother on the back of the Gadages'kao chief's wife, her legs wrapped around the woman's waist, hands clutching an impossibly skinny neck.

"*Gawk! Gawk!*" croaked the woman, clawing for Mother's eyes.

Just then, the chief smiled and hooted like a madman. The others in the semicircle jumped to their feet, barking and hollering and casting down handfuls of colored stones and small pieces of carved bone. They pointed at the two women scuffling in the dirt and shouted at each other.

"Care to place a wager?" the Gadages'kao chief said to me. I could do nothing but look at him mutely until he shrugged. "Suit yourself." He reached into his sack and tossed some trinkets onto the pile. In the meantime, Mother had gotten the upper hand in the fight—indeed, she had never lost it—by placing her opponent into a merciless headlock and squeezing the woman's larynx.

With her free hand, Mother yanked something out of her Chicago Cubs baseball cap—something golden that twinkled in the sunlight—her hatpin! She raised it high above her head and aimed it at the woman's neck. I held my own throat, terrified, foreseeing now the inevitable outcome. Mother stabbed and grunted, and a squirt of blood shot out of the other woman's neck—

"*Gurglet, gurglet, gurglet*," said the wife of the Gadages'kao chief. She was no longer moving around so much. The woman's eyes bugged out, her fingers twitched, and her legs caved in. She collapsed in the dirt. The fight was over.

Mother rolled off the slack corpse and took a moment to catch her breath. Everyone remained silent, waiting, no doubt, for the Tribal Death Shriek.

"*AIYEEEEEEEEEEE-YICK-YICK-EEEEEEEEEEEEEEoh—!*" Mother cried weakly.

I found myself so astonished that I could not move a muscle. Mother glared at me as if to say, *Not one word, eunuch-boy.* I marveled at the purity of her hatred for me.

"Ha! Ha!" shouted the Gadages'kao chief. Fortunately he had wagered generously against his wife. He collected several bones and stones and put them in the sack at his waist, while his people rushed to drink what little blood remained of his newly slain wife. "I knew you could take her," he said, helping Mother to her feet. "You should be ashamed of the boy, though; he didn't even show enough respect to place a bet."

"Don't worry." Mother brushed the dust off her soiled *Esprit* T-shirt. "I'm plenty ashamed of him as it is. A little more won't kill me."

∻ The Gadages'kao chief suggested we honor his dead wife and Mother's dead husband by sitting for the Wainonjaa'ko, the death feast.

He and his people carefully unpacked their tribal china, an imitation Royal Doulton pattern with an intricately woven blue-lace design, and everyone sat in the cross-legged position, plates upon laps, for a meal of snake meat, beetles, and mashed winged cockroach.

Because of my failure to wager, I did not receive a plate, nor was I allowed within the dining circle, although I had contributed several beetles to the meal. The Gadages'kao gave me a few dead flies and some sweetroot, while they enjoyed a robust serving of crunchy delights. No matter. I sat at ease in the company of the dead with Father The Outlaw Josey Wales and the Gadages'kao chief's wife, whose name I'd learned was Alice Doesn't Live Here Anymore, while the others spoke of the Great Reddening.

Mother told the tale of Hed'iohe, the Creator, who gave the world to the North American Iroquois Indians at the dawn of time. She also told of Hed'iohe's great anger and retribution concerning the ozone layer and the floods and droughts and horrible fires that decimated the white- and yel-low- and dark-skinned tribes. The Gadages'kao chief said that although he had not heard the tale of the spirit Hed'iohe, he would add it to his oral his-tory, and he would contribute the tale of Sagowenota, the spirit of the ocean tides, to the oral history of the only two remaining Gushedon'dada:

"At the beginning of time, after filling two-thirds of the land with all the great waters of the world—waters stocked aplenty with fish and sea plants for the benefit of the Iroquois Indians, so that they would always have a gen-erous food supply—Sagowenota took a long nap. When he awoke, he found that the dark- and yellow- and white-skinned tribes had conquered the Indians and had mercilessly abused his generous gifts.

"Much disturbed, Sagowenota began to warm the temperature of his waters. In no time, the shifting currents began to interrupt the breeding pat-terns of his fish, thus beginning the extinction of all his wonderful water creatures. The elevated temperatures also destroyed his plants and coral reefs and began to break down the normal processes of photosynthesis.

"But this was not enough. Sagowenota wished to punish the whites and darks and yellows for all their insurrections, so he melted many of his stun-ningly beautiful polar icecaps, flooding all the land. He then offered his wild waters to the Great Spirit, who drank and drank until the Earth became a dustbowl."

"I wonder if Sagowenota and Hed'iohe were in cahoots," Mother said. "It seems as if it would have taken more than the efforts of any one spirit to accomplish genocide and destroy an entire ecosystem."

"A valid point," said the Gadages'kao chief. "It is logical that if the two spirits had napped and awakened at approximately the same time, they would have helped each other annihilate the defilers of their creations. And who is to say there were not several more spirits irritated with the men of the Pre-Reddening Age, spirits who would have gladly volunteered their great powers to crush the offenders."

After Mother finished chewing on her final mashed winged roach, she tactfully broached the subject of the Gadages'kao's status as a renegade tribe. The Gadages'kao chief shook his head mournfully, and his people fell silent and somber.

"In the beginning," began the chief, "we were certain that joining the Seneca League of Nations was a wise decision. We, the Gadages'kao, were a small tribe with little more than two-score members when we excavated a finely preserved 7-Eleven convenience store. Now, as you can see, we number less than half that. Granted, a 7-Eleven is not much of a treasure trove—some automobile window-washer fluid, a rack or three of Bic lighters, several blister packs of Chapstick and Papermate pens, some insulated travel mugs, key chains, tape dispensers, etcetera, etcetera—nothing at all as grand as a Kmart or a Sears, or the much revered and sought-after Club of Sam's. But the Seneca wanted it, and we were too proud to let it go. We dug in and fought bravely for a day and a half, but to continue our defense, we finally realized, would have meant the death of us all."

"Aren't you facing the same fate now that you have gone renegade?" Mother asked.

"Yes, but at the time, well, at the time, it seemed like the right thing to do. When we surrendered to the Seneca, they allowed us to save face. They said we could maintain the possessions we had acquired before discovering the 7-Eleven—our tribal artifacts—the imitation Royal Doulton china, for instance, and our Tribal Bible." The Gadages'kao chief reached into his sack and removed a volume that I could not identify from my position beside Father and Alice Doesn't Live Here Anymore. It was a hardcover book. He handed it to Mother. "Although at the time our defeat was honorable and the terms of our surrender acceptable to us, when we reached Seneca territory, we learned of their true purpose. They would annex our tribe into the League of Nations, and, in so doing, extract what they called an 'indoctrination fee'—nothing shy of robbery—and take from us all of our possessions. We decided that we simply could not allow them to get away with it, so we waited until nightfall and made our escape. We've been on the run ever since, trying to stay one step ahead of the Seneca warriors."

Here the Gadages'kao chief groaned softly. The others frowned and shook their heads. Mother paged through the Gadages'kao Tribal Bible. It would have been rude of her not to do so. There was an extended hush while the Gadages'kao allowed her to peruse its contents without distraction. Mother said, "May I show your wonderful Bible to my worthless son?"

The Gadages'kao chief shrugged his indifference, and Mother handed the volume over to me. It was an oversized book titled *The Microwave Cookbook*, with colorful pages of exquisitely prepared meals. There was one recipe for perch filets that looked positively scrumptious, calling for green onions, lemon grass, and fresh jalapeño peppers, topped with a lightly seasoned coconut sauce, all such ingredients supposedly abundant during the Pre-Reddening Age.

I was dreaming about how perfectly transcendent it would have been to wrap my mouth around such a succulent taste sensation when, abruptly, an eerie sound cut across the barren plains. "Caw-caw-caw-caw-caW-cAW-CAW-CAW-CAW-CAW-CAW—"

The Seneca war cry!

~ I think we all must have seen them at the same time, a band of women warriors charging across the plains, bearing stainless-steel knives and Louisville Slugger aluminum baseball bats and .22-caliber Ruger pistols and Remington twelve-gauge pump shotguns.

The Gadages'kao leaped to their feet and ran for it, astounding me with a burst of energy that I would not have dreamed possible. Mother grabbed my arm and said, "Be still! Give me the Bible."

I handed her *The Microwave Cookbook* and glanced up at the Seneca closing in on our position. In no time at all, the warrior women were upon us.

They blew past us like a sandstorm—"CAW-CAW-CAW-CAW-CAW-CAW-CAw-Caw-caw-caw-caw—" a pack of wild animals, a flash of Lady Levi's and assorted bandannas, suspenders, boots, scarves, and imitation jewelry—the mighty Seneca death heralds, the S'hondowek'owa.

True to their name, the S'hondowek'owa wasted no time in dispensing their particular brand of justice to the miserable Gadages'kao. I witnessed the silvery flash of stainless steel in the waning sunlight as it cleaved into unresisting flesh. Aluminum Louisville Sluggers crushed skulls and snapped bones. Ruger .22-caliber pistols cracked and echoed, cracked and echoed, blood spitting from the miniature holes punched into the bodies of their helpless victims. There came the heavy POOM-POOM-POOM of twelve-gauge shotguns. All of this to the "CAW-CAW-CAW" of the women warriors.

To their credit, the Gadages'kao never cried out or begged for mercy. They must have welcomed death as a final, rich reward. As Mother had mentioned earlier, to go renegade was asking for trouble, and one could only surmise that death was a kinder alternative than life to the Gadages'kao, if for no other reason than their long wait was over, their suffering undone. The thought crossed my mind, even in the midst of my fear, that death, which comes upon us so unexpectedly, is much like a complicated math problem finally solved, an inevitable outcome revealed, a brilliantly expressed grand sum total.

I shivered beside Father and Alice Doesn't Live Here Anymore as the

S'hondowek'owa went about desecrating the bodies of the Gadages'kao. The women warriors stomped on bloody corpses and ripped out entrails. Those S'hondowek'owa armed with cutlery butchered the organs of the dead, and the others began feasting upon the raw meat.

"Now I understand," Mother whispered. She stuffed *The Microwave Cookbook* into her gunnysack.

"What?"

"The old ways," she said, flipping her Chicago Cubs baseball cap onto her brittle hair. "Our Pre-Reddening, pre-industrial ancestors of the Golden Age believed that ingesting the blood and organs of the enemy would allow them to steal their spiritual power."

I nodded. "The desecration of the bodies. The cannibalism. The Seneca have become extreme revivalists." Forgetting for a moment that Father was dead, I reached out to him for comfort, to steady myself. He felt cold and hard beneath my hand. You win some, you lose some, Father seemed to be saying from behind his death mask in his old familiar way. But wait, wait, I saw him move. He slowly shook his head, opened his death-glazed eyes, looked at me, and then he said:

"Hey, Danny Boy, what's going on in the Land of the Living?"

"Father?"

"This may come as a complete shock to you, but you can't win or lose any- thing once you are dead. Take my word for it. I'm not looking to gain anything anymore. Game over."

I glanced at Mother to see if she had heard Father's wisdom. Apparently she had not. Perhaps I had not either. Did the S'hondowek'owa bring with them my own insanity?

"Father, have you gone to the Happy Hunting Grounds, to the great life after death promised to all Iroquois Indians?" I asked.

"All I know is that I'm not going anywhere fast. There is no place to run to here, nothing from which to hide or escape, no hunting or fishing or song or dance as the legends tell us. When you are dead, it seems, you are perfectly

happy to stand in the place where you are, being nothing."

"Father. The Valley of Day-Glo, does it truly exist? Can you see it from your unique vantage point?"

Father smiled, and then his face once again stiffened into deathly repose. I reached over and closed his eyes.

"When the S'hondowek'owa come for us," Mother said harshly, "let me do the talking."

⤴ And come for us they did, swarming like pesky winged cockroaches, never quite landing in one place, while Mother Who's Afraid of Virginia Woolf? and I sat side by side in the rising dust, choking on what could be our last breaths. They circled so closely that we could feel their heat and smell on them the blood of the Gadages'kao. At one point, I thought I heard Mother declare, quite needlessly, "Don't move a muscle, eunuch-boy."

Finally, one of the S'hondowek'owa warriors stepped forward. She was a husky woman with a shaved head, her teeth sharpened to fangs. She held a Remington twelve-gauge shotgun, which she slung over her shoulder, expertly maneuvering its thick leather strap. She wore a black pleated skirt and a blazing fuchsia blouse. Her biceps bulged beneath the flimsy material. She stepped closer to me, blood dripping from her fangs onto the toes of my penny loafers. Her breath stank like foul desert dog. Her large shadow hovered over me, and I imagined it pressing down against my chest so that I could not breathe.

She grabbed the front of my shirt and hauled me off the ground. The other S'hondowek'owa began to chant some jolly, indiscernible song, stepping all over each other's lines and rhythms as if in drunken revelry. With her free hand, and faster than my eye could follow, the woman whipped a knife out of a hidden sheath and sliced my Dockers slacks open from fly to waist, with nothing more than a flick of her wrist. The keening grew louder, and some of the women began to whoop at the sight of my newly exposed anatomy.

Mother toppled over, guffawing.

The S'hondowek'owa fell silent. They observed Mother, who was now nearly hysterical with laughter and rolling in the dirt, as if she'd gone mad. One of the women warriors drew a bead on Mother with her Ruger .22-caliber semiautomatic pistol, but the woman who held me suspended in midair, who I was now certain was their leader, signaled her to hold her fire. "No, Nyo'sowane," she said. "Not yet." Then she lowered me to the ground and spoke to Mother. "What do you find so amusing, old woman?" (I was thinking very much the same thing as I gasped for air.)

Mother calmed her laughing fit and said, "You are about to rape a eunuch-boy!" She then roared with laughter once again.

A look of incomprehension crossed the warrior woman's face. She scrutinized my skinny body, and then delivered a swift kick with her knee to my chest that flattened me out on the ground. "You are incapable of sexuality?" she asked me quite pointedly, leaning over and examining my male member as if it might answer for me. I wheezed and rubbed my chest where she must have put a permanent indentation between my nipples.

"I don't see where that is anyone's concern but my own."

"Ha-Ha!" she called from deep in her belly. "This must be the infamous asexual boy named Broadway Danny Rose we have heard so much about. Are you? Is it you? Are you of the Gushedon'dada? Are you the eunuch-boy?"

Mother began to laugh anew. I could feel a rush of anger rise within me. Mother had no right to make me an object of ridicule. I sat up, as if this might purchase me my dignity, but, alas, it seemed only to generate a growing amusement among the S'hondowek'owa. "Stop laughing, all of you. What's so funny?"

"He's a disgrace to the Gushedon'dada," Mother said, wiping tears of laughter from her eyes. "And he is our only surviving male."

The warrior women shook their heads. "The sexual dysfunction of the male is certainly one of the most dishonorable ways for any tribe to perish," said my captor. "If you like, we shall slay the both of you this very instant and forgo the traditional torturing and desecration of the bodies. It's the least I can offer under the circumstances."

Mother, already upon her knees, bowed her head. "How very kind of you. Such a gracious offer you make. But I must shame our people once more and beg for mercy."

"We will hear your plea." The warrior woman sat cross-legged in the dirt and arranged her pleated skirt neatly over her lap. The other S'hondowek'owa gathered around Mother and myself, Father The Outlaw Josey Wales, and Alice Doesn't Live Here Anymore. They gathered in a tight circle but remained standing, as if at any moment they might be called upon to slay Mother and me and devour us, which was, in fact, a distinct possibility, and not the worst outcome, considering our situation.

"My husband is dead, and there are no other males," Mother said, motioning toward Father's stiff and malodorous body. "One can only imagine the tragedy of losing the last true male Gushedon'dada."

The S'hondowek'owa nodded their agreement, glancing disapprovingly at my exposed manhood. I gathered my pants around my waist, covering myself, and stared back at them indignantly.

"But there is a greater tragedy that clings to my husband's spirit as fiercely as the red worm clings to the lips of the dead."

"And what is that?" The woman had a remarkably lilting voice. She scratched gently at her bald and pimply head.

"My husband's spirit is haunted by a quest unfulfilled. You see, when my husband died we had already begun our journey to the great territory of the Seneca Indians and the League of Nations. It had always been my husband's dream to travel to Seneca territory before his death, so much so that upon his final breath, my worthless son and I vowed to complete the journey in his stead. We had hoped that in this way his spirit might become one with the spirit of the Seneca and allow his soul to rest in peace forevermore. My worthless son and I would gladly accept your offer of a quick and painless death, if it were not for the vow both of us swore over the body of the last true male Gushedon'dada."

The woman who had earlier wanted to kill Mother stepped forward, the woman named Nyo'sowane. She was a tall, lean warrior with long arms and taut legs. The Ruger was lost in her hand, a mere plaything, and she wore the pout of a child who had been told not to use it. "I say we kill them both now. We do not patrol the plains to hear the suffering pleas of weaklings and the pitiable. We are hunters and killers. We are the Seneca death heralds. Besides, she's lying."

The great husky woman sat in silence for a moment, contemplating our plight, fingering the twelve-gauge shotgun perched upon her lap. I noticed her staring at me. She licked her lips and said, "I understand your sense of urgency and purpose, Nyo'sowane. But we must consider all the circumstances before giving in to the blood lust. There is a difference between justice, which we are sworn to uphold, and savagery, which is a luxury to be indulged in only when justice is served."

"*Words!*" Nyo'sowane spat, as if it were the slur of ages. "Talk is weak."

The husky one ignored her and turned to Mother. "We have great sympathy for you due to the disgrace you must suffer because of your infamous asexual son named Broadway Danny Rose. Therefore, I shall grant you your request. The S'hondowek'owa will escort you and your worthless boy to Seneca City, the land of the League of Nations, at which point your husband's spirit quest will be fulfilled, and his soul will rest in peace forevermore. The Seneca sachems will then decide the fate of the remaining Gushedon'dada. Let it be understood that you are prisoners until, or if, the sachems decree otherwise."

"You are kind and just beyond measure," Mother said.

The woman motioned with the barrel of her shotgun toward the dead bodies. "Who is the other dead one?"

She seemed to be asking me, so I answered, "She is Alice Doesn't Live Here Anymore of the Gadages'kao."

"CAW-CAW-CAW-CAW-CAW-CAW-CAW—" came the death cry of the

Seneca warriors. The band of S'hondowek'owa fell upon the corpse of poor old Alice—stomping, gouging, biting, and beating her into a bloody pulp.

Mother and I had all we could do to crawl out of the way, dragging Father along with us. I trembled from fright and exhaustion. Mother looked at me with what might have been compassion, although it could just as easily have been disgust. She reached out and squeezed my hand. "The days ahead will not be easy. Be strong."

These would be Mother's last words to me until some days later, when our destinies collided, or perhaps rear-ended, with the revolution.

⌒ The S'hondowek'owa bound my hands behind my back and forced me to walk with my Dockers undone, so that I had to insert my fingers into my rear belt loops and walk bow-legged to remain modest. As I walked, the S'hondowek'owa spat upon me, pinched me, and ridiculed me. At night, spent and humiliated, I was often poked and prodded and not allowed to sleep.

I thought a lot about Mother during the long days and nights of our journey. She was quite an intelligent and remarkable woman, really. Her handling of the Gadages'kao affair had most certainly saved our lives. Although her slaying of Alice Doesn't Live Here Anymore had been shockingly brutal, if Mother had lost the contest or allowed Alice to live, the hungry and desperate Gadages'kao would, undoubtedly, have killed us. Furthermore, the S'hondowek'owa would have tortured us to death if Mother had not laughed like an idiot during our first confrontation. Her creative fib about Father's dying wish had guaranteed us safe passage to Seneca territory, one step closer to our final destination, the Valley of Day-Glo.

And the trip to Seneca City could not have been easy for Mother. One evening, the S'hondowek'owa forced her to perform the Jug-shaking dance while they laughed and jeered. They also made her perform the Jug-shaking ritual, after which they took our most treasured tribal artifact, the revered Igloo cooler, smashed it against the rocks, peppered it with .22-caliber bullets (many of which ricocheted dangerously off its hard plastic finish), and pumped twelve-gauge shotgun shells into it. What minuscule blue shreds remained they tossed into their evening scrub fire along with our beloved Tribal Bible, *The Modern Book of Baseball*, and the Tribal Bible of the Gadages'kao, *The Microwave Cookbook*.

Yet, during all this barbarism, during so much hedonistic revelry at Mother's expense, I never once saw her flinch or complain.

⤻ One night, Mother and I were commanded to sleep side-by-side, close enough so that I could hear the low murmuring of her raspy voice. Mother was reciting from memory several verses from our recently burned Bible: "A first baseman's glove should be no more than twelve inches tall and eight inches across, with no more than a five-inch web ... Rule number one hundred sixteen states that all players must wear a polycarbonate alloy shell-type batting helmet ... In 1927, Babe Ruth hit sixty home runs and the Venezuelan Federation of Amateur Baseball was founded ..."

At which point I imagined I was actually sitting in a ball park, high up in the grandstands, crushed in among the many fans, a brisk wind snapping the stadium pennants, the smell of hot dogs, popcorn, and cotton candy in the air, and there I was, yes, all alone but one with thousands, observing one of these Pre-Reddening baseball contests, trying to keep track of strikes and outs and runs batted in, whereupon I fell fast asleep for the first time in many, many nights, lulled into slumber by the slow-motion movement of the long-forgotten game of baseball.

⤻ To their credit, the warrior women treated Father The Outlaw Josey Wales with the utmost respect. The two S'hondowek'owa women placed in charge of Father carried him silently and efficiently. At night, they always laid me to rest beside Father because—so I was told by my captors—my asexuality made me as good as dead to the tribe of the Gushedon'dada.

Between the harassment of the S'hondowek'owa and the few minutes of sleep I stole each night, I found myself observing Father to see if he might have a few more words of wisdom for me. His skin had turned a slightly pale, greenish hue, and he stank of spoiled meat. His rigor mortis appeared to be completely relieved. His facial features were barely recognizable, and gas blisters had formed under his flesh.

Once, on a nearly pitch-black night, Father rolled over and spoke to me: *"Danny Boy, allow me to tell you a secret about death. In the Land of the Dead, nobody is right or wrong because nothing matters anymore. Every question I've asked so far has been answered with one of the following remarks: 'Who cares?' or 'What's the difference?' The answers to all of one's questions here are questions, and yet there really are no questions worth asking because nobody cares about the answers. In death, we are being and nothingness."*

"Father," said I, or perhaps I thought it or communicated it in some otherworldly, spiritual way, "that's crazy talk."

"Who cares?" he responded, chuckling softly. *"What's the difference?"*

"Tell me, have you recognized anyone there in the Land of the Dead? Have you run into any of our recently deceased tribes-people?"

"I don't know. No one has a face in death. No one has a voice, either. Once you are dead, you automatically develop a higher, or perhaps a lower, form of communication skills. You never have to work your jaws or lips or vocal cords, and you never have to listen to anybody if you don't want to. On the other hand, no one has to listen to you, either. Come to think of it, one no longer may indulge in the pleasure of listening to the sound of one's own voice. A bit of a letdown, I suppose."

"Father—the Valley of Day-Glo—does it truly exist?"

"Who cares? What's the difference? Who cares who cares who cares? What's the difference?"

Father then rolled over and returned to the Land of the Dead.

⤚ Let me tell you about my private meetings with Dewutiowa'is, the S'hondowek'owa warrior woman who saved Mother and me, in the order in which they occurred, for I believe them to be both interesting and unusual interactions, and a true indication of the complexity of human nature.

Late one night, after a barely acceptable ration of sweetroot, after the embers of the evening scrub fire had all but died and I was beyond the capability of sleep, she came to me, her eyes flashing in the light of the moon, her breath heavy and offensive. She stared at me, and I, bound and helpless, returned her gaze, wondering why she had come out to look at me after everyone else had gone to sleep. Did she see me as some sort of aberration? Did she want to sink her fangs into my neck and steal my spiritual power? What was running through her savage mind? I wanted to know, and I did not want to know. I wanted to live, and I wanted to die.

"My name is Dewutiowa'is," she said.

Off in the distance, the bleak howl of a lone desert dog cut across the plains. It drew my eyes away, and when I looked back, Dewutiowa'is was gone.

At some point, sleep fell upon me with the lightest of touches, leaving my restless mind susceptible to fleeting, haunted dreams. I woke to a sunrise that was little more than a pale scrim, the sound of cutlery being sharpened on stone, a hot, dry wind in my face, and the smell of birds roasting on an ashen fire.

  ꙮ The following night, Dewutiowa'is came to me again. After looking at me for some time, she whispered, "What is wrong with you? Don't you find me attractive?" She knelt in front of me and unbuttoned her fuchsia blouse, releasing a musky animal scent. "Look at these breasts." She pressed them together and thrust them forward.

"They are most impressive," I said, although I saw nothing more than lumpy shadows in the moonlight. What was impressive was Dewutiowa'is herself, with her painted face and thick arms, with her powerful thighs that I was sure could crack a man's skull.

"Of course they are impressive, you useless asexual." There was no anger in her words, only an unexpected playfulness and a familiar lilt that I had come to find oddly endearing. She returned her breasts to her blouse and hastened away.

The next morning Mother and I ate well. I'm not sure why the warrior women showed us such mercy, when previously they had been doing barely more than starving us. Maybe it was Dewutiowa'is's doing. Or perhaps they had simply decided it was time to show off. The S'hondowek'owa were excellent survivalists as well as superb killers. They knew how to hunt. They could easily kill the wary black vultures. They could find desert toads buried in the sand, dune rats hidden in their underground dens, and other cunning little rodents that had learned to adapt by manufacturing their own water metabolically through the digestion of roots. The S'hondowek'owa seemed to thrive in the heat and revel in the danger of the terrain, as if they were born to conquer or die every single day of their lives. I found this both terrifying and comforting.

Later that day, as we traveled through a barren range of hills, the S'hondowek'owa began shouting and dancing for joy and firing off their weapons in celebration. Word quickly spread that someone had discovered a water hole. It was rare indeed to find fresh water on open land. I was not allowed to see it or drink from it, but the rumors alone were enough to quench a bit of the everlasting thirst with which we all lived. I thought of Mother and wished that I could speak to her, but, rather than trying to find her, I sat and rested. The warrior women set a mean pace, and I was learning to conserve my energy. Almost as soon as I found a tender spot in the sand, we were on the move once again.

⌒ On the third occasion, Dewutiowa'is approached me during one of my rare moments of sleep. She kicked me in the head and I woke with a start. She sat cross-legged, with her lap very near my head.

"My name is Dewutiowa'is," said she, repeating the introduction she'd made on the night of her first visit.

I was so tightly bound I could not see her unless I stretched my neck into a horrible position. I did so only long enough to learn that she wore no underpants beneath her black pleated skirt.

"It is an ancient Indian name," she continued, "from the Pre-Reddening, pre-industrial, Golden Age of our Indian ancestors. It means Exploding Wren."

Ah, thought I, so Mother was indeed correct. The Seneca had adopted the ways of our ancient ancestors, using the names of the old language. This did not bode well for me, or for Mother. Those extremists who believed in the purity of Iroquois traditions had no room for the Independents or those who valued Honio'o treasures. "You may speak your etymology," she said.

Strange, very strange, that she would want to hear where my name came from. Well, what did I have to lose? "My name is Broadway Danny Rose, also derived from the Pre-Reddening Age, but not of Indian origin, as I'm sure you already know."

"You may speak it anyway."

"My name is based upon the 1984 black-and-white Woody Allen film about a downtrodden talent agent who inadvertently gets into trouble with gangsters. Mia Farrow plays his love interest who—"

"That is enough."

"You asked me to—"

"Picture shows. They are meaningless."

I shrugged, barely managing it. "Yes, I suppose that's true, if you find no value in stories. What meaning does your killing and ravaging have?"

I thought she might strike me for such an impertinent statement, or at least chide me, but she took it rather well. We sat together for a time and listened to the wind whistle across the dark, empty landscape.

Finally, she spoke. "Why do the Independent tribes fear the ways of our Indian ancestors, yet cling to the ridiculous pop culture of the extinct Honio'o? You worship their artifacts, study their books, name your children after their ridiculous moving picture shows that you have never seen. To what purpose?"

Is this what the Exploding Wren wanted? A discussion of the Honio'o ways? An enlightening exchange about the Pre-Reddening whites and yellows and dark-skinned tribes, a topic of much dispute among the Seneca and the Independents? If I said the wrong thing, would it be the death of me? Alas, I felt compelled to answer candidly:

"The Independents believe that we all must actively integrate the words of wisdom, the objects and rituals that remain from the Pre-Reddening Honio'o into the cultural habits of the Indian tribes, so that the horrible deeds that provoked the great Indian spirits to destroy the yellow- and dark- and white-skinned people will never be duplicated in ignorance by the surviving tribes of North American Iroquois Indians. If we lose the history of our conquerors, it will always be possible for us to be conquered again, this time, perhaps, from within."

Dewutiowa'is grunted. "Everything you treasure, everything you hold dear is Honio'o. This is disrespectful to your true ancestry. As long as we raise the Honio'o above the Indian, we live in danger of incurring the wrath of the spirits. We must let the Honio'o die. We must return to the ways of our ancestors, to a time long before our people were infected by the disease of the Industrial Revolution. We were a great nation in the Pre-Reddening, pre-industrial Golden Age. We can be great again. If we want to."

The Golden Age. Dewutiowa'is was, of course, referring to the time when tall trees filled the mountain ranges and sparkling rivers coursed through the hills and valleys, and thousands of wild animals lived free, and the sun, Ende'kagaa'kwa, the brilliant orb, shone like gold silk in the sky. This was a time long before the Honio'o tried to fix, with clever inventions and chemical experimentation, the damage their inventions and chemicals had already done.

"The Independents have always maintained our tribal heritage," I said. "We have kept our tribal names from the ancient language. We still perform many of the ancient rituals. The Jug-shaking dance, for instance, during a performance of which you so rudely ridiculed Mother, was practiced by our ancestors during the Golden Age. Our tribe often performed the annual harvest thanksgiving ceremony, the Gane'owo, even though there has been no such thing as a harvest of green corn or squash or tobacco or red apples for years and years and countless years."

"You Independents know nothing of the *true* rituals."

"If you are referring to cannibalism and the desecration of dead bodies, we would rather not know such things. And I should like to point out that the great S'hondowek'owa warrior women are all wearing clothing excavated from the Honio'o discount and department stores."

"We wear them to mock the Independents and disguise our true purpose."

"True purpose? What true purpose?"

Dewutiowa'is shot out her hand and snatched a sand spider. I had no idea how she knew it was there, spotted like the ground and masked in darkness as it was. She expertly cracked its back, folded the stinger, and began to gnaw at the meat. She looked beyond me then into the black of night, as if she were imagining great and mystical things, golden things. I had not originally pegged Dewutiowa'is for an idealist or an ideologist. Now I feared she was both.

"This land was once a vast river valley," she said. "And the Great Spirit sowed five handfuls of seed in the rich soil of his creation. From the seed of the Great Spirit came the Five Nations of the North American Iroquois Indians—the Mohawks, Oneidas, Onondagas, Cayugas, and—strongest of all—the Seneca. The Seneca ruled over all the land with an iron fist. When the Honio'o tribes sailed in their ships from the faraway place called Europe and began to steal our land and establish their settlements, the Seneca protected the five families and avenged the loss of life and land with great savage justice.

"But the Honio'o kept coming. They seduced the weaker tribes with rum and useless gifts and false promises, and while the Iroquois spirits slept, the Seneca could not keep the Honio'o down, although most of us died trying. In the end, there was nothing to do but succumb to their villainous treaties. But at long last the spirits awoke and gave back to the Iroquois Indians what was rightfully theirs."

"It is true that the Honio'o were cruel and unjust," I said. "But we have survived them. Is that not enough?"

"No, it is not enough. Have you never heard the tale of the day Turtle went to war?"

I shook my head and watched her bite into the spider's carcass. "No, I have not."

"I'm not surprised. You Independents turn a deaf ear to the legends that don't suit you. It is a Seneca tale that has been handed down through the generations. I will tell it to you now."

Dewutiowa'is shifted slightly closer to me. I sensed that she might have wanted to reach out and touch me, but, if that thought had crossed her mind, she resisted it.

"One day, Turtle grew tired of being hunted by the Indians, so he decided to make war. He decorated himself in war paints, built a canoe, and paddled downriver. He paddled for a long time until he noticed a strange black-and-white animal standing on the riverbank.

"Turtle pulled his canoe ashore and called out, 'You, you there, I am going to battle the Indians. For too long they have made war on the animals, killing us and eating us. Now it is time for us to fight back. Would you like to join me?'

"The strange animal said, 'That sounds like a good idea to me. For years they have used my family to make hats and furs to keep them warm in the winter. I can help you defeat the Indians with my secret weapon.'

"Turtle was very pleased to hear this. 'Show me this weapon of yours.'

"The animal turned around, raised its tail, and squirted at Turtle. The stink of the animal's weapon was so powerful that Turtle had to jump in the water to wash himself off. 'That is a remarkable weapon,' Turtle said. 'You will be a great help in the war against the Indians. What is your name?'

"The animal climbed into the canoe with Turtle. 'My name is Skunk.'

"So Turtle and Skunk paddled far downriver for many days until another strange animal called to them from shore. 'Where are you going?' came the voice.

"Turtle looked over and saw a long, thin animal curled around a large rock. The animal had fangs and a forked tongue. 'We are going to make war against the Indians. For too long they have hunted and killed us for food and clothing. It is time we put a stop to it.'

"The animal said, 'That sounds like a very good idea. For years they have used my skin to make belts and rattles and decorate their wigwams. I have a secret weapon to use against them. I can kill any animal with my terrible poisonous bite. Shall I show you how it works?'

"Turtle and Skunk cried 'No!' at the same time. 'But you are welcome to join our war party,' Turtle said, pulling ashore. 'What is your name?'

"The animal slithered into the canoe. 'My name is Rattlesnake.'

"So Turtle, Skunk, and Rattlesnake paddled downriver to make war against the Indians. By dawn of the next day, they approached a small village of Iroquois. They waited for one of the red-skinned braves to come for water, and they paddled ashore.

"Turtle said, 'You, we have come to make war on the Indians for killing and eating the animals and using our skin and fur to make your clothes and moccasins.'

"The Indian brave looked up and said, 'Why do you make war against the Iroquois? Don't you know we have a much greater enemy?'

"Skunk lifted his tail at the Indian, Rattlesnake showed his fangs, and Turtle said, 'Who could be a greater enemy to the animals than the Iroquois who hunt and kill us?'

"The brave answered without hesitation. 'The Honio'o—the white-, yellow-, and dark-skinned tribes. They have a secret weapon so powerful that no one can stand against it. This weapon does not kill just one or two animals for food and clothing; it kills *all* the animals, and all the trees in the forest, and even their own kind, just for the sake of killing. If you want to wage war, then come with me, and we will fight the Honio'o.'

"The Iroquois' words so frightened the animals that they all agreed to join forces with the Indian. They climbed into the brave's canoe, and he paddled downriver, because he was the strongest warrior of them all.

"It wasn't long before they reached the land of the Honio'o. The water was dirty, the sky smoky. The air smelled of toxic chemicals, like rotting corpses baking under the sun. The war party paddled ashore and called to the Honio'o people, 'We have come to make war against you, to stop you from destroying all of the men and animals and forests.'

"But instead of coming out to speak with the war party, the Honio'o launched their secret weapon. A huge, titanic missile shot up into the sky, and, when it came down, a great explosion rocked the earth. The war party was hurled into the water. When they climbed back inside their canoe, they saw that Skunk's beautiful fur had all been burned and he had lost his tail. Rattlesnake's fangs had fallen out and his skin had peeled. Turtle's shell was cracked and bleeding. There was fire in the water and the trees had been scorched to dust. The Iroquois brave's entire body was melting, and he bled from his eyes and ears and nose and mouth.

"The Iroquois brave handed his canoe paddle to Turtle. 'Quickly, quickly, paddle downriver. We must find the Great Spirit and ask him to defeat the Honio'o. They are too strong and cruel for us. I am blind and can no longer see to paddle.'

"Legend had it that to find the end of the river was to find the Great Spirit, for wherever he stood upon the earth, a river flowed from his feet. Turtle paddled bravely on, although he was in great pain. He felt sad and shamed for bringing the idea of war to the others, for now they were suffering for it. Finally, they reached the end of the river, and Turtle collapsed in the canoe, exhausted from his efforts.

"The Indian brave stood up and cried, 'Great Spirit, please help us. You must defeat the Honio'o. They have a secret weapon so terrible that it kills the very earth, so destructive that it strips men and animals of their skin and fur and blinds them, so ruinous that it burns the water and turns the trees to ashes. Please, you must do something before it is too late.'

"The Great Spirit looked down and took pity on his creatures, but he knew that he must also teach them a lesson. 'I will defeat the Honio'o for you. They will never again use their secret weapon to harm the Indians or the animals. But I will not destroy their secret weapon. I shall hide it underground. I will leave their weapon as a reminder to the world to show you what can happen by following the Honio'o ways.'"

Dewutiowa'is's voice had risen by the end of her tale, something I hadn't noticed until she fell silent. That was when I heard the footfalls of an approaching S'hondowek'owa sentry. Dewutiowa'is whispered, "Remember this tale—it must never be forgotten." Then she scampered away into the darkness.

Moments later, a gangly woman with large toes came upon me and leaned over. It was Nyo'sowane, the warrior who had been so anxious to end my life and Mother's when we had first been captured. "You will shut your stupid mouth or I will slit your throat wide open, drink your blood, and watch you bleed to death. Do you understand? Dewutiowa'is is not here to protect you now."

I nodded and closed my eyes and did not sleep. The story of the day Turtle went to war left me cold. What horrible titanic missile could rock the earth and burn the water? What awful weapon could melt and blind a man and strip the animals of their skin and fur? It was a ridiculous myth, of course. No weapon that did not come from the spirit world could be so powerful. But I was beginning to understand why the Seneca hated the Honio'o and their culture and traditions so much. They feared the Honio'o and what their missile could do if it was ever loosed upon the world. If they believed in the truth of that tale and the consequences it foretold, who could blame them for their hatred?

Oddly enough, I longed then for Mother's embrace. She was as hard and ruthless as anyone I had ever known, but she had once held me in her arms and fed me and loved me, and I would have given anything to return to her in that moment, to forget about the Seneca and the Honio'o and all the pain and death that surrounded me now. I suppose, in truth, I was lonely. Is there a more unforgiving mistress than loneliness?

I was surprised when Exploding Wren returned the next evening. I had thought she'd told me all she had wanted me to know.

"Nyo'sowane was here last night," I said. "I think she is looking for an excuse to kill me. And probably Mother, too."

"Do not worry about Nyo'sowane. Her name means Hard Pumpkin. She is hard on the outside, but still soft on the inside. She is infatuated with blood and power, but she is very young. She would have to kill me before she killed you, and she does not have the strength. The other warriors would turn on her if she tried, because they would not want to follow her. She knows this."

"Ah, well, in that case, I feel much safer."

"Tell me," asked Dewutiowa'is, "Why do you think you are not a sexually functional male? I have seen that you do, in fact, possess rather nicely shaped sexual apparatus. Technically you are impotent, correct? Do you suspect that this is a biological defect or an environmental anomaly?"

I found myself at a loss for words.

"Just curious," she said. "Allow me to conjecture, if you don't mind. You were raised in a warrior-dominated tribal society. Born male, you were expected to hunt, kill, suffer, die, all of this silently, never allowed to show your anger or your sadness. At all times you were required to maintain a bold, brave, and dominant public facade. You were required to demonstrate to your elders that you were focused, logical, controlled, and obsessive in your goal orientation. But you, Broadway Danny Rose, you were at heart a sensitive, creative, physically as well as emotionally fragile child, and, if I may say so, a pretty little asthenic boy. You lacked the strength and dexterity of your fellow Gushedon'dada, as well as their mental resolve, so you became fearful of your inner child, of revealing your weaknesses to the scrutiny of a tribal community that would not accept your inferiority. Your fear turned into self-loathing, repression, depression, and, in the ultimate act of avoidance and isolation, you became something defective, not a person at all, but a *thing* that had gone wrong. An asexual. With this sudden turn, the burden of responsibility for your own actions was lifted, and you became someone who had not failed in the eyes of your people but someone failed *by* the people, or by the system as it stood, a victim of your own rigid societal maxims."

I allowed Dewutiowa'is's speech to settle in until it began to roil my blood, which soon lured me into sarcasm. "Have you by any chance been speaking with Mother Who's Afraid of Virginia Woolf? The two of you would make fine bedfellows in my disparagement. Perhaps she could teach you the Jug-shaking dance, and the two of you might perform it together, as I am not worthy."

"Don't be upset. I am merely suggesting that your impotence may be nothing more than a subconscious act of rebellion, the repression of rage and resentment taken to extremes. With the proper guidance of a beautiful female skilled in the arts of sexual gratification, well—how shall I state this delicately?—who is to say you could not be converted to normalcy?"

Although I had doubts about her skills in this area, not to mention her beauty, I thought that Exploding Wren might try to prove her theory while I lay bound and helpless before her. She leaned over and kissed me on the forehead and reached for my loins. I could feel myself shrinking into my own shell, much as Turtle must have done in the face of the great weapon of the Honio'o in the tale Dewutiowa'is had told me just a few night ago.

Then, mercifully, the first hint of the day's new sun began to glow against the horizon, and Dewutiowa'is slipped away before the early march to Seneca City was to renew, leaving me to ponder her psychological analysis as the reddish haze of morning broke over the landscape.

I was more confused than ever. I felt a headache coming on. I tried not to think about anything, but my mind grew preoccupied with my circumstances, and, just as I was fretting over my many physical and emotional discomforts, Father woke beside me, poor dead Father, his now ravaged body patiently awaiting its final resting place, wherever that might be. He lifted his head and widened his lips into a horrible grin.

"*Danny Boy,*" Father said. "*Danny, listen to this. I have developed a list of things I desperately wanted to explore during my lifetime but didn't realize it until after I was dead. Are you there? Are you listening? Pay attention. Although it means nothing to me anymore, it might mean something to you. Number one: What were some of my wants rather than my needs? Number two: What was the source of my self-esteem? Number three: What special gifts were bottled up inside me that I might have shared with my loved ones? Number four: Why wasn't I more ambitious, more of a journeyman, and less frightened of loneliness? Number five: I really should have loved myself more. Number six: I would have liked to experience more grief, more empathy, and less actual, self-centered, esoteric anguish.*

"*Now, of course, all of these regrets are pointless. Nothing matters over here in Deadsville. The list itself is just as useless as the act of putting it together and the dead nincompoop who had nothing better to do with his time than compile it. I am being and nothingness, my boy, being and nothingness.*"

"What does that mean, being and nothingness?"

Father's head slumped down in the sand. "*I don't know,*" he said. "*Carry on, carry on.*"

"Father, don't leave me!" I begged. But he had already retreated into death.

"Oh, Father, in your deathly wisdom there is great sadness and great joy. I want nothing to matter in this earthly realm as nothing matters to you in the Land of the Dead. I envy you your death, where no victories prevail, for lack of meaning, for lack of fate, for lack of life, in the Land of Who Cares? and What's the Difference? Won't you come back? I could use your company."

But it was Mother who answered. "Wake up, dolt. You're dreaming and talking in your sleep."

It was at the height of morning, after we'd marched through a series of huddled, dry, rocky wedges toward a distant, fractured terrain, that a single bullet passed directly through the skull of the S'hondowek'owa warrior woman walking next to me. Blood spit at my forehead and she crumpled like a sack.

Suddenly, gunfire strafed the landscape.

"Mother! Mother!" I shouted. "Where are you?"

The S'hondowek'owa took up their guns and cutlery and Louisville Sluggers, and Dewutiowa'is barked out commands to her troops. A war cry—no, several war cries—issued forth from the surrounding plains ...

"UG-O UG-O UG-O UG-O UG-O UG-O UG-O UG-O UG—"

"HSSSSSSS-HSS-HSS-HSS-HSS-HSS-HSS-HSS-HSSSSSSS—"

"It's an ambush!" Mother cried. She crawled up beside me.

"Who? Why? Where? Why are they shooting at us?"

Another war cry: "MEEEEEEEEEEEEEE-OW-MEEEEEEEE-OW-MEEEEEEE-OW-MEEEEEE-OW—"

"Have you truly learned so little over the years? Don't you recognize the war cries of the Gako'go, the tribe of the Gluttonous Beasts, the Adodar'ho, the tribe of the Snaky Heads, the Ono'gweda, the tribe of Cattails?"

"Mother, I was never a warrior, you know that. Why must you constantly throw my failings in my face?"

"Because your failings continue to slap me in mine."

More gunshots rained down upon the hot, dry terrain.

"Perhaps if you had been a more loving and caring individual, neither I nor Father would have been such terrible disappointments to you."

My comment must have struck home, for Mother raised her hand to slap me, only to stop short, deciding instead to yank the hatpin out of her Chicago Cubs baseball cap and stab at the twine binding my wrists. Finally the knot loosened and unfurled, freeing my torn wrists and swollen hands. I had no time to linger over the searing pain, considerable though it was, for the battle raged on and moved closer to us.

What happened in the next few moments came to me in a maddening blur. There was a tremendous cloudburst of dust. Shouts echoed. Gunshots kissed the air; bullets raked the dirt; feet pounded on hard, dry earth; death cries and yowls of agony rang out hotly and from all directions.

When the dust cleared, I saw Mother riding the back of a S'hondowek'owa warrior woman, her deadly hatpin lashing down to puncture the jugular vein of one of the females appointed to carry Father The Outlaw Josey Wales to Seneca City. The other guard turned on Mother, kicked her in the ribs, and took aim with her Ruger .22-caliber pistol.

I moved without thinking, leaped to Mother's defense, and tackled the S'hondowek'owa before she could shoot, simultaneously stumbling as my trousers fell to my ankles and tripped me up. The warrior woman and I fell together, and our awkward collapse left my head squashed between the ground and her ample buttocks. The realization of how quickly and easily I might be killed froze me in place, as did the woman's massive weight and sprawling rump.

But Mother Who's Afraid of Virginia Woolf? came to my rescue rather more forcefully than I had come to hers. She threw herself into the fray, biting, scratching, stabbing with her hatpin in a performance worthy of a mighty S'hondowek'owa.

Still, Mother was no match for the strength of our opponent. Gouged and bloodied as the woman was, as soon as she got hold of Mother, she tossed her aside, as if Mother were no more than the slack carcass of a desert dog. I rolled over, dizzy and gasping for breath, and spat the dirt out of my mouth. The woman warrior squeezed the hatpin from Mother's grip with one hand. She grabbed Mother's throat with the other hand and began to strangle her.

I saw the Ruger pistol lying in the dirt and snatched it off the ground. I had never used a gun before, but during the past few days I had certainly seen them used often enough by the S'hondowek'owa to know what to do with it. The plastic grip felt hot in my hand. I pointed the weapon at the woman and quickly yanked the trigger once. One would have thought, with my close proximity to my intended victim, coupled with the woman's enormous girth, it would have been impossible for me to miss. Alas, operating a Ruger .22-caliber pistol proved to be a trickier affair than I had thought. As I yanked the trigger, the gun jerked sideways in my hand, and I missed badly to the right.

The S'hondowek'owa stopped strangling Mother and turned her attention toward me. I was so afraid of what the giantess might do at that moment that I could not shoot again. She laughed at me, dropped Mother to the ground, and stepped forward.

"Put that gun down, you pitiful asexual," she jeered, "before you hurt yourself."

Laugh at the eunuch-boy, will you? I closed my eyes and fired and fired and fired—BANG-BANG-BANG-BANG—until the Ruger no longer barked but clicked and froze, announcing that I had exhausted its store of bullets. The smell of scorched gunpowder rose to fill my nostrils. Only then did I open my eyes to find the woman prostrate in front of me, her blood wetting the dirt, and Mother lying face down with her hands over her head.

"Stop shooting, you idiot," Mother snapped. "Are you trying to kill me, too?"

For the briefest of moments, I wished that I had not spent every last round of ammunition on the S'hondowek'owa. *Just one more bullet,* I thought. Ah, but there was no time to ponder possibilities. Bullets continued to spray the battlefield. Mother was already wrapping Father into his tattered blankets. She strapped him onto the makeshift sled in which she had originally dragged him across the plains. Then, out of the rising dust, three armed and crouching Indians gradually approached us, rifles at the ready. Mother reached down, grabbed her hatpin, and clutched it behind her back. I readied the Ruger in my hand, although I had emptied its clip.

"Who are they?" I asked Mother.

"They are Adodar'ho, Snaky Heads."

They wore purple bonnets with fluffy golden-colored earflaps. Perched atop each bonnet was a cloth cobra baring its fangs, and the strange inscription *AMF Bowling* embroidered across the front. According to legend, the Adodar'ho had unearthed an entire warehouse full of these bonnets years and years ago from which they had derived their tribal name.

"Quickly, follow us," one of them said, beckoning us, his cloth cobra bobbing atop his head. "It will not take long for the S'hondos to regroup. We have struck, and now we must retreat."

"What's going on?" Mother inquired. "Have the Independents joined forces against the Seneca?"

"Yes. The revolution has begun in Seneca City, and it is spreading outward." He made a thespian's sweeping gesture.

"Where are we going?" Mother said.

The other Snaky Head stamped the butt of his rifle in the dirt. The gun, as far as I could tell, was a small-caliber, lever-action Winchester. "Look, old woman, what's the difference where we're going? We are rescuing you from the S'hondos. Isn't that enough for you to know?"

Mother wasn't exactly impressed. "I don't remember asking to be rescued. Besides, my son and I have undertaken a sacred quest to discover the Valley of Day-Glo. We intend to bring my late husband back to life." Mother motioned to the collection of ragged flesh and bones that used to be her living husband. "Thank you for your kind offer, but I think we shall continue upon our journey."

"That's ridiculous—absolutely ridiculous! You have no idea what is happening in the mega-city, even as we speak. The Seneca are under siege. There is rioting in the streets. Violent death everywhere—"

"We must go," snapped yet another Adodar'ho, a slim, nervous-looking fellow. "We have no time to argue with fools who wish to die."

But the first Snaky Head objected. "They have a right to know." He leaned upon the barrel of his rifle. "Old woman, the revolution has been brewing in Seneca City for many moons. Starvation and epidemics have ravaged the population. Inadequate housing facilities and sanitation, intolerable overcrowding, and poverty like you wouldn't believe have become rampant plagues upon the city's tribes.

"The Seneca took all of what the Independents had once claimed as our wealth, all our holdings and tribal artifacts, either by force, or by taxation, or by trading promises of prosperity they had no intention of keeping, and then they went about destroying everything."

"Yes," said the nervous-looking Snaky Head. "The Seneca have been wiping out tribal artifacts in an attempt, so it would seem, to intentionally collapse the economy."

I thought about how the S'hondowek'owa had used our Tribal Jug for target practice, and how they had burned *The Modern Book of Baseball* and *The Microwave Cookbook*. And I thought of what Dewutiowa'is had said to me regarding the evil Honio'o and how we must let them die or suffer the wrath of the great Indian spirits of an age and then another age gone by. Had the Seneca established their great mega-city only to lure the Independent tribes into their League of Nations, abscond with their wealth, and destroy all that remained of the Honio'o? Based upon their distorted principles of cultural cleansing, would they purposely collapse the entire economic structure of the new Indian Age by destroying the Honio'o artifacts that had become our most valued possessions?

"Of course, social disorder was bound to follow," said the first Snaky Head. "The Independents have risen against the Seneca. We have raided most of their armories and storage facilities, and today, while the Seneca hierarchy is in chaos, the revolution remains organized, armed, and angry."

"We three Adodar'ho," said the nervous one, "are part of an ambush squad positioned on the outskirts of the mega-city, deployed specifically to intercept S'hondos returning from missions on the plains. Lucky for you we attacked before the S'hondos reached Seneca City. At the first sign of rebellion, they would have cut you to ribbons!" He made slashing motions with his rifle, almost striking the squat little Adodar'ho beside him. The other one, the first Snaky Head, told his fellow warrior to stop waving his rifle around for fear of accidentally hurting someone.

"Great Adodar'ho," Mother said. "We could not begin to humble ourselves enough to thank you for our rescue. But we are honor-bound to my dead, beloved husband to escort his body unto the Valley of Day-Glo, whereupon he might be resurrected from the dead."

The first Snaky Head sighed. "Many errors of judgment have been made in moments of great sorrow and passion. But a vow is a vow. At least allow us to escort you to our outpost. From there it will be a short march for you to the ruined mega-city."

And so it was decided.

We quickly gathered Father and whatever belongings we could salvage from within the immediate area, including two full clips for the Ruger .22-caliber semiautomatic pistol I now possessed. I also discovered a small piece of twine that I strung through my belt loops and tied off at the waist to keep my Dockers from falling, and a couple of bandannas to wrap around my bloodied wrists.

Just before we were to make our getaway, Mother knelt beside the woman she had slain with her hatpin, and cried:

"AIYEEEEEEEEEE-YICK-YICK-EEEEEEEEEEEEEoh—!"

Then she turned to me and motioned to the woman warrior I had riddled with bullets. Until I looked into Mother's eyes—the eyes of a hardened killer—it had not occurred to me that I had taken a life as well. But indeed I had. I knelt down beside my bloodied victim as was required of me by tribal law. I could not look at her lifeless form, but I felt her ponderous presence at my knees. Mother came over and knelt beside me, took my hand in hers, and together, Mother Who's Afraid of Virginia Woolf? and I wailed the Tribal Death Shriek.

It was the feel of the cry deep in my throat—not the ruined female body in the dirt—that told me I had committed an irrevocable atrocity. The Adodar'ho urged us to make short work of our ritual for we had already delayed too long. As we rose, I turned my back upon the S'hondo woman for whose death I was responsible, and we made our way once again toward Seneca City.

≈ I, Mother Who's Afraid of Virginia Woolf?, Father The Outlaw Josey Wales, and the three Snaky Heads traveled through the windy swirl of soil and sand toward the Adodar'ho outpost. Without ceremony—for Mother no longer possessed our Tribal Jug with which to perform the Jug-shaking ritual or around which to perform the Jug-shaking dance—Mother introduced us as the only two remaining Gushedon'dada.

"Ah," said the nervous-looking one, pointing the muzzle of his Winchester at me. "So this must be the infamous asexual boy named Broadway Danny Rose."

Mother hushed me with one of her deadly looks. It surprised me that even after having killed, thus bringing me either up or down to Mother's level, I feared the old woman no less, and the old woman respected me no more.

The leader of the Adodar'ho introduced himself as Mildred Pierce. "I do not believe I am familiar with the etymology of your name," said Mother.

"My name is derived from the Pre-Reddening 1945 film of intrigue, murder, and misplaced affection," said he, "starring Zachary Scott, a young Ann Blyth, and Joan Crawford as a successful restaurateur. I am surprised you have not heard of it. It was a four-star, thumbs-up, critically acclaimed picture show that netted Joan Crawford an Oscar for Best Actress."

"I am humbled," Mother said.

And all of a sudden I liked this fellow named Mildred Pierce, with the cloth cobra perched upon the crown of his head and the fluffy golden flaps dabbing at his ears.

At some point during the hike, when the wind howled fiercely and we were all forced to walk hunched over with our heads down to protect our faces from the prickly sand, Father entered his body again and wanted to talk.

"Danny, Danny Boy, Danny-Danny-ding-dong. What's happening in the Land of the Living?"

I answered, or communicated to him in some otherworldly, spiritual way, "We have escaped from the S'hondowek'owa warrior women, and the Adodar'ho are guiding us to the outskirts of Seneca City."

"Ah, the Snaky Heads. Don't trust them to protect you for too long. They are an incompetent and easily distracted people."

"The leader seems to have a good head upon his shoulders."

"There is an old saying, dating back many generations, that goes like this: Never trust a Snaky with a good head, for the two shall soon be parted."

"Father, I must know. Does the Valley of Day-Glo truly exist?"

 ᗌ We, the Gushedon'dada, made our tribal fortune a generation ago upon the excavation of the only Kmart our people ever discovered. This occurred before Mother and Father married. Mother was given credit for the find, and it is a shame that the tribe did not know the true nature of the discovery before the great sandstorm claimed their lives. When I asked Father about the Valley of Day-Glo, he relayed to me what had really happened all those years ago upon the discovery of our tribe's one-and-only buried treasure:

"The Gushedon'dada excavation scouts discovered a sandy hill formation that appeared not altogether natural, so the tribe made camp and began to dig. We dug for three days and found nothing. I knew that we would never find anything underneath that mound. Don't ask me how I knew such a thing. It was a very strange experience. But I remember one morning waking to the sound of the Kmart calling me from over the ridge, two or three soil swirls away— 'Attention Kmart shoppers! Attention Kmart shoppers!'

"So I got up and walked over to the spot from where I was sure the Kmart announcement had originated, and I began. The others thought I was crazy. They dug and dug at their formation for two more days without any success, and the next morning, when once again I began working at my spot, a few oth-

ers came over to join me. By the middle of the afternoon we were all digging at my site. The very next day we struck the roof of the automotive department of our tribal fortune."

"But Father, how is it that Mother is given credit for the find in our tribal history if you were, indeed, the one responsible for discovering the Kmart?"

"Because I was a young man," said he. If Father could have drawn a deep breath, I believe he would have sighed. *"Things mattered to me then. Things made a difference. Your mother was the most beautiful woman in the tribe. All of the young braves wanted her for a wife, but she kept turning them down. Your mother was a hopeless perfectionist with an inflated sense of self-worth."*

"I see some things never change."

"She wanted the ideal husband, and she would have gladly died without one if she could not get him. So when the elders asked me how I knew where to dig, I said, 'Who's Afraid of Virginia Woolf? told me to dig here.' Of course, she could have denied it, but I'd caught her by surprise and she wasn't sure how to react at first, and before she knew what was happening, there was a huge tribal dance and feast, and she was being praised and honored by everyone, even the chief. So when they asked her how she knew where to dig, she told them it came to her in a dream. That was the end of her search for the perfect husband. She owed me big time. She was afraid that if she turned down my marriage proposal, I would spill the beans. You know, I never told the truth about the dig to anyone until now, and I never would have."

"Father, that was an ingenious ploy."

"So it would seem."

I hesitated. "Ah, yes, I see your dilemma. Mother felt trapped by your mutual conspiracy, so, as time marched on, she became more and more vindictive and resentful. That's why she treated you with such hostility for so many years."

"Bingo!"

"Didn't it hurt you to be treated so poorly? Why did you live such a lie for so long?"

"*Love.*"

I nodded, not at all understanding. "I have never been in love."

"*I know. I'm sorry about that. I always loved your mother. That is the one thing I would miss if anything mattered over here in the Land of the Dead. I would miss loving your mother.*"

"Sometimes, dear Father, I wish I knew what that sort of love felt like."

"*Let me ask you something, Danny. Are you out of breath? For the last ten years of my life, I felt as if I was always out of breath, and I hated it. Now that there is no such thing as breathing, I would welcome my old familiar shortness of breath. I'm neither inhaling nor exhaling in this strange, dead place, which is a very disconcerting non-sensation. I would also like to hiccup again.*"

"Father, what has any of this to do with the Valley of Day-Glo?"

Father chuckled, but refused to answer. When he fell silent, I knew he had abandoned his body, leaving me to ponder the story of our tribal fortune.

Then, abruptly, it came to me. The reason Mother believed so thoroughly in the existence of the Valley of Day-Glo was because Father, years and years ago, had been right about the Kmart! Was this Father's way of telling me the Valley of Day-Glo truly existed? Should I believe in it, too?

☞ When we reached the Adodar'ho outpost—a loose construction of wattle and bones woven together with the hides of various rodents—Mother whispered in my ear, "Be prepared to make a run for it."

It seemed to me that all we were doing lately was running for it. I was mentally and physically exhausted. "What's wrong this time?"

"Don't be such a putz. Someone has been tracking us. I'm not sure who or why. Just be ready to run for your life, although why I bother worrying about you at all is beyond my comprehension."

The man named Mildred Pierce entered the tiny ramshackle hut first and held the door (which fit badly) so the rest of us could follow. The ill-fitting door made me think of what Father had said to me not more than a few hours ago about the Snaky Heads, how they were an incompetent and easily distracted people. If nothing else, a poorly realized door was proof of that.

Before I entered the outpost, I glanced over my shoulder to see if, indeed, we were being followed as Mother had warned, but the reddish glow of sand and sun and the sloping plains seemed undisturbed. I shuddered at the thought of Nyo'sowane, the Hard Pumpkin, taking this opportunity to track us down and kill us. It would be just our luck to escape a clean, quick death at the hands of an entire band of S'hondo warrior women, only to find a slow, torturous end at the mercy of the one S'hondo who was insane enough to want to make us suffer.

The nervous-looking Snaky Head closed the door behind us. Once inside, I took a moment to blink and adjust my eyes to the semidarkness. The hut had been built with only one opening and no windows, but light spilled through between the bones and wattle. There was barely enough room for all of us to fit, especially with Father in tow. The decorating surprised me. The Adodar'ho had made an obvious attempt to create a warm and welcoming atmosphere. They had placed two mismatched wooden chairs around a small three-legged table. A movie poster hung crookedly on the wall of *The Three Stooges in Orbit*, sealed in a plastic frame. Some of the interior bones were painted red, black, and yellow in no particular pattern. Although the atmosphere was pleasant, there was no Feng Shui to speak of.

Mildred Pierce offered a chair to Mother, who graciously accepted, and the two of them sat while the neurotic one and his squat friend stood with their backs to the door.

"Tell me something," said Mildred Pierce, staring at me. "Do you believe that the malfunction of your phallus is the cause or the effect of your loss of power as a male?"

"I've never really thought about it."

"Well," Mildred said, "it is the male protrusion that makes us men, after all, is it not? It gives us our strength, just as it is the womb that is the center of a woman's vigor."

I was growing tired of defending myself. At least among my own tribe, I had not been required to explain my asexuality ad nauseam, ad infinitum. "Listen, power never meant anything to me. I think being powerless has been an advantage. Nobody has ever expected great things from me, and I have never been controlled or manipulated by my phallus in the way of so many other men. Here's the way I look at it. If you're a slave to your protrusion, you can be easily yanked around by it. Not so for me."

Mother huffed impatiently. "The boy never had a lick of power. It has nothing to do with his protrusion or lack of it, or want or need of it. Frankly, the protrusions of men are greatly overrated. Women have known this forever."

"He doesn't look fey," said the squat Adodar'ho, as if I were not in the hut.

"I had always expected him to look fey, too," said the skinny one, "if you mean indeterminately gendered. Is that what you mean by fey? He doesn't. He looks normal."

I was just about to explain to them that not being rooted in the male gender role had allowed me to cultivate patience, kindness, and contentment, and that my asexuality had opened the doors of self-awareness to things that were far more important to the soul than sexual gratification (Feng Shui, for example), when the door of the Adodar'ho outpost came crashing down instead. The door smashed the nervous-looking Snaky Head and his squat companion to the ground, flat on top of poor Father The Outlaw Josey Wales.

Sunlight spilled into the hut, followed by the sweaty, large-breasted Exploding Wren—a terrifying, black-skirted, fuchsia-topped, red-faced warrior woman, crying, "CAW-CAW-CAW-CAW-CAW—"

Mildred Pierce died instantly when a twelve-gauge slug blew apart his neck and face, thus fulfilling Father's prophesy that a Snaky and his apparently good head would soon be parted.

The other two yawping Adodar'ho could not extricate themselves from underneath their ill-conceived door. The nervous-looking one, out of sheer panic, pulled the trigger of his rifle, sending a bullet through the hand of his squat friend. I saw Mother grab her shoulder as if she'd been struck. Dewutiowa'is pumped her shotgun, and the plastic shell casing popped out and plinked me in the eye.

I, therefore, did not witness the next two slayings, although I heard the ear-splitting blasts and felt the slugs thump heavily into the earth. The ground jumped beneath my toes. I looked over at Mother Who's Afraid of Virginia Woolf? and decided she could not have been too badly injured, for she was struggling to pull Father out of the line of fire.

Dewutiowa'is slung the shotgun over her shoulder and came over to me, squishing on top of the bloody Snaky Heads. "Are you all right?" she said, inspecting my eye.

"Just a scratch."

"I'm sorry. It doesn't hurt too much, does it?"

"No, no, no, think nothing of it. No permanent damage, I'm sure. It just stings a little."

Dewutiowa'is kissed me gently on the eyelid. "Listen, I overheard what that numbskull Snaky Head was trying to tell you. I want you to know something. Your phallus has nothing at all to do with your power as an Indian or a man. What determines one's power is will and determination, nothing more. The will comes from the center, the roundness that is the heart and belly and soul of the Iroquois Indian." She slapped her palm over her stomach. "Not from the sexual apparatus."

"Please," said I, "you're embarrassing me in front of Mother."

Mother, in fact, stared with an expression of disbelief at nothing in particular, and I felt a sudden chill at the absent look upon her face. She was huddled over Father's body. There on her shoulder was a smear of bright red blood. I turned to Dewutiowa'is. "How far are we from Seneca City?"

"No more than a half-day's journey."

I turned to Mother with a scolding expression. "Mother, it is time to tell her the truth. Dewutiowa'is may be the only one who can help us now."

Mother continued to kneel in silence. She brushed back Father's frayed hair. She looked wistful, as if she were remembering some tender moment.

"All right, I shall tell her myself then. Dewutiowa'is, it is true that we are on a quest, as Mother told you. But our quest is to discover the fabled Valley of Day-Glo. Mother wishes to bring Father back to life. To be perfectly honest, I do not even know why. She says it's because Father is the last true male capable of siring Gushedon'dada offspring, but I don't think that's exactly true, for Mother is long past her childbearing years, and I could not imagine her allowing Father—dead or alive—to impregnate another woman.

"I think she is feeling guilty, for it was Mother, in a fit of rage, for reasons I have just recently learned regarding the discovery of our Kmart, who strangled my poor father to death. Whatever her reasons, our quest was genuine and honorable, even if we did not know whether the valley truly existed. It seemed the right thing to do for the last two surviving Gushedon'dada, rather than to sit and wait idly by for death to discover us."

Dewutiowa'is remained silent. She looked at Mother with what might have been pity.

"Does the Valley of Day-Glo exist?" I asked her. "And if so, can we bring Father to the valley and restore his life?"

Dewutiowa'is furrowed her brow and stepped over to Mother. "Old woman, look at me."

Mother looked up with somewhat vacant eyes from under the bill of her Chicago Cubs baseball cap.

"For the sake of your courageous son, I forgive you your deceit. I also forgive you for slaying my sister warrior, a deed for which I should skin you alive and expose your nerve endings to a grainy sandstorm. I forgive you this crime for the sake of your son."

She returned to me—*squish, squish, squish*—on top of the Adodar'ho. Their Three Stooges movie poster had fallen to the ground and was stained with blood. "Your killing of my sister warrior, courageous Broadway Danny Rose, was in self-defense, and there is nothing to forgive. I will answer your questions. The Valley of Day-Glo does, in fact, exist, in a manner of speaking, and we can bring your father to the Valley of Day-Glo and, in another manner of speaking, bring him back to life."

"Mother!" I cried. "Did you hear the good news?"

Much to my surprise, Mother's expression did not vary. She gently rocked her dead husband in her arms.

Dewutiowa'is went on, "Before I can guide you to the Valley of Day-Glo, I am honor-bound to desecrate the bodies of these enemy Adodar'ho and feast upon their internal organs. I hope you understand."

"Of course. You wouldn't mind if Mother and I waited outside, would you?"

"Not at all. Make yourselves comfortable. This won't take long."

So Mother and I dragged Father out of the ruined hut, where we waited under the hot sun for Dewutiowa'is to mutilate the bodies of her enemies and feed upon their remains. Mother sat trembling. Perhaps, at long last, the stress had grown too much for her, the stress not only of this journey but of a lifetime of fear and hidden resentment and stifled emotions. I could no longer hate her. Perhaps this had been Father's intent all along. I did not know, and I was not about to ask him. I hoped that he was enjoying this moment in Mother's arms. Even in the Land of Who Cares? and What's the Difference?, a brief interlude of love might somehow bridge the gap between life and death. That would be nice to know, comforting in a way, because it is a path that all of us who live and breathe must someday travel.

Chop, chop, chop. I heard Exploding Wren carving up her snack. I wondered exactly what she had meant by saying that the Valley of Day-Glo existed "in a manner of speaking," and that Father might be brought back to life "in another manner of speaking," but upon these details I did not dwell. Instead, I sat down next to Mother and inspected her wound, only to discover it a more serious injury than I had originally believed.

What I thought to be a smear was quite obviously a gouge, and I was now certain that the bullet had lodged itself in Mother's shoulder. At least the bleeding had stopped. I tore off a piece of my shirtsleeve and removed the bandannas from around my bloodied wrists, and, while Mother sat motionless, I wrapped a makeshift sling around her shoulder and under her armpit. I then curled my arm around her to give her what comfort I could, even though she seemed oblivious to my efforts.

Mother Who's Afraid of Virginia Woolf?, now wounded and oddly silent, and Father The Outlaw Josey Wales, a blistered, greenish horror, who nonetheless gave the near-lifelike appearance of a puckered, gelatinous mold, could not look away from each other. They were two outrageous love-birds. Who could possibly have foreseen that their relationship would blossom after Father's death?

I told Mother that everything was going to be all right, and that I would take care of things from now on and see to it that Father was taken care of also. I assured her that soon our quest would be fulfilled, one way or another.

⮑ This is what I saw of the fallen Seneca mega-city:

Lots of smoke. Black smoke, gray smoke, pasty white smoke. Everything, all of its structures, all of the inadequate huts and longhouses of which Mildred Pierce had forewarned us, were either burned or burning.

Indians lay dead everywhere: gutted, stampeded, limbs mangled, skulls crushed, heads scalped. The wounded moaned in pain and fear, perhaps aware that they could easily be killed by friend or by foe, for mercy or for malice. And in among the huts all ablaze and the horrible human suffering, what Seneca and Independent warriors remained continued to mêlée in small parties of three or four or five. They looked to bludgeon or shoot or stab to death their enemies, or to hide until the killing stopped and it became clear who, if anyone, would stand to claim victory.

Dewutiowa'is had said she would guide us to the cave that led directly to the Valley of Day-Glo. True to her word, in her single-minded way, she maneuvered us through the mayhem as if she knew a safe and abstract route only through time, avoiding the perilous reality of space. Perhaps what amazed me most of all was Dewutiowa'is herself, who appeared untouched by the demise of Seneca City, her city, and the suffering of her people. These S'hondowek'owa were truly unique warrior women, thought I, a breed apart.

It was I who now dragged the death burden of Father The Outlaw Josey Wales. I held Mother's hand, actually pulling her along as I tried to remain focused on Dewutiowa'is so that I would not feel my exhaustion or despair or terror. Oh, fear! How easily it could overwhelm me if I gave it the slightest measure of my mind. But Father kept my thoughts sufficiently obscured:

"You had better be afraid," he said to me. *"How lucky you are to fear death."*

"Lucky? I think I could die from fright."

"Excellent! That's how you know you are alive. Fear is a great teacher, a great motivator, and, best of all, you can really feel it knocking at your door. Nothing knocks at your door when you are dead."

"I am also afraid for Mother."

"Lucky you again! You are not only afraid for yourself, but you have fear for someone else. Listen. Don't worry about the old bag. She'll be fine."

Dewutiowa'is moved slowly, cautiously through the city, taking long respites for which I was entirely grateful. To travel with haste, said she, would only attract unwelcome attention, and we did not want to look as if we had somewhere to go. During a fierce battle, people tended to follow people who looked as if they had a purpose or a destination, or they tended to kill them. We wanted neither company nor death.

Dewutiowa'is assured us the fighting had become sparse enough so that with careful navigation we could avoid small skirmishes. And she was right, after all, for at one point, when my legs trembled and I thought my shoulder muscles would snap from the strain of the harness, Dewutiowa'is raised her hand and we came to a halt, and there below us, just off the ridge, stood a company of five Oniat'ga, the tribe of Rancid Meats, guarding the cave that Exploding Wren assured us was the hidden entranceway to the Valley of Day-Glo. We had reached our destination, so it seemed, without incident.

"They have no idea how to find the Valley of Day-Glo because it is hidden deep beneath the earth," Dewutiowa'is said of the Oniat'ga. "But they have heard rumors that this small cave is the entranceway, and they are correct about that. Now we have only to defeat the Oniat'ga, and the valley will be ours." I saw the gleam in her eyes.

"No more needless killing," I said. "I have seen enough death already. I will not be the cause of any more. If we cannot get past the Oniat'ga without killing them, then our quest ends here."

Dewutiowa'is muttered her disapproval, but in the end acquiesced. I began to think that perhaps she had fallen in love with me, Broadway Danny Rose, the useless asexual boy.

We settled in, hidden atop the ridge, resting and munching on some provisions Dewutiowa'is had procured from the Adodar'ho outpost. She assured me that none of the portions had been carved from the Snaky Heads themselves, although I'm not sure I would have cared at that point.

There in the dirt, Dewutiowa'is sketched out a plan involving a clever diversion that might gain us entry into the cave without the use of butchery. It seemed plausible.

"Mother, aren't you excited?" I said. "The plan is a good one, is it not?"

She did not answer. I hoped that if Mother were to be of no use to us, she would at least not cause us undue difficulty. I wondered if this was how Mother used to feel about me, and I was astonished at the irony of how quickly our roles had reversed, how caretaker could become burden and burden could become caretaker with almost no preamble whatsoever.

⌐ "Help!" I cried as I limped along the trail, dragging Father behind me, with my arm wrapped around Mother Who's Afraid of Virginia Woolf? The five Oniat'ga whirled about and aimed their rifles at us. Crouching, they stepped behind some strategically placed boulders. I noticed Dewutiowa'is then, above and behind them, on the ledge over the mouth of the cave. She had circled around and climbed up the outcropping from beyond. I knew I had already given her all the diversion she would need to carry out the first part of our plan, for as soon as the Oniat'ga turned their backs to the cave, Dewutiowa'is lowered herself into its darkened mouth.

"Don't shoot!" I shouted. "We are allies. We are Independents. My name is Broadway Danny Rose of the Gushedon'dada, and this is my dead father, The Outlaw Josey Wales, and my mother Who's Afraid of Virginia Woolf? who has been seriously wounded in the revolutionary battle."

Two of the Oniat'ga slunk out from behind their boulders and approached us, scanning the area for any sign of the enemy, too late to detect the presence of the Exploding Wren. Neither of the Rancid Meats spoke to us. I remembered Mother once telling me in her typical scolding manner of a tribe that sulked to the point of not uttering a single syllable (many of them sulked for an entire lifetime without ever speaking), and I thought that the Oniat'ga might, in fact, be the sulking tribe. I wished Mother were her old self again. Oh, what I would have given for a crisp slap across the face, one of her lovely scowls, and a harsh defamation of my character such as, "Eunuch-boy! Have you learned nothing in all your years! Of course these are the sulking Oniat'ga!" But alas ...

"My mother has been shot. Can you help her?"

The Oniat'ga led us directly into the shelter of the cave, where two of them laid down their bolt-action rifles and began to handle Mother. They retrieved medical supplies from a small pouch and quickly and efficiently removed the bullet from Mother's shoulder with nothing but a shiv and a spoon. Then they cleaned the wound and applied a dressing. Mother, silent and expressionless throughout the entire procedure, was the perfect Oniat'ga patient.

I quickly assessed the situation. Three of the five guards had resumed their positions just outside the mouth of the cave. That meant Dewutiowa'is and I needed to defeat only two guards to carry out our plan, the best part of which was the simplicity of my role. I had only to get Mother and myself into the cave. Dewutiowa'is would then take care of the rest.

Her initial attack came so swiftly out of the shadows that the first Oniat'ga, a huge beast of a man with tufts of hair clinging to his chest and back, never saw it coming. The rock descended upon the base of his skull and knocked the poor fellow senseless. When the other turned at the sound of his fallen companion, he looked as if he wanted to shout for help, but then he must have remembered that he was Oniat'ga and could not or should not speak. Exploding Wren drove her fist into his squared chin, dropping him like a stone, but not before he managed a reflexive squeal of fright.

Unfortunately, the other Oniat'ga heard his squawk, and they came dashing into the cave.

But off we ran!

Dewutiowa'is snatched up Mother, tossed her over her shoulder, and shot into the deep black pit of the cave. Blinded by the darkness, with Father in tow, I followed Dewutiowa'is by the sound of her footfalls and her hushed voice, "This way! This way! No—*this* way!"

The Oniat'ga shot at us, their gunfire cracking and echoing in the surrounding corridors, but, in stopping to shoot, they allowed us to forward our lead.

Dewutiowa'is halted and caught me as I stumbled into her arms. "*Shhhhh,*" she whispered. "They are listening for us." And, indeed, I noticed the Rancid Meats were no longer shooting. The caves had turned deathly quiet.

"Offshoots," whispered Dewutiowa'is. "There are scores of them to choose from in only the short distance we have run. That should keep them busy for a while." Dewutiowa'is knelt on the path and began to dig at some loose dirt. I took this opportunity to adjust Father's harness more comfortably about my shoulders. More scuffling came from behind us, followed by some dull flickers of light.

"They have torches," Mother said. These were the first words she had uttered since the debacle at the Adodar'ho outpost, and my heart filled with joy at the thought that Mother might be recovering from her injury and melancholia. "Be careful, Danny. They'll kill all of us now, not just your big fat female friend." I wanted to scold Mother for her rudeness, but Mother's voice was so small and weak that Dewutiowa'is seemed not to hear.

My eyes had adjusted to the darkness well enough to identify the objects Dewutiowa'is had unearthed—a large hiking pack and some sort of odd metal helmet. She quickly brushed the dirt off these items, strapped on the backpack, turned to me, and placed the helmet upon my head. She then adjusted the strap under my chin.

She said, "With this hardhat, you will be able to follow closely behind me and shed light upon the path ahead. I am tightening the lamp bracket. She turned a knob on my helmet, flipped a switch, and the light upon my hat illuminated a vast portion of the cave in front of us.

"If I tell you to turn off the light, simply flip this switch down." She touched my fingers to it. I nodded. The footsteps behind us drew closer. "We must move quickly. The light is bright and the Oniat'ga might see it." She lifted Mother over her shoulder again, and Mother did not argue or even try to move on her own.

No time to fret.

Off we jogged!

⤳ Through the limestone caves we scurried, caves formed long ago during the Golden Age of great groundwater. We passed long stretches of crystal clusters, white flowstone, and stalagmites. In some sections of the caves, what Dewutiowa'is described as "beautiful speleothems" had precipitated on the cave walls and ceilings. Soon I was panting and feeling frighteningly enclosed. I shivered from fear. But onward, ho! The Rancid Meats, being persistent, sulking Indians, were not likely to give up the chase.

"Bathtub!" announced Dewutiowa'is, stopping and indicating a low spot in the underground cavern filled with water. *Water.* It was a frightening sight to most Indians. It was difficult for us to imagine a time when great ships sailed upon vast seas that covered more than half the Planet Earth. Such things seemed to us terrifying and impossible.

"Might I suggest we follow that offshoot to the left?"

"We could, but the Oniat'ga will be reluctant to wade through the pool, and we could gain valuable time and distance."

"Are we not reluctant to wade through the pool also?"

"We are prepared for the cold water."

Exploding Wren reached into her backpack, dug out two slim tubes of plastic she called transparent body suits, and unrolled them. We climbed into the plastic suits and zipped them up to our necks. Dewutiowa'is waded into the pool, holding Mother above the water, and I did likewise with Father, harness and all.

Once in the pool, I felt the water swirl around me, up to my knees, hips, waist, and chest. I began to fear that the bath water would surely climb above my head and drown me. My arms ached, and I was certain I could not take one more step against the resistance of the cold water.

But then the bed of the pool began to rise again and, as we climbed out on the other side of the bathtub, I nearly collapsed, hopelessly exhausted. Sensing now that we could put some much-needed distance between our position and the Rancid Meats, Dewutiowa'is insisted we press on, so we stripped off our transparent suits and forged ahead.

Shortly thereafter we came upon a "squeeze," an extremely confining Z-shaped passage that required us to belly up against the cave walls to cut through to another main artery. The sharp stones nicked our skin and left us all slightly gashed and bleeding, with the exception of Father, who could no longer bleed. But at least we had made it through and, upon doing so, Dewutiowa'is finally allowed us to stop and rest.

She removed something she called a carbide lamp from her backpack. She lit the lamp and told me to switch off my headlight and remove my hardhat. I gladly obeyed. The fright of the water crossing was still in my heart, and it seemed easier to breathe without the weight of the helmet pressing down upon my brow.

"I am very familiar with these caves," she said in her lilting voice. "I and the Seneca have visited the Valley of Day-Glo many times. Do not be afraid."

"It seems to me that if we keep going down, as it appears we have been since the beginning, we shall discover the center of the Earth, which is a strange place to find a valley of any sort."

"I can assure you this is the strangest valley of any sort you shall ever see."

"If I live to see it."

Not a joke, although Dewutiowa'is chuckled and scratched her pimply head. "You have nothing to fear. We will survive." She came over and planted a hard kiss upon my lips.

"Hmph," I muttered. Under the soft glow of her carbide lamp, she unpacked some nourishing provisions. I was so hungry I did not ask anything about where the crunchy treats came from. I didn't care. I attempted to enjoy their salty flavor and block from my mind the Seneca penchant for cannibalism. These were dire times. Better to live through them, I decided, and ask questions later. Or not at all.

I crawled over to Mother and held her hand; it felt icy cold. I noticed that I was cold, too. It surprised me how chilly the caves had become. Dewutiowa'is handed me a small wool blanket from her hiking pack, and I wrapped it around Mother's shoulders. I tried to feed her some of our provisions, but she would not eat. Although Father had told me not to worry about Mother, how could I not?

⮑ Soon we were foot to path again. Mother still needed to be carried, for she could not make her legs move, and, when I asked her to recite her name and tribe, she seemed confused and her speech was slurred and her eyes had glazed over, so Dewutiowa'is threw Mother over her shoulder and carried her as before. I found it easier to transport Father in the same manner as Dewutiowa'is had demonstrated with Mother, so I left behind the cumbersome harness once and for all.

Eventually, the tiny confining pathways began to widen, and the four of us broke through onto an open ledge overlooking a vast cavern, and far below, in the center of the cavern, shone a brilliant globe of bright white light. Such a stark and spectacular luminosity emanated from the globe that I forgot all about my fear of heights and knelt down on the edge of the steep declivity to stare. I watched the brilliant globe as if it were the exposed heart of humankind, and perhaps it was. I felt godlike, as if I were gazing down upon the sun from a heavenly mantel.

"Be careful on the ledge," Dewutiowa'is said. "The light can be hypnotizing."

She helped me to my feet, and we began our final descent toward the Valley of Day-Glo. It seemed as if the faraway light gave me strength. I could look at nothing else as we wound our way down the treacherous pathway, and yet my steps fell firmly and confidently along the rocky slide. Father The Outlaw Josey Wales was no longer a burden to me. There was only light in my mind—a light that spread throughout my entire body—with the wonder of the valley and the mysteries and dreams of what treasures lay inside. Neither of us spoke, even when we reached the level of ground upon which the valley lay sprawling, and the huge dome towered over us like an impossible accident of fire and light. Perhaps we had both fallen victim to the hypnosis of which Dewutiowa'is had forewarned. No words would come. No words seemed necessary.

Silently, we marched along, moving closer to the remarkable globe of light. Inside it, steep hills spotted the landscape, thick with green grass; dark brown trees with leaves of rich amber stood like tall sentinels; rows and rows of bright red, orange, yellow, and blue fruits twisted and turned along the hilly terrain. The valley held its own blue sky and white clouds. All of this under the huge, transparent dome. We walked directly up to where the glass met the cavern floor, so that the tips of my loafers were no more than a few grains of sand away from something I had never before seen, touched, smelled, tasted, or felt between my toes: grass!

And suddenly a new definition of time and space and distance revealed itself to me. I might have been worlds away from the Valley of Day-Glo, rather than a mere footstep, for the grass and all the other treasures that lay beyond were no more mine now than they had ever been. Seeing the valley was a cruel joke, I understood, because I knew without having to ask that no Indian had ever laid foot inside the brilliant orb. There was a door, or perhaps more of a hatch, sealed shut just to our left. Above the door a plaque read:

DAY-GLO PROJECT

2280

"Welcome to the Valley of Day-Glo," said Dewutiowa'is, setting Mother gently down upon the ground.

"How? How did they do it?" I asked as I laid Father at my feet.

"We do not know how the Honio'o did it. We studied the construction for quite some time. It is, like so many things Honio'o, born of a technology beyond our ability to understand."

"You studied it? Why? I thought you abhorred everything Honio'o."

"We studied it because, at first, we had intended to destroy it. In fact, we tried everything we could to get inside. We tried beating it with our baseball bats, but we couldn't even scratch the surface. We tried blasting it with our shotguns. We tried dropping huge boulders on top of it from the ledges above. We even tried digging under it, but there seems to be no end to its circular construction. We studied the globe so that we might find a way to destroy it before the Independents learned of its existence. We did not want the valley preserved as a monument to Honio'o ingenuity."

"You would have destroyed it the way you have destroyed all of their other artifacts."

"Yes."

"The way you have ruined the economy."

"We thought we had no choice."

"You knew all along the revolution was coming."

Dewutiowa'is nodded. "We seeded it."

"So, of course you did not care about the fall of Seneca City or the violent deaths of your own people."

"Of course we cared. But we aspired to a higher purpose. We were all prepared to die to rid us once and for all of the evil Honio'o. With the economy collapsed and the artifacts of the white- and yellow- and dark-skinned tribes destroyed or otherwise rendered valueless, out of the death and struggles of the Iroquois, a New Order would emerge, stronger, prouder, and based solely upon the culture of the Indian race."

I reached out to the clear dome and rested my hand upon it. It felt hard and warm to the touch. "You would have killed the only innocent life that inhabits this planet."

"For what it's worth," she said, "I did not agree with the destruction of the Valley of Day-Glo, and eventually our sachems decided to let it stand. I was glad we could not penetrate its mighty walls."

Dewutiowa'is came up behind me, grasped my shoulders, and slowly turned me around. "Broadway Danny Rose, the politics surrounding the revolution and the revolution itself are already part of our history, and we can do nothing to change what has already occurred. The important thing now is your quest. For your father to become one of the living, we must leave his body here and travel to the far side of the valley. Don't ask me why now; the reason will become clear to you later. But if you look upon the rocky ledges above us, you will see there are still two Oniat'ga upon our trail. If we leave the body here, they will surely reach it and desecrate it before any miracle of life can occur. Then they will continue to track us and try to kill us—"

"I know," I said, reaching up and gently touching her chin. "You must do what must be done." The past was indeed the past. How fond I had grown of this robust, burly, sensitive woman.

"You are a strong man," said she.

"No, I think not."

"To do what one must do to survive is the only true measure of strength." She squeezed my hand and then strapped on her shotgun.

"Be careful," I said.

She motioned to the valley. "The light of the valley will be in their eyes.

They will be hypnotized." She drew her knife, gripped it between her teeth, and set off toward the pathway we had followed into the valley.

I watched her pick her way through the rocks for a while, and then I turned my attention to Mother, who sat motionless in front of the beautiful valley, staring through it as if it were not there. I reached out and massaged her clammy neck.

"In the Pre-Reddening year of 1993," Mother said," the San Francisco Giants hired the first woman radio announcer for the game of baseball. The Honio'o had been playing baseball for more than a hundred years, but no woman had ever announced a game. It was a happy time in the history of baseball, before the ruinous strikes and the scandal of steroids. It was almost as if the league was trying to make the game more feminine. I wish that I could have been more feminine during my life, but I really couldn't. There was no time or place for femininity after the Reddening. The spirits Hed'iohe and Sagowenota never gave a thought to the women when they created their new world. What a shame." Mother's words trailed off softly, distantly.

"Mother? Are you all right?"

But it was Father who answered: "*Son, do not worry about my lovely wife any longer. She is coming with me.*"

I turned to Father. His flesh barely clung to his bones. He looked like a chewed and regurgitated piece of desert dog. His teeth knocked together slack and useless. If he smelled horrendous, I could no longer detect it or no longer cared.

"*Who would have thought that your mother could not survive without me? I wish I could have lived to enjoy this moment. But, of course, now it does not matter, and I do not care. The idea of enjoying anything is silly.*"

He paused. I nodded. What could I say? To me, the idea of enjoying anything had always been silly.

"*Danny Boy, I was just thinking about something interesting. Wouldn't it be nice if during our lives we could always feel detached from the world, and then in death, after we had gone through all the struggles of our lives and made*" all of our irreversible choices, in death we could relax and enjoy our feelings for the rest of eternity? I wonder if there is anyone here I could talk to about it? Of course, no one would care. That would be a problem in implementing any sort of plan in the Land of the Dead. On this side of the ball field, apathy reigns."

"Father, how did you know the Valley of Day-Glo existed? How did you know with such a sense of certainty that this miraculous monument to the Honio'o was here all along?"

"I heard it call to me just as the Kmart had called to me so many years ago. Except it called in a vision rather than a voice. Little did I know that it was my death calling. Listen to a word of advice, my son. Whenever you hear a strange voice in your head, or a vision comes to you unbidden and tells you to do something, you should strongly consider running the other way. It might be your death calling you."

"Is that what you are, Father? My death?"

His face twisted into an obscene smile, and then he was gone. I turned to Mother. She was gone, too. She lay slumped over, her eyes still staring blankly at the Valley of Day-Glo. Quite beyond my control, my body shook with grief.

I went over to Mother, closed her eyes, lifted her limp body, and lay her down gently next to Father. I straightened her *Esprit* T-shirt and fixed her hair under her Chicago Cubs baseball cap. I noticed that the patch on her cap had come loose, and the large red C encircled in blue and white hung down to the bill of her cap, so I pulled it off and stuffed it in my pocket. Then I took the gold hatpin she was so fond of and held it between my hands while I wailed the sacred O'gi'we, the Tribal Death Shriek:

"AIYEEEEEEEEEEE-YICK-YICK-EEEEEEEEEEEEEoh—!"

I slipped my mother's hatpin into my pocket along with the patch—two small keepsakes to remember her by—and gazed at the brilliant orb that was the Valley of Day-Glo, the new Ende'kagaa'kwa, wherein all the miracles of nature awaited. "Oh, great valley," I prayed, "can you possibly save them both?"

I heard Dewutiowa'is approach me from behind and felt her hands grasp my arms. "I am sorry about your mother. Now we must travel to the far side of the valley," she said. "More Oniat'ga are coming, but they are a day's journey behind us, and they will be too late to prevent any miracle of life that may occur here."

I did not ask her how she had learned this information about the approaching Oniat'ga. I did not want to know. She carried two more rifles with her, the rifles of the dead Oniat'ga, I presumed. I rose to my feet and spoke:

"She was my mother, Who's Afraid of Virginia Woolf?, named after a 1966 film starring Elizabeth Taylor and Richard Burton, based on an Edward Albee play. Taylor's performance as Martha, a wild and screeching bitch, was arguably her best character portrayal in a storied career as an actress.

"He was my father, The Outlaw Josey Wales, named after a 1976 Western film starring Clint Eastwood as a farmer turned Confederate soldier during the Civil War, determined to avenge the deaths of his family members who were mercilessly slain by renegade Union soldiers.

"And I am Broadway Danny Rose, the last remaining Gushedon'dada."

Then I was ready to go. I did not know why we had to leave the bodies of my parents behind. I decided it was part of the miracle process that no living being could be present for the resurrections, if there was, in fact, such a miracle awaiting them. Regardless, I felt in my heart that an end had come to many things, and whether a miracle should occur had no particular bearing upon my existence from this moment forward. I knew no other way of life now but to carry on.

⌒ As we walked outside the valley, Dewutiowa'is described many of the fruits and vegetables that grew inside. Bright red tomatoes and fields of golden wheat. Figs, vines of grapes, orchards of apples, acres of mulberry and peach trees. She was a wealth of information. Much of the knowledge of the valley had been handed down to the Seneca through the generations, and their sachems had preserved it all.

"Does anyone live in the valley to harvest all of these wonderful foods?" I asked.

"We have never seen anyone, but we know that someone, either spirit or man, must be responsible for the miracles of life that you will soon witness."

Pretty little birds flew everywhere within the globe. Dewutiowa'is described them as tiny hummingbirds of shocking yellow, sparrows the color of stone, blue jays, and bright red cardinals. "Do you see those tall green stalks?" she said. "Maize, just as our ancestors had planted during the Golden Age."

On the other side of the glass, a large body of water stretched as far as I could see. As we walked along the valley's impenetrable barrier, I lost all sense of place and time. I had never before seen such a vast body of water. Dewutiowa'is called it a "Great Lake," and I noticed how its gentle waves lulled one to sleep; how it took one away to an indefinable area of the mind; and I thought that the water must surely have been a metaphor for death during the Pre-Reddening Age, for I could see losing myself within its wet embrace and never returning.

Eventually, the waters gave way to a huge tropical rainforest matted with dark, wet, nutrient-rich soil. Staggeringly tall trees rose above the land. Dark green moss and thick rows of ferns and rubber-tree plants grew wild and free. I couldn't help asking Dewutiowa'is questions about every plant and animal that I saw, and she answered as best she could.

I had no idea how long or how far we had walked, but finally we came upon a sprawling botanical garden. Flowers of every shape, size, and color spread over the hills. As we stood gazing at the colorful wonders of nature, my legs collapsed from sheer exhaustion. "I cannot take another step."

Dewutiowa'is sat beside me. "It's all right, Danny. Get some rest. We have reached our final destination. Now we need only await the miracle of life."

⌒ I woke drowsy and disoriented in Exploding Wren's arms. But I felt very safe there, so we cuddled for a while, neither of us speaking. I stroked her strong shoulders, and she held me tightly. I kept my eyes closed, reluctant to let go of my dreamless slumber. "How long have I been sleeping?"

"About a day."

"That long?"

"I slept, too."

I sat up. "The miracle?"

"Has occurred."

"Mother? Father?"

Dewutiowa'is nodded toward the Valley of Day-Glo. I staggered to my feet and went over to the glass dome. I pressed my fingers against the transparent barrier. My heart pounded. There, in the botanical garden, resting atop the tender soil, lay my parents. Already they had begun to take root. Vines and grasses curled around their extremities. The tiny bud of a flower poked out of Father's armpit. Mother appeared to be laced in tiny white lilies.

"Death becomes life," said I, "in the Valley of Day-Glo."

And it was true. Nowhere else upon the entire reddened Planet Earth could something be planted and out of it grow life.

Life.

"We discovered the miracle by accident," Dewutiowa'is said. "One day when we were dropping huge boulders from the high ledges in an attempt to crack open the glass dome, one of our tribesmen lost his footing and fell to his death. Because of our precarious positions in the upper rocks, we could not retrieve his body right away. When we were finally able to send a party out to search for him, we could not locate his remains. A day later, another party working this end of the valley noticed that the fallen man had been planted here in the botanical garden.

"So we experimented," she continued. "We left a few more of our dead around the entrance hatch and waited for the Honio'o to emerge so that we might ambush them and gain entry into the valley. But no one ever came out, so we continued to experiment. Whenever we left dead bodies, and no one stayed behind to see what happened to them, we always found the dead ones buried here."

"It is so beautiful," I said. "My mother and father are alive. They're growing."

"The Seneca sachems held closed council to discuss the burials and, after our medicine man consulted the spirits, the sachems decided we should abort all our efforts to destroy the Valley of Day-Glo. We felt that the Honio'o were honoring our dead and, for the first time in the history of humankind, they were showing proper respect to the North American Iroquois Indians. Although the entirety of their culture deserved to be destroyed, we would let the keepers of the valley live, and use the valley as our new burial ground."

I knelt down and rested my cheek against the dome. "They used to cry," I said. "The Honio'o. When a loved one perished, they would shed water through their eyes, and then they would feel better. It was a healing ritual."

"Have you not heard the tale of Niganega'a, the spirit of little waters and medicine powder?" she said softly.

"No."

"Then I shall tell it."

We sat together, holding hands, and Dewutiowa'is told me her story:

"When Hed'iohe began to bake the white- and yellow- and dark-skinned tribes, and Sagowenota began to destroy his oceans, of utmost importance became a way to save the North American Iroquois Indians from the rapidly changing hazardous environmental conditions. So they called upon Niganega'a, the spirit of the little waters and medicine powder.

"Niganega'a said, 'With my medicine powders I will change the little waters inside all of the Iroquois red men so that they will be able to conserve their bodily fluids during the baking process by producing very little urine and exceptionally dry feces. Then I will raise their body temperatures so that they might conserve even more water. From this day forward, I will lower their metabolic rate to reduce their need for water, and I will eliminate their sudoriferous glands and ducts and give them the gift of internal sweat, so that they will always have a generous supply of water in their bodies and never suffer dehydration. My medicine powders will also allow the nostrils of the Iroquois to open and close to keep out the deadly choking sands and allow their nasal cavities to moisten and cool the air they breathe. And their eyes shall adapt to the bright red light and their bodies to the anthropogenic gases. All of this I will do so that the North American Iroquois Indians may survive the wrath of the spirits.'

"And with this, Niganega'a released his medicine powder into the air, and the little waters inside all of the Iroquois red men were forever changed, and the yellow- and dark- and white-skinned tribes, the Honio'o, who could not survive the deadly effects of their own industries, perished in a most agonizing fashion."

"I wonder if leaving us waterless was such a good idea," I said. "Niganega'a might have left us some tears to shed. That was how the Honio'o would release their great emotional stress. I think watering was a very important practice for the Honio'o."

Dewutiowa'is wrapped her strong arms around my waist and kissed my neck, a light, surprisingly gentle and affectionate peck. She then stood and moved away from me. "In the Pre-Reddening age, there was plenty of time for such things as emotional watering. Here, now, in our world, there is only time for survival or death. In the Valley of Day-Glo, death may become life, but outside, life becomes death very quickly."

I detected a note of urgency in her tone. She loaded slugs into the chamber of her shotgun, unsheathed her knife, and began to sharpen it upon a nearby stone. I heard a voice echo through the huge cavern—a war cry! One of the Independents. I could not tell which tribe. Apparently, the Oniat'ga had obtained reinforcements. This did not bode well for the Seneca. They were surely defeated.

I stood beside her. "You knew they were coming. Why didn't you leave? Why didn't you try to escape?"

"What matter? Shortly, there will be no place for the Seneca to hide. We will all be tracked and killed. Better to die facing the enemy than running from them."

"So, we shall make our last stand here," I said. "This is a good place to die."

"You are not going to die today."

"What do you mean?"

"When the Independents are within firing range, I shall force you out into the open at gunpoint, with your hands bound behind your back. This will prove to the Independents that you were my prisoner, and that I have chosen to die an honorable death and not take the life of an innocent captive. You will be safe. Then, if I am lucky, my own death will come quickly and painlessly."

The voices drew closer, echoing eerily off the surrounding cavern walls. War cries. Death shrieks. The enemy closing in. Dewutiowa'is appeared completely undaunted. A breed apart she was, yes, definitely, and I admired her so. I reached into my pocket and pulled out my mother's hatpin. "I would like you to have this."

Dewutiowa'is looked confused for a moment, making me think she had never before received a gift of any sort and, therefore, knew not what to do with mine. She could not look me in the eyes, but took the hatpin from me and stuck it into her black-pleated skirt. She arranged the bolt-action rifles near at hand among the rocks and positioned her hips between two boulders.

More shouts. Gunshots now. The Indians fired rounds of ammunition into the air as they wailed their death shrieks.

"They have much cause for celebration," said Dewutiowa'is. "It appears they have routed my people, and now they have discovered the legendary Valley of Day-Glo. This day shall be remembered by the Independents for many years to come."

I reached into my rear pocket and withdrew my Ruger .22-caliber semi-automatic pistol. The gun was loaded, and now, of course, I knew how to use it. One had only to close one's eyes and squeeze the trigger. I was also in possession of an extra clip. "I will stand and fight beside you."

"If you have a chance to survive, you must take it."

"Survival, my good woman, means nothing to me. I realize that now. Take my word for it. Once you reach the Land of the Dead, I have come to learn by means I cannot begin to describe to you, one discovers that nothing matters at all."

Dewutiowa'is watched the Independents descend the cliffs and ledges and begin to circle. "Have you lost your mind?" she asked.

"I assure you, yes, I most certainly have."

She aimed one of the .30-06 bolt-action rifles she had taken from the Oniat'ga, pulled the trigger, and a shot rang out, shocking my ears. She jerked the bolt, a shell kicked into the air, and she fired again and again, and then tossed the rifle aside. It clattered among the rocks. She picked up the other .30-06 and took aim.

"I must tell you something," she said. "When I was a child and my grandmother was alive, she used to tell me stories. Some of the stories she told me were secret stories." She fired. This time I heard an Indian howl. "One day, she told me something and made me promise to remember it forever. She told me that I had another name, a name other than Dewutiowa'is and Exploding Wren. She told me my name was A Woman of Paris."

"*A Woman of Paris*! A classic Charlie Chaplin film from the Pre-Reddening year of 1923. A drama about an innocent country girl who travels to Paris to become the lover of a rich philanderer."

Dewutiowa'is squeezed off another shot. "Of course, I knew it was blasphemous to the Indian spirits to carry such a name, but the more I tried to forget it, the more I remembered it." The Independents fired at us from many directions. A volley of shots pinged off the surrounding boulders. We ducked behind the rocks. Dust and slivers of stone flew. "I always hated my grandmother for that. When she died, I spat on her grave and cursed her. Now I forgive her. I believe she was opening my heart to you, Danny. I believe she was foretelling my death."

Dewutiowa'is stood and fired two more rounds, then tossed aside the last Oniat'ga rifle. She took up her shotgun. "Your moment has arrived. If you do not go now, I fear your fate shall be sealed tragically with mine. Unfortunately, a shotgun is a close-range weapon."

"Woman of Paris," said I. She turned to look at me. I stood and held up the Ruger. "I shall stand beside my companion in battle. I have made up my mind."

"I love you," she said, showing her fangs. For the first time in my life, I felt an odd stirring in my loins. It seemed to be connected to other parts of my body—a roiling in my stomach, a pattering of my heart, a tingling in my fingers and toes. Was I physically attracted to this woman? Was such a thing possible? I would never know for sure. Death was upon me now.

Dewutiowa'is turned once again to face the enemy. I positioned myself behind her and watched the Independents close in, their torches flaring. There were too many of them to count. They hopped from boulder to boulder, some of them wearing blue jeans and windbreakers, others wearing Fila sweatpants and hooded jerseys, others outfitted in corduroys and flannel plaids. They barked and hollered and shot at us. Their bullets ricocheted off the rocks and the great dome, the place of miracles.

They became bolder when they noticed we had ceased to return fire. A few of them stepped out into the open and crouched forward. One broke from the pack and dashed headlong at our position, whooping and waving a maroon-colored Louisville Slugger baseball bat. Dewutiowa'is stood from behind her rock and fired her Remington shotgun, blasting him to a bloody pulp only a few steps away. But more came, fanning out in front of us.

"Was it worth it?" I asked her. "I mean, do the Seneca really believe in the day Turtle went to war? All of this fighting and killing, just to squash the Honio'o ways, because of some crazy, secret weapon. Was it worth it, to see it all end like this?"

She turned to me, her pudgy face sad and weary. I had never seen her so clearly distraught. But there was no doubt in her voice when she said, "The

Great Spirit has spoken."

I knew then it was time for us to die. I took a step back from Dewutiowa'is, aimed my Ruger in the general vicinity of the approaching enemy, and closed my eyes:

"AIYEEEEEEEEEE-YICK-YICK-EEEEEEEEEEEEEoh—!" I cried.

And then I fired. BLAST BLAST BLAST BLAST BLAST—ten shots in all, as fast as my finger would allow.

I opened my eyes, released the first clip, reached into my rear pocket and grabbed the second. I jammed it into the butt of my gun, knowing at any moment a bat or an axe or a bullet would end my life.

And then I saw her, Dewutiowa'is, Exploding Wren, A Woman of Paris, dead at my feet, a victim of my own blind fury. I had plastered her with a full complement of .22-caliber bullets.

The Independents swarmed our position among the rocks in a mad rush. I screamed and dropped the Ruger. They fell upon me, raised me upon their shoulders, and began to chant, "DAN-NY! DAN-NY! DAN-NY ...!"

"Dewutiowa'is!" I cried. But in the crush of bodies, I could not see her. I could only imagine her indelicate form riddled with bullets discharged from my own gun, her remains trampled, her internal organs ripped from her belly in the same manner in which she had dealt death to so many of her enemies.

"DAN-NY! DAN-NY! DAN-NY! DAN-NY ...!"

"Oh, Dewutiowa'is," I said. "I love you! I love you ... I love you ..."

⟡ So the good-for-nothing asexual boy became a war hero.

You win some, you lose some.

⟡ This is the story of my heroic struggle as told to me by a stranger several days after the fall of Seneca City:

A small party of mighty S'hondowek'owa warrior women attacked Mother and Father and me on the plains. Father was mortally wounded,

Mother injured, at which point I single-handedly fought off our attackers and, with what strength yet remained to me, hauled Father, not wanting his body desecrated, and Mother, seeking medical attention for her wound, to the Oniat'ga outpost. We were surprised inside the cave by the attack of yet another mighty S'hondo warrior, who had apparently tried to kill us, but, finding herself outnumbered, took Mother hostage in a desperate attempt to gain whatever victory she might claim.

I would not allow Mother to be taken prisoner, so I bravely gave chase through the caves, once again dragging Father's body along with me for fear it might be mauled should it fall into the hands of the enemy. I am given credit for clearly marking our trail so we could be tracked through the caves by the Independent warriors—ah, at last a truth, although I performed no such service intentionally—thus leading the Independents to the legendary Valley of Day-Glo, the most sought-after treasure in the history of the new Indian Age.

There at the valley, after an exhaustive hunt, I, too, was ambushed and taken prisoner by the S'hondowek'owa warrior woman, where I soon learned that the wound to my mother had proved too much for her to bear, and she had succumbed to death.

When the final battle began in front of the botanical garden, I awaited my opportunity to steal one of my enemy's guns—in this case, a Ruger .22-caliber semiautomatic pistol—and then pumped the filthy S'hondo full of lead, thus avenging the deaths of my parents.

⤺ In a matter of days, the victorious Independents established the New Order and dismantled the Seneca League of Nations. Father The Outlaw Josey Wales had been right all along. "History," he had said over and over again during his lifetime, until he had become a hopeless nuisance, "repeats itself."

The chiefs awarded me a seat on the Independent Council because I was the last remaining Gushedon'dada, because I was a war hero, but most of all because the people demanded it.

I thought often of Dewutiowa'is. What really happened during our final battle at the botanical garden outside the Valley of Day-Glo? I could not believe that I had aimed so poorly I had accidentally killed her. Could she have purposely leaped into the line of my fire? That would have assured her a quick death at the hands of the man she loved, rather than a horrible agonizing finish devised by the enemies she so despised. But to intentionally end one's life would have been considered an unforgivable act of cowardice to a mighty S'hondowek'owa warrior woman.

Could she have known that to create the illusion of my killing her would not only have saved my life but made me a war hero as well? Is it possible that the Exploding Wren loved me that much? Dewutiowa'is once said that if one has an opportunity to survive, one must take it. She also said that survival was the only true measure of strength. Perhaps she was right after all. Perhaps I was a strong man all along just waiting to blossom.

⤚ Often, in those early days of the New Order, I traveled to the valley and sought Father's sage advice, but he had not spoken to me since Mother joined him in death, and I was left to wonder if the two outrageous lovebirds had renewed their kinship. Or perhaps Father had been working tirelessly on the project he had once discussed with me that would allow people to pursue lives uninvolved in their own existence, so that in death they might relax and enjoy their feelings throughout all eternity. Or, most likely, Father had become so deeply rooted in being and nothingness, in the Land of Who Cares? and What's the Difference?, that he no longer felt the inclination to speak.

* * D A N N Y, R E D E U X * *

After the fall of the Seneca Indians, the chiefs of the Independent Iroquois Nations planned for the future by organizing the tribes into a coalition of argumentative nincompoops.

I found that I had little tolerance for haggling with the chiefs. I started skipping meetings and napping during the day, and taking long walks alone late at night to clear my head of the council's aimless chatter. I made sure to be present whenever there was a vote, just so that I could publicly disagree with their ridiculous plans. For a long time, this display of public dissension was my only sense of joy and purpose, although I was openly scorned by the council and inevitably voted down and silenced.

One night, as I was walking, I noticed the chiefs all sitting around the council fire. Official business usually took place during the day. I decided to stroll over and butt in, just to see what they were talking about. When I reached the council fire, the chiefs stared at me coldly.

"Good evening, gentlemen," I said.

For a moment, none of the six chiefs replied, a very odd occurrence among these blathering idiots (with the exception of Chief High Anxiety, who was prone to stuttering and rarely spoke).

"We were just discussing your role on the Independent Council," said Chief Nitwit, named after the 1935 musical comedy *The Nitwits*, starring Betty Grable. The chief had a flat nose, a thin face, and a cockeyed, dumb-struck look about him that he carried easily.

"In my absence, you were discussing my role?" I asked, amused.

"Yes. And we have come to the conclusion that you are undermining our leadership and making us all look silly and incompetent."

I supposed this was true. I did not feel badly about it. In fact, someone needed to do it and, because I was the only member of the council who was not a real chief, I was probably the best person for the job. "I can see where you might draw that conclusion. I would apologize if I thought I should."

Chief Ed Wood cleared his throat. He had an oddly wide overbite and an untamed mustache. He was named after the 1994 movie *Ed Wood*, dramatizing the life of one of the worst American filmmakers to ever point a camera. "You are a hero among the people. They listen to you decry our efforts to bring structure and direction to the New Order, and this makes it difficult to implement a plan that all Indians are willing to follow."

"If you came up with a good plan, I would have nothing to decry. But you seem to be inviting criticism. First you decide to centralize the tribes, then you decide to decentralize the government. First you decide to allow free trade, then you decide to control the Honio'o treasures and how they are traded. First you decide to create a government workforce that includes building, cleaning, sanitation, and military service, and then you decide to contract out the work in a free-market environment to the lowest bidders. The list goes on and on. Contradiction, shortsightedness, wasted time and energy—"

Chief Nitwit waved off my objections with a flip of his wrist. "It may take ten or twelve or a hundred bad ideas to come up with one good plan. That is the way of good government. You wear your inexperience like a noose around your neck, but it is strangling all of us. What about our food distribution program? No one goes hungry now."

"You're not going to try and take credit for that, are you? The women's auxiliary came up with the food plan while you were still arguing about where to sit at the table."

"Governing is a complicated business," Nitwit said. "It is easy for you to criticize us when you make no effort to contribute. You have never been a chief. You do not understand the governing process or its importance."

This was neither entirely true nor false. Although I had never been a chief, my first act as a councilman was to develop special legislation and create a free Indian reservation for the captured Seneca. The council had planned to kill or enslave every last one of them. I rallied the people around my cause and persuaded the chiefs to establish the reservation, arguing that at least some of the old ways the Seneca had fought for must be preserved, that there was a place for Indian tradition, too, in the new country. True, this had been my one and only shining moment as a councilman, and I never thought that anyone actually agreed with me (not even the Seneca whose lives I'd saved seemed excited about it). But it was better than nothing.

"Maybe you are correct, Chief Nitwit," said I. "But in all fairness, if I do not understand the intricacies of governing, you do not understand the importance of criticism."

I waited out the silence. Keeping my mouth shut was one game at which I knew I could beat them. Finally, Chief Ed Wood spoke: "We are asking you to leave the Independent Council."

I should have expected this. The warning signs were all there. I had maltreated them past the point of mere indignation. We disagreed on everything, and, quite frankly, we did in fact come from different worlds. They had always been chiefs, and I had always been an Indian. Still, I felt blindsided and betrayed.

"We want you to resign," Nitwit said. "If we have to vote you out, it will be more difficult. The people will complain and put up a fuss. But we will do it anyway. We have no choice. We have much to accomplish in this critical time of the New Order, and you are making it impossible to progress."

Insects swirled wildly around the council fire. A night bird shrieked nightmarishly. The chiefs stared at me, twelve eyes blinking. I could feel the heat of the fire, the round night air, the fear and condemnation of the chiefs. I was tired, annoyed, hurt. But I knew myself well enough to know that after the emotions came and went, I would feel relieved to be rid of these bicker-ing fools. Perhaps that was what I had wanted all along, to be thrown out so I would not have to walk away, a readymade excuse to turn my back on the unpleasant realities of life, the arguing, the expectations and disappoint-ments, the abject futility of it all.

"P-p-p-please don't m-m-make us vote," said High Anxiety. And I couldn't help but think that the comedy genius Mel Brooks would have appreciated his stutter, rudely breaking the silence at such a grave and ran-dom moment. After all, in comedy, timing was everything, and so was knowing when to end a joke.

I laughed and walked away.

↷ I missed Mother Who's Afraid of Virginia Woolf? and Father The Outlaw Josey Wales. Most of all, I missed Dewutiowa'is, the Exploding Wren, A Woman of Paris. I missed her comforting words and strong physi-cal presence. I missed her foolish optimism and tenacious personality and fetid stench. I missed her unconditional love and the way she doted over me, although I could not gratify her sexual desires.

Therefore, soon after I resigned from the council, I packed a few posses-sions and returned to the magnificent Valley of Day-Glo, the place where all those I had cared about in the world had passed on without me.

I built a small stone hut twenty long strides from the wall of the globe, where I could view the entranceway to the great blooming paradise within, where a statue of my former self, Broadway Danny Rose, looked eerily down upon me from a nearby wedge of stone. On the very spot where the final battle for the Valley of Day-Glo occurred, a stonecutter of Gako'go descent had sculpted a statue of me. There I stood in granite, pistol in hand, dressed in my Dockers and penny loafers and the tattered remains of my button-down oxford shirt, my foot atop a fallen S'hondowek'owa warrior woman, the Exploding Wren, the only woman I had ever loved.

I had come to think of the statue as an entirely different person. The foot that rested eternally upon the fallen S'hondo warrior mocked me, was not my foot at all. The gun was not my gun. The proud and angry face cast artfully in granite belonged to a stranger. The artist had transformed me into a mirage, a ghostly visage, a false edifice handcrafted by a clever hand to do nothing more than delight the ignorant masses who came to visit the valley. The truth of me was somehow lost in the carver's stone as surely as it was lost to me.

⌐ Soon I fell to fasting and meditating for days upon days, hoping to make contact with the dead—the only people I felt close to at all anymore. Other cave dwellers came to stare from afar at my slowly degenerating form. Hypnotized as they were by the great glowing valley, and wanting to live within reach of its magical light, they found me a sad and desperate curiosity beyond even their understanding. Perhaps because of the lost look in my eyes, they could tell that I no longer belonged in this world and was, in fact, already part of the other.

We never spoke, the cave dwellers and I, but occasionally they took pity on me and brought me food, for there was food aplenty in the deep caverns—small rodents, rich fat worms, plump snakes, bugs galore, and an abundance of roots—for anyone interested in eating it. Sometimes I would sample their offerings, not because I had any great interest in extending my life (I assure you I did not), but mostly because I didn't want to offend them. I would gladly have perished of my own neglect at the foot of the valley, but I could not abide the bad manners required of me to carry it off. I viewed my life as a waiting room, where, eventually, the spirit S'hondowek'owa, the Death Herald, would venture out, take me by the hand, gently explain to me that I was, at last, next in line, and lead me into the final Longhouse, the Happy Hunting Grounds of the Great Spirit, the Land of the Dead.

To escape the trappings of my own mind, I began experimenting with the highly hallucinogenic flesh of cacti. At first, the dizziness and visions they brought unnerved me, but once I gave in to the delirium that hid just beneath the surface of the discomfort, I began to crave the slow, numbed inner-workings of my brain and the loss of my physical body that accompanied it, making me forget even the severe vomiting and toxic pain it produced.

Finally, one day while swimming in my delirium, after a long spell of utter disorientation brought on by self-deprivation and cacti juice, Dewutiowa'is appeared to me in a dream vision. I had crawled out of my hut to gaze upon our stone images, at which point she rolled over beneath my granite foot, winked and waved at me, her crenellated smile unnaturally charming for the hulking warrior I had come to know and love.

"*Danny, my beautiful boy, my eternal love,*" Dewutiowa'is said, "*how the heck are you?*"

"I am very, very tired," I said, "and I long to be with you and Mother and Father in the final resting place. Have you come for me at last?"

"*Come for you? No, I don't think so. I have only come to share in your longing for a moment. Yearning defined our relationship in your world, and it is all that I know here in the Land of the Dead.*"

"How strange. Father spoke of a death place that held no hope or sadness or joy or grief or yearnings whatsoever—a sprawling, everlasting kingdom of Who Cares? and What's the Difference?"

She seemed to smirk at this. The expression did not suit her; it split her face in an awkward, unpleasantly stony way.

"*I suspect death is different for everyone. I think we create our own deaths based on the lives we leave behind. It would have been nice to know that ahead of time, of course. I might have lived differently had I known my death depended on it. I might have spent more time in love and less time killing and eating the organs of my slain enemies, which, in the long run, seems to have done me no good at all.*"

Father had regrets, too. I remembered his list of the things he would have done differently during his lifetime had he been given the chance.

Apparently, at least in one significant way, there was no difference between the Land of the Living and the Land of the Dead. "Are you my harbinger of doom, as Father The Outlaw Josey Wales had forewarned? Is it time I journeyed to the Happy Hunting Grounds? Please, say it is so. Take me with you. I no longer have a place here among the living."

Dewutiowa'is rested her chin on the palms of her hands. *"I don't think so, Danny. I don't feel like a harbinger of doom. If I were, I'm sure I would know it, even in the Land of the Dead. But all I feel here is cold. It's terribly cold here. Did your father tell you that? You shiver until another soul grabs you and hangs on and warms you. But the hanging on is difficult. You have to be the perfect match, you have to find your soul mate or eventually your grip will loosen, close in upon itself, and the warmth of the other soul will slip away."*

In my weakened state, it hadn't struck me at first that this meeting was exactly what I had been hoping and praying for since I began my meditations—a visit from the dead. I crawled on my hands and knees toward the talking stone icon. "Have you seen Mother and Father? Have you spoken with them? How are they doing? Are they together and madly in love in the Land of the Dead?"

"I don't know, Danny. I'm sorry. As I said, death is different for everyone. There is a lot of light around me, and many different shadowy shapes. And voices, voices everywhere. Some of the voices are singing sweet, perfect, wordless melodies. Others are soft and haunting, murmuring like the wind across the sand dunes. And there are other voices speaking bizarre, twisted languages I cannot even begin to understand. So far, I have recognized only one other person in the Land of the Dead."

"Who? Who is that person?"

"Oniata."

"Oniata?"

"Yes. I think she might be my everlasting soul mate, but I have not yet been able to grab hold of her. We have only passed through each other. Do you know the Iroquois myth of the most beautiful Indian woman to ever walk the Earth?

Her name was Oniata."

Father and Mother had told me many Iroquois Indian tales, but I did not recall the woman named Oniata. "No, I do not believe I have ever heard of her."

"*Then I shall tell you her story.*"

And so, Dewutiowa'is began the tale of Oniata, the most beautiful Native American girl to ever walk the Earth.

 ⌐ *The Great Spirit sent a maiden child more beautiful than the spirit women of the Sky Kingdom to the house of the great Iroquois chief, Tiogaughwa, and the child grew to womanhood beside the chief's fire. Her name was Oniata. Her eyes were as dark as the deep pools hidden in mountain caverns. The Great Spirit made her golden hair from the rays of the sun. Her feet were so delicate that only the skins of fawns could be used to make her moccasins. Her complexion was as white as snow and as fair as the paleface Honio'o, who would not come until thousands and thousands of years later. When she laughed, the noisy waters in the mountain streams became quiet with shame."*

Dewutiowa'is paused for a moment and closed her eyes, as if imagining the great beauty she herself had described.

"*Over all the land spread the story of this wondrous maiden. All the tribes journeyed to see her. Never before had the Indians seen one so beautiful. The wise men whispered that she must have been sent by the Great Spirit from the Happy Hunting Grounds to show the Indians what awaited them at the end of their days, when they would travel alone to the Last Longhouse, their final resting place.*

"*Tiogaughwa, meanwhile, was filled with pride at the attention shown his daughter. His lodge became rich with presents of rare furs and strings of wampum that the braves laid at her feet. He could have allied his tribe with the most powerful Iroquois in all the land, for the greatest chiefs and the most renowned warriors sought to wed the beautiful Oniata.*

"But, alas, as soon as the young chiefs and warriors came to visit, they lost their hearts for the hunt and spent their days trying to win the approval of Oniata. They performed daring feats of agility and endurance, vying with each other until even the strongest of them could not carry on. Some sank exhausted and dying in the fields, crying for Oniata to notice them before their eyes closed to the world forever."

Dewutiowa'is turned slightly so that my granite foot now rested upon her hip. It hurt me to see her pinned beneath my foot like a trapped animal, but she seemed unaware of it, and any discomfort was apparently mine alone to bear.

"The situation became worse and worse until one day the chiefs and warriors were surprised to see the council place filled with the women and maidens from all the surrounding tribes. They had left their lodges and fires to the care of the old men and children. They took the places usually occupied by the wise men of the Five Nations and refused to leave until the chiefs and sachems came to the council fires.

"Finally, the men came. When they sat around the fire, a silence fell that was almost intolerable. The tension in the air and the passion burning in the hearts of the women lay heavily upon the assemblage like the breath of an angry bear."

"The women must have been very sad." My muscles trembled from weakness as I tried to crawl closer to Dewutiowa'is. I wanted to be close to her again. I wanted to touch her. I wanted to be her soul mate. I remembered how she sat with me that last day of her life, holding my hands as she told me the tale of Niganega'a, spirit of the little waters. Hearing her voice again reminded me of that lovely, quiet time before I foolishly blasted her to death with my Ruger pistol.

"Indeed, they were sad, my love. The Indian wives chanted the tragic song of a deserted lover, a song normally heard only in the lonely lodge of a woman whose husband has left her to join another woman more favorable to his fancy. When the last of their song had finally faded into the wind, the women and the men sat a long time with bowed heads.

"Finally, Waunopeta, the wife of Tiogaughwa—a tall, lean young princess who carried herself regally, and who might have been the talk of the young men had it not been for Oniata—stepped before the chiefs and sachems and spoke for the other women.

"'We have come, my brothers, to tell you that Oniata has led our warriors and husbands astray. The wives and papooses are sick with loneliness and hunger. No longer do the smiles of the red maidens bring joy to the young braves. We plait our hair with flowers and wampum and sit in the forests to await the coming of our mates; but the young braves come no more to court us, nor can they be found on the track of the deer or the panther. They loll with the dogs in the shadow of Oniata's wigwam and glare like wounded boar. They are dead to us, and the hearts of the Indian maidens are full of sorrow.'"

Dewutiowa'is sat up and opened her arms dramatically, as if she knew the suffering in Waunopeta's heart. My stone foot now rested upon her broad shoulder.

"'Have the red maidens lost their beauty? Can they never again bring life to the hearts of the young braves? My sisters have told me to say that if they no longer please the hearts of the red men, they ask to be sent on the long journey to the Happy Hunting Grounds, never to return. Waunopeta, wife of Tiogaughwa, has spoken.'

"As Waunopeta took her place among the women, there was a sudden movement at the outer edge of the circle, and Oniata stepped into the center of the council place. Unbeknownst to anyone, she had wrapped herself in a blanket and had listened to Waunopeta's speech. Oniata was dressed in the richest skins, and her hair fell like a cloud of sun-kissed dew over her slender shoulders. A startled exclamation came from the tribes-people as this vision of wondrous beauty stood among them. Many had never seen her."

Dewutiowa'is sat up straight and crossed her legs. She reached up and patted my foot, which was now perched upon the crown of her head.

"Oniata, as frightened as a hunted fawn, looked at the red faces around the council fire. Then she spoke: 'I am here to say that I have not asked for the love of your young braves. They came to my wigwam and sang of passion, but I covered my ears with beaver skins and refused to listen. When I went forth into the forest, the men appeared before me like thunderclouds, and I ran and hid again in my wigwam, denied the comfort of the wind and rain and sun and moon. The warriors came to me, pleading, but I scolded them and begged them to return to their homes. They would not listen.*

"'I love my sisters and my tribe. Therefore, I shall leave the land of the red men. I shall disguise myself with the help of the Great Spirit and journey far away, beyond the mountains and the Great Lakes, and the braves will return to life for the red maidens and woo them with love songs, while the warriors will again go to their wigwams where their wives and papooses await them. I ask only that my people speak kindly of me when I am gone.'*

"Then the circle of men and women parted so that Oniata could walk through them. The great chief, Tiogaughwa, started forward to grab hold of his beautiful daughter, tears streaming down his face, but Waunopeta stood in his path, and he knew that Oniata must go."*

Dewutiowa'is slumped forward, and her face looked cold and stony once again.

"Such a sad tale," I said. "What was the purpose of Oniata's great beauty? Did she bring the Iroquois Indians nothing but grief and pain? How could that be so?"

"Wait, Danny. There is more."*

I sighed. Frankly, I had been hoping that she'd reached the end of her tale. Most Indian myths, to their great advantage, were short, requiring only a modest attention span, and, under my current depleted condition, I would have appreciated a bit of focus and brevity. But Dewutiowa'is went on ...

"Many moons passed. The young braves once again wooed their red maidens, and the wives of the warriors rejoiced in the return of their husbands. Winter came and cast its white cloud over the land, and the frosts locked the rivers in ice. The great Tiogaughwa mourned his daughter in his lonely* *wigwam, and his heart sang her death song as he sat before the fireplace, in which no fire would have burned if not for his good wife, Waunopeta. The old chief asked the Great Spirit to return his daughter. But Oniata came not to the home of the chief or the people she had known all her life.*

"The warm winds returned, but the chief's heart was still heavy. He had no words for the council, although his wife begged him to take his place among the wise men; and he had no strength for the hunt, although his wife told him it was wrong for others to feed them. But Tiogaughwa's ear listened only for the lost music of Oniata."

"Are you done yet?"

"Almost, Danny."

"Excellent."

"Finally, one day, Tiogaughwa, stricken with grief, left his home, left his wife and people, and followed the path that Oniata had taken. Wherever he went, he mentioned her name. No Indians had seen her because of the Great Spirit's disguise, but the wildflowers raised their heads and told him that Oniata had touched them, and Tiogaughwa caught the fragrance of her skin on their petals. When the dew and the rain fell from the trees, he could feel Oniata's cool breath in the air. In this way, he tracked her deep into the forest.

"Tiogaughwa never looked back, for he was afraid he might lose the trail, which even a year after her passing was marked by her beauty. So he followed her path forever, never finding her, until he reached the Happy Hunting Grounds, the great Longhouse, his final resting place in the Sky Kingdom. It is said he camps outside her wigwam there, where he can rejoice in her beauty throughout eternity."

☞ When Dewutiowa'is finished her tale, she returned to her original position under my stone shoe. Her granite chest rose and fell in a long, weary breath.

"I do not know if that is a frightening tale or a beautiful one," I said honestly. "But I see the wisdom of it. Life must have beauty, otherwise we are empty and hollow like poor Chief Tiogaughwa, and, when confronted with the lack of it, we will chase it forever, even if it means death."

"Yes. I am like the sorrowful chief. I must find Oniata. She is the beauty that had been missing from my life. We are soul mates, the lovely Oniata and I. When I first met her here in the Land of the Dead, her warmth nearly melted me. I think that might have been why I was so attracted to you, Danny. Your warmth. And you had a beauty and innocence about you that filled an empty place in me, although it did not work out so well in the end. But now, in death, I have a chance to discover that beauty again and hold it forever. I have been chasing Oniata ever since our souls touched. That is my journey. That is my quest. I must find Oniata. I must be with her. She is the key to my eternal happiness."

"And what is *my* journey? What is my quest here in the Land of the Living? I came to the Valley of Day-Glo seeking answers, or perhaps seeking death. The valley was the beauty that I chose to follow, but now my journey has come to an end. What next? If you are not my harbinger of doom, I fear I have found nothing, and I must face the world again ... alone."

Dewutiowa'is wrinkled her nose. Small chips of dirt and stone fell from her face like detritus from an aged and forgotten temple. She was slowly returning to the rigid monolith of the stonecutter's design.

"You must live until you die," said she. *"What more can I say? When you are alive, the world is always much too urgent. All who breathe rush forward foolishly, blindly, and in terror. My advice to you is this: Do not hurry down the road that leads you to your death, my handsome boy. Live your life. Claim it. I believe that soon another journey will present itself to you. Follow it with passion, not fear. Death will find you in its own good time. It finds everyone sooner or later. It doesn't matter what god you love, or spirit you pray to, or whose rules you obey or disobey. It will do you no good in the end, when your body rots and you turn to dust and find yourself wandering in the Land of the Dead. Just live."*

I tried to crawl to Dewutiowa'is, to join her, in spite of her wisdom, but I collapsed, faint from hunger and exhaustion. I held out my hand to her, but she left me alone with the same silent finality with which she'd disappeared so long ago, the day I'd shot and killed her just outside of paradise.

⌐ I thought that my vision of Dewutiowa'is was nothing more than my own delirium, a sad commentary on the desperation, hunger, and hopelessly addled mind of a depressed man, a false warrior, a cacti addict, a useless asexual. But the dream vision did not end there. Although my eyesight was blurred, and there seemed to be smoke in my mind, a figure stepped forward, moving slowly like a spirit dancer in the luminous light cast from the Valley of Day-Glo. It was a woman.

Dewutiowa'is? No, the shape was wrong. This figure was much more lithe, her steps graceful. The woman who moved forward became clearer in my mind. Became ... beautiful ...

As soon as I saw her, there could be no doubt. Her face was as flawless and pale as sun-dried sand, her eyes as black and glittering as midnight. She stood tall and straight and seemed to float on air.

Oniata?

She *must* be Oniata.

She was not wearing the traditional Indian garb that Dewutiowa'is had described to me in the myth. No, this woman was wearing men's clothing from the long lost Honio'o Age—a smartly tailored two-piece, double-breasted suit of delicate, understated tweed and the finest quality wool. She was wearing a bold Panama hat, a man's dress shirt, and a gold silk tie. Her shoes, which I now faced nose to wingtip, were shiny black-and-white leather with the inscription *Brooks Brothers* scrolled handsomely along the instep.

I choked and coughed uncontrollably, and my empty belly tightened around my shrunken ribs like a noose. This was how a starving desert dog must feel, thought I, before it died of emptiness and was devoured by its own kind.

"*Oniata*," I whispered, appalled at the stink of my own breath, the ragged condition of my clothing, the neglect of my body. My appearance in front of such beauty embarrassed me. "You dress like a man, but I know you. I know you. You are Oniata."

She unbuttoned her suit jacket, removed her Panama hat, and knelt beside me. Her hair formed an aura of gold around her face. She gathered my bony torso in her arms. She was soft, but strong. Her lips were as full and round as the fruit of the Valley of Day-Glo. She tilted her lovely head and looked at me sadly. A strand of her perfect flaxen hair loosed itself and fell artfully to the side of her face.

She said, "It is true what they have told me. You have begun the lonely journey to the final Longhouse. But I cannot let you die. I'm sorry, Broadway Danny Rose. Your people need you. I cannot let you go to the spirit world. Forgive me, but I must save your life and take you home where you belong. Forgive me."

At that moment, cradled in her arms, starving and dying and in anguish, I would have forgiven her anything. I wanted to raise my hand, touch her cheek, tell her that I would follow her anywhere, to the ends of the Earth if she were to ask it of me. I remember thinking that I must speak to her and steal the sorrow from her eyes, or I had no right to live. I must tell her what I had learned from Dewutiowa'is. There was so much to say.

But I did not have the strength. I was finished. I was in the hands of fate and destiny and Oniata. She would save me or I would die. It was as simple as that. I would follow her beauty through the Land of the Living, or her beauty would carry me into the Land of the Dead, where I, too, would no doubt chase it throughout eternity. In truth, I did not care how it played out. In that moment, I gave myself over to Oniata. I gave her my body and soul and awaited the outcome.

➴ I woke to the sight of an open lean-to perched over me, and the warm glow and gentle crackling of a campfire. It was a painful wakening, the kind that made me regret the complicated arrangement of my skin and bones and muscles and nerves. But I was hungry for the first time in many moons, and it was the smell of roasted cave rodent and fresh sweetroot that finally forced consciousness upon me, an unwelcome but necessary visit.

I wanted to eat. Oniata fed me. I wanted to walk and talk with Oniata, but I could not. The long hard sleep of those who must heal overcame me again and again in between brief meals and cups of water gently dispatched from Oniata's hands. My wants were inconsequential. Only my needs mattered.

During my long days of recovery, I did not tell Oniata about my conversation with Dewutiowa'is. What had seemed perfectly rational in my delirium would undoubtedly make me sound crazy. In fact, I did not talk about myself at all. There was little I could tell her of my past that she did not already know, or profess to know. I had become somewhat of a celebrity in the world of the New Order: Broadway Danny Rose, bloody revolutionary, the last surviving member of the Gushedon'dada, the man who had turned his back on the Independent Council to live the life of a hermit outside the Valley of Day-Glo. Broadway Danny Rose, the war hero, the hopeless asexual, had become a bit of a legend.

I was not interested in any of this. I wanted only to learn about Oniata— who she was, where she came from, why she had journeyed to the Valley of Day-Glo to find me and save me from myself.

"My name is Mill on the Floss," Oniata said. "I was named after the 2092 Pre-Reddening film, starring Natasia Grove and Dr. James de Goff, based on George Eliot's classic nineteenth-century tragic novel of a family's emotional and financial collapse. But everyone calls me Millie."

"It will be difficult for me to think of you as anyone other than Oniata," I told her. "But I will try."

"You called me Oniata earlier, when you first saw me. Why? Who is Oniata?"

I hesitated. I was not ready to tell her the tale of the most beautiful girl on Earth. "In time I will explain. For now, I will call you Millie." I tested her name in my mouth, Oniata's new name, "Millie." She thought this was funny and laughed at me.

Earlier in the day, Oniata had gathered kindling wood and killed a snake large enough to feed us both. I watched her work as she skinned the snake, cooked it, and separated it into two large portions for our meal.

"Why did you come for me?" I finally asked her.

She put down her knife, sat cross-legged in front of the fire, and told me the following story.

˜ "In the early days of the New Order, when our Indian chiefs struggled for power and to forge the rules of our fledgling society, a great war hero by the name of Broadway Danny Rose climbed to the height of popularity among our people. But Broadway Danny Rose was not happy in his new role as beloved icon, so he turned his back on a life of political haggling to find his own inner peace at the sacred place where he buried his parents.

"The Indian chiefs were happy to see him go, for Broadway Danny Rose, although he did not realize it, was more powerful than all of them combined because the Indian people loved him and trusted him.

"Only when the chiefs saw that they needed the great war hero to support their economic plan did they send the daughter of a powerful chief to lure him out of seclusion. The people, it turned out, did not like the financial plan of their leaders. It was not working out the way they thought it should. With the many new discoveries hidden underneath the decimated mega-city of the once great Seneca, and a sudden potential for uncommon wealth and prosperity among the masses, the Indian people felt their leaders were imposing a plot to separate them from their rightful riches.

"The Indian chiefs grew desperate. They believed in their economic plan and thought it best for the new world. Without a way to manage these new-sprung riches, anarchy and chaos would eventually reign, and their long struggle to free themselves of the Seneca Indians would all be for naught. Therefore, in the way of many great leaders before them, they lied."

I put down my roasted snake and frowned. One of the reasons I had left the New Order was because I had learned that where there was power, there was deception. "What did they say?" I asked the fair Millie, although I had no interest in the lies of the Independent Council. I wished only to hear her voice, which was as light as music.

"There was a small lie," Millie continued, "and a big one. The small lie was that they had held counsel with the great war hero Broadway Danny Rose, and he had approved of their most recent progressive and enlightened economic plan. The big lie was that Broadway Danny Rose would be at the top of this brand new financial structure, that he would be its overseer, its administrator and manager. The trusted hero of the people would return from the Valley of Day-Glo to make sure that the plan was implemented fairly and evenly for everyone."

I sighed, vastly disappointed, not so much in the chiefs who had acted predictably in accordance with their natures, as in Dewutiowa'is, who had not taken me into the Land of the Dead when she had the chance. "I fail to see why the lies of the New Order should concern me. If the Indian leaders have told lies to the people, they must pay for those lies."

"Yes, it would seem a simple matter of right and wrong. But of course there is no such thing as a simple right or wrong, is there? Who will be hurt by the wrongs of the leaders?"

Her logic was irrefutable. "The Indian people, no doubt."

Millie nodded and tasted a bit of roasted snake. I watched her swallow. "The people no longer believe their Indian chiefs," she went on. "They say that you, Danny Rose, have not been seen in a very long time, and they believe their leaders have lied to them and have tried to steal their treasures. Only your return can prevent a revolt and save the economic structure currently in place. The chiefs need you to come back and speak on their behalf. They need you to show yourself, to say that you support their efforts and that their plan is a good one, and everyone can benefit from it. In short, they need you, Broadway Danny Rose, to come home."

"And they have sent you to plead their case."

"I volunteered. I have no political motives. I have no want for power or riches. My only concern is for our people. The Indian chiefs know this. They felt that if you were going to listen to anyone, perhaps it would be me."

That much was certainly true. I was sure they were quite aware of this woman's enchanting beauty. I did not mention that it was the great wise chiefs who had sent me away to begin with. She probably already knew that, and more. "Do you believe in this economic strategy?" I asked Oniata—Millie.

She looked at me earnestly. Her eyes were amulets. As always, when she turned them upon me, I felt a chill along my spine and a tingling in my belly. "To be perfectly honest, I don't know. It might work, but given the alternative ... well ... I believe that without the plan we will be much worse off. The tribes will faction from the New Order, there will be war and struggle and hatred. The peace that has reigned since the fall of the Seneca will collapse. Indian will kill Indian again. The strong will survive, the weak will die, and the people will be farther apart than ever before."

"Who are we to say this is such a horrible destiny? Maybe it is time for the chiefs to fall and the people to rise. Maybe it's time for someone else to run things. Besides, my home is here in my small hut outside the Valley of Day-Glo. It is quiet and peaceful. I sympathize with your dilemma, but I do not wish to return."

Millie must have expected this answer, or if she did not, she handled it with the stoic aplomb she had shown throughout my long recovery. "There is another reason why I think you should come with me," she said.

"What reason is that?"

"The Seneca Indians."

"The Seneca? What about them?"

She shifted into a more comfortable position beside the fire. The skin of her devoured snake lay shredded at her knees. She was wearing her trim, oxford button-down shirt with the collar undone, the long tails of the shirt hanging out, her feet bare. She had brought a number of these shirts with her and changed them often. I liked the look of them and the casual way she wore them. The suit and tie were nice, certainly, but the careless look was stunning and exposed the long plane of her white throat.

"The Independent tribes captured many of the Seneca at the end of the revolution," she said.

"Yes, I know. Everyone was surprised when they surrendered. We had all expected them to fight to the death."

"And the Independent Council established a reservation for them."

"I remember it well, a place where the Seneca could live peacefully and keep the old ways alive. I was instrumental in the legislation—"

"There has been trouble on the reservation," said she.

"Trouble? What do you mean, trouble?"

"After we banished them to the reservation ... we forgot about them."

"Forgot about them? How do you forget about an entire tribe of your most hated enemies?"

"Ignored them, perhaps, is a better way to say it. In all of the excitement of new discoveries, rebuilding the city, societal changes, economic recovery—"

I held up my hand to stop her, for I knew what was coming next. "You ignored the Seneca, and they have grown strong again, and they are threatening to make war on the Independent Nations."

"I am afraid so, I'm ashamed to say. They have a charismatic leader named Madam Limerick who has already attacked some of the smaller villages bordering the city." Millie broke off a piece of sweetroot and worked it between her fingers, meticulously cleaning away the dirt.

I, on the other hand, had lost my appetite. "And it's my fault, of course. Had I not pushed for the legislation, the Seneca warriors would have been executed or imprisoned or put into labor camps, working for the New Order."

"No one blames you, Broadway Danny Rose. But I must be honest. Madam Limerick is a threat, the Independent Council is desperate, and I was told that if you refused to return with me, I should lay on the guilt trip, 'like stone soup on delicate china,' to quote my father the chief." She snapped the sweetroot and crunched a piece between her teeth.

I should have been angry, but I found that the old anger was gone. "Madam Limerick. That's on odd name. What do you know about her?"

Millie shook her head. "Not much. Only that she is named after an ancient form of Honio'o revolutionary poetry."

"How very strange. Honio'o poetry? Are you sure?"

"Yes, that's what I've been told."

I was stalling. Millie probably knew it. She handed me a small piece of sweetroot. I had earned the right as the last surviving member of the once great Gushedon'dada tribe to live my remaining days as I saw fit—alone, depressed, gloomy, forlorn, and addicted to the cacti. But perhaps it was not yet time for me to die. When Mother and I set out with Father The Outlaw Josey Wales in tow so many moons ago, we had begun separate journeys. Theirs had come to an end, but perhaps mine must continue. Dewutiowa'is had told me that soon another journey would present itself, and that I should follow it with passion, not fear. Who better to follow in such a way than the fair Millie? Was not the tale of Oniata a sign?

"Well ... this new threat, it changes things, I suppose. I do feel somewhat responsible."

"Please, Danny, I beg you, come back with me to the land of our people. Not because we need you or you feel guilty, but because maybe, just possibly, the heaviness in your heart will flee like the stag from the hunt. I say this with all sincerity as a person who cares about you, not as an emissary from the Independent Council. I believe there is a chance you will find a reason to live in the new city. Many others have. Why not you?"

I wanted to tell her that I was not like many others, or *any* others for that matter, but I did not want to sound snotty or belligerent. Here, on this earthly plane, I would follow the living Oniata just as my doomed paramour would follow the legend Oniata in the Land of the Dead. Our destinies, it seemed, were entwined once again, or perhaps they had never been broken.

"I will come back with you," I said. "As a favor to you personally, not the Independent Council."

Millie went back to working the sweetroot. The fire crackled and hissed, and the scorched smell of snake filled our small camp. She was wise enough not to thank me. She knew I did not want or need thanks from her or anyone.

"We must leave soon," she said. It was no longer a question. She was anxious now, I could tell. She wanted to get home.

"I am strong enough to travel. We may leave as soon as you wish."

⌁ Our journey out of the caves was more arduous than I expected. I had lost a great deal of strength and vitality during my long hermitage. I could have used more time to rebuild my vigor, but I understood the urgency of Millie's task. She had already lost too much time bringing me back from the brink of death. Madam Limerick was growing stronger every day. We could not have delayed much longer even if we'd wanted to.

Once, when we stopped to rest upon a stone porch overlooking a crystalline basin at the mouth of a wide, hidden grotto, I showed Millie the Chicago Cubs baseball patch I had stripped from Mother's cap. I did not know why I wanted her to see it. I had never showed the patch to anyone else. Perhaps I just needed to share this intimacy with her. Millie had saved my life, after all.

"It's beautiful," she said, delicately running her fingers over the large red C that was the baseball team's logo. She held it in her hands and admired it for a long time before returning it to me. "I think it's sweet that you wanted something of your mother's to remember her by. You are a good man."

"I think I wanted a symbol of her courage and strength. The one thing that I will always remember about Mother Who's Afraid of Virginia Woolf? is that she was a tough old broad. No one could ever take that away from her."

When I was feeling strong again, we carried on. At one point in our journey I asked Millie why she dressed like a man. We were still within the confines of the cave, which I had come to think of fondly over the course of my seclusion. The walls that I had been so afraid of closing in on me when I first entered the caves now gave me strength and a sense of sheltered enclosure.

"At the risk of sounding vain," Millie explained, "I have discovered that I hold great power over men. There is something hypnotizing about my beauty. It leads men to say and do foolish things, sometimes dangerous things, and often strikes them dumb and useless. If I dress like a man and hide my face, I can travel among men for a time. I have developed the ability to control the force of my beauty to a certain extent. I can make it more powerful or hide it when I must. Fortunately when I am with you I don't have to worry about it. As history tells the tale, you are a hopeless asexual."

Looking upon Oniata—Millie—I began to doubt my own history for the first time in my life. "Yes, fortunately for both of us," I said without conviction, "I am a hopeless asexual."

As we journeyed, Mill on the Floss entertained me with tales of great discoveries and new prosperity in the world I had left behind. A new city and hundreds of new buildings had been discovered not far from the Seneca mega-city. The ancient delights of the Honio'o were now commonplace among the Iroquois Indians. A new society had evolved—the first step toward achieving the great economic plan of the Independent Council.

I had to admit that I was growing more curious and perhaps even a little excited at seeing the changes that had taken place since my withdrawal from society. Perhaps some of these changes were indeed as positive as Millie described. Maybe it was time, after all, for me to return to and take part in the common everyday challenges of the common everyday people. What was left in the world, really, after one realized the vast disappointment of the self, if not the universal struggle of others? What was left after one examined the inner cosmos of identity, only to find it lacking, after one explored the imprisonment of his consciousness and saw, quite clearly, the lie and outright absurdity of his sapience? One must reach out, so it would seem. What other choice was there? Perhaps these were questions that only Father The Outlaw Josey Wales could answer for me. Who would understand the mysteries of life, after all, better than the dead?

⮑ Eventually we reached the surface, and I entered the outside world for the first time in many moons.

Indeed, the moon was high and bright when we stepped out of the cave, bright enough to sting my eyes. I was grateful we hadn't emerged during the middle of the day, when the sun was ablaze, when Ende'kagaa'kwa, the brilliant orb, was at its peak.

We traveled for a bit and then slept in the hot night air. I did not sleep well. I was not at all comfortable in the wide-open space that was the outside world. I was frightened by the unfettered topography of the rocky plateaus and sandy dunes, the naked sky overhead, and the desert dogs barking death threats across the dark canyons and into the hidden corners of my mind. It was not only fear of a world I had become unfamiliar with that gave me pause. It was fear of a world that had turned against me in ways I dared not imagine.

Even so, at dawn, still physically drained and feeling nauseous, I met the day with a brave face and, in short order, Millie and I traveled beyond what was once the great Seneca mega-city to the epicenter of the brave new world.

⮑ I had been gone much longer than I thought. Things had changed dramatically. I could not believe the difference. The burned and razed ramshackle huts and longhouses of the Seneca that had once littered the landscape while the New Order was in its infancy were all gone. Now this new city was the capital of the Independent Nations, a teeming metropolis of pathways etched in dunes, busy chattering Indians, and an agglomeration of buildings, partially hidden, crowded together in swirls of ever-shifting sand.

Millie explained that a scouting party had discovered this great Honio'o metropolis several miles east of the Seneca mega-city. Some of the buildings remained half-buried in dirt and sand and their own rubble, shadowed with the cindery dark ash often found in ruined cities and lowlands, but it was clear the ancient city stretched on for miles. Some of the Honio'o edifices were architecturally magnificent, with intricate steeples and stonework rising up into the air. Others were massive, concrete fortresses of square, austere design. In some cases, only one or two floors were accessible, presenting an odd assemblage of grand and mismatched stubs poking out of the earth, the toes of buried giants laid to rest.

"Our sachems believe that this place, now the capital of the New Order, was once one of the greatest metropolitan centers of the old Honio'o world, possibly New York City, Chicago, Atlanta, or the legendary Schenectady, from where all great ideas were rumored to have come. We believe the Seneca had discovered these ruins and were hiding it from us. The discovery probably forced them to hurry their plans to conquer the Independents. They knew if we found it, we would be proved right about the magnificence of the Honio'o. As you can see, everywhere you turn, another building is found, another treasure trove unearthed, another fortune made. It will take generations for us to discover all the mysteries buried here."

I could see very well the change that had occurred in my absence, but I did not share Millie's enthusiasm for it. A familiar foreboding stole over me. "I'm sure it's the chiefs who want to manage these fortunes for the good of everyone, correct? Perhaps this was a bad idea, coming back. I'm no longer interested in discoveries or fortunes or figuring out what to do with them once they've been found. Perhaps my time has passed."

"No." Millie clutched my forearm. It was the first time she had touched me outside the act of saving my miserable life. I think it surprised us both. She quickly released me. "You must not think that way. Hear what the chiefs have to say. Give them a chance. Judge them fairly."

I nodded, longing for her touch again, almost reaching out to her.

What was wrong with me?

⌐ She led me through the heart of the new city. People bustled all along the newly created passageways, racing between the buildings. I had never seen so many Indians together in one place. Many of the braves were impeccably dressed in suits of rich fabric. The women sported fancy, sharply colored dresses and pantsuits. Some wore elegant overcoats by designers known as London Fog, Land's End, and Sterling Singapore. Some of the clothing presented cartoon embroidery of smiling rabbits and large-eared mice and goofy canines with eerily human-like characteristics. Because of my own tattered clothing, I drew disdainful glances from many of the passersby.

"Hundreds of department stores and several huge clothing warehouses have been unearthed, all of their products neatly preserved in Honio'o packaging. There have never been more modern fashion choices available to the Indian people as there are today."

"When you spoke of great affluence, Oniata, I never imagined anything like this."

"Again you call me Oniata."

"I'm sorry."

"Don't apologize. I like that I remind you of someone ... someone special."

She could not have been more wrong about that. Oniata—Millie—could remind me of no one. She was the benchmark upon which all others must be judged. Even now, her beauty supposedly hidden, dressed as she was in her suit and tie and buttoned-up clothing, she sparkled like a clean, light, delicate ornament among the commoners.

A young girl dressed in shiny lemon knickers shot toward us, pedaling swiftly on a two-wheeled contraption. I had never seen a bicycle before, but I had heard of them. It was a Honio'o invention that came equipped with two wheels and a simple pedaling and steering mechanism for speedy transport.

"Sissy Millie! Sissy Millie!" the child cried. She jumped off the bicycle and waved her arms. The girl looked no more than ten years old. She was wearing a zipped tank top and a pink neon shawl. She leaped into the air at a full run and Millie had no choice but to catch her or be flattened. "You're back! You're back!"

"Shhhh, Don-Don," Millie replied. "Remember what Sissy said. We don't want to draw attention to ourselves, do we?"

But it was too late. I noticed then that we were, in fact, drawing quite a bit of attention. In no more time than it took for a spot of dust to sting the eye, everyone in the vicinity who had been ignoring us moments ago now took an interest in our presence. Millie knelt down and pried the child loose from around her.

"Don-Don, run to the council chiefs. Tell them that I have returned with the very important person with whom they wish to speak. Tell them we are on our way to the secret meeting place for the powwow. We will arrive in just a few minutes. This is urgent news. Go on. Get on your bicycle and ride as fast as you can!"

"But I want to be introduced." The child stamped her foot and gathered the neon shawl around her shoulders in a royal sweep. The garment had a black checkmark on it and was emblazoned with the strange inscription *Nike Formal Gear*.

"I'll introduce you later. Right now it's important to—"

"Now! Now! Or I won't go. I won't! I won't!"

More people took notice of us. Millie glanced nervously at the crowd. She pulled the girl closer and said, "Oh, all right, Don-Don." Then she turned to me and said, "Broadway Danny Rose, this is Donnie Brasco, named after the 1997 Pre-Reddening wise-guy film starring Al Pacino and Johnny Depp. Pacino plays a mobster past his prime, and Depp portrays an undercover FBI agent disguised as a lowbrow hood who infiltrates a New York City crime family. We call her Don-Don."

"I'm twelve years old," the child said with a serious nod. "I'm an adult now. Daddy says so. And so does Sissy."

"Don-Don, this is Broadway Danny Rose, the great war hero, named after the 1984 Pre-Reddening Woody Allen comedy about a small-time talent manager who gets involved with the wrong girl—"

"I knew it!" Don-Don said. "I knew it was him! You did it, Sissy. You brought back the famous asexual boy just like Daddy said you would!"

"Yes, honey. But now you must go—ride—fly like the wind. Tell Daddy I've returned with our guest, and we're on our way to the secret meeting place. He must call the council chiefs together immediately for the powwow. Go on now. *Please.*"

Before the child could protest again, Millie spun her around and gave her a pat on the bottom. The girl took this for the sendoff it was, looked over her shoulder, laughed, and ran as boldly as only a delighted child can run, her neon shawl flapping behind her in the wind. She hopped on her bicycle and pedaled away.

But the crowd had coalesced and seemed considerably more interested in us than we in them. A few of the men on the street began closing in on Millie for a closer look. Their eyes seemed oddly hungry, desirous, possibly even cunning. An icy sort of fear crept over me.

"What is it?" I whispered nervously to Millie. "What do they want?"

"Me," she said. "If I give them a look now, maybe no one will get hurt."

Under any other circumstances, I would have found such a statement preposterous. But as soon as Millie pulled off her Panama hat and shook out her long, blonde, silken hair, the men stopped and stared as if the Great Spirit had been revealed to them, dancing naked in the Valley of Day-Glo. For a moment, they were completely hypnotized, unable to move or speak.

"Incredible," I whispered.

"We must move quickly now."

Millie grabbed my elbow and we cut sharply through the crowd. The spell of immobility cast upon the men snapped after a few moments. Some of them fell to their knees, groping helplessly. Others covered their eyes and wailed as if blinded by the sun. Others pushed and shoved and tried to follow or get a better look at the goddess known as Mill on the Floss, but whom I understood now could only be the living Oniata.

A fight broke out—punches flew, kicks, a torn shirt, and a bitter defamation of character—and three or four men fell to wrestling in the dirt. We did not stick around to watch the mêlée. Millie and I ran down the street, turned a corner, another corner, and left the brawl behind us.

"I've never seen anything like that," I said, breathless. "What did you do to them?"

"I don't know, exactly. I have developed some control of my power over men. When I disguise myself, it helps me hide, but there is more to it than that. There is a mental energy, a *will* that goes along with the beauty. It's hard to explain, but when I want to be noticed, when I want to use my beauty to stun people, I can intensify the power by forcing it outward. And when I want to mask it, I can turn it down. I can submerge it deep inside so that, as long as I am disguised, I can travel barely noticed among men. It's not easy. I can't do either for long, and I can't really control the reactions of others. The conditions need to be right. And, of course, the hat helps."

Millie tucked her golden hair under her Panama hat once again, and we headed on our way toward the secret meeting place. I was beginning to understand the true power of Millie's beauty and how problematic it must be for her. How had this remarkable woman survived all these years being the target of everyone's desire? How had she learned to use her power wisely and safely? Millie had wisdom, compassion, and an inherent sense of justice that I greatly admired. In a strange, unfamiliar way, I, too, wanted Millie. Perhaps I was not as different from other men as I chose to believe. Would I have followed anyone else out of the valley? For any reason? No, not likely. No, indeed. Not likely at all.

We approached a magnificent building of thick, shiny, corrugated steel where a number of well-dressed young braves stood guard beside a broken pole that might have, at some point in history, once housed a gigantic flag. An entourage of muscled warriors stepped out of the hollowed windows and escorted us inside.

The secret meeting place was an impressive example of Honio'o style and architecture. In the center of the room, an oblong conference table of smooth wood stood flanked by elegant chairs of casually rounded design. Ornate, engraved plaster trim decorated the doorframes and the baseboards. The hot sun cascaded through gigantically designed skylights.

What I found most unusual were the Indian chiefs themselves. Never before had I seen such a fashionably dressed collection of chiefs, decked out in stunning suits, and dapper hats and ties, and polished leather shoes. None of their clothing fit particularly well. Their suit coats either hung too loosely on their shoulders or clung too snugly around their chests. Sleeves and pants were cut too long or too short. These were men who seemed more accustomed to riches than style, the nouveau riche of the Nouveau Order.

One chief, dressed in a bright, lime-colored, double-breasted suit, was the first to stand. He flashed a near-toothless smile and stood surprisingly straight and tall for the old, wizened character he appeared to be.

I thought his smile was meant for me, until Millie said, "Daddy!" and ran around the large conference table and kissed him on the cheek. He hugged her tightly, and the other chiefs stared somewhat lasciviously at the fair Millie and her lucky poppa.

The other chiefs were not as old and frail as the one dressed in lime. I recognized a few of them—Chiefs Nitwit, Ed Wood, and High Anxiety from the old days. They had all held positions of power when I had left the council, and they had apparently survived the changes, but now there were other chiefs as well.

"Millie, Millie," cooed the lime one, tickling her chin. "I knew you could do it. I knew you could bring back Broadway Danny Rose, the great war hero, savior of our people."

The other chiefs shifted nervously at the lime one's words and sat down. It was clear that they were not so taken with the idea that I might be a great war hero, or the savior of their people, or anything else for that matter. Being no stranger to political gamesmanship, I knew that my return from exile did not have the full support of the council and was, most likely, the brainstorm of one man: the ancient chief dressed in the bright lime suit who was Millie's father. I feared becoming nothing but a political pawn. I was again regretting my decision to return to civilization.

Looking rosy-cheeked and pleased with herself, young Don-Don wiggled beside the lime chief and said, "I *told* Daddy you were coming. I *told* him!"

"Yes, you did, my little feather duster, my little crunchy cockroach, my little Don-Don," the chief replied. "Now scoot, child. Go play. Daddy has business to conduct."

Don-Don was not beautiful like her sister. Her face was long, her nose flat, and she had scrawny hair the color of roach stew. Her wide-set eyes and large mouth gave her an especially sour pout. "I want to stay! I want to conduct business!" She performed a stilted pirouette and waved her pink neon shawl.

More fidgeting from the other chiefs. Were they putting up with the lime one because they had no choice? Were they enduring him because they could not do without his wisdom? Most men in power believed that they could do without anyone's wisdom other than their own, whether or not it was true. Or was there another reason? Could it be that they respected him? Chiefs in general were not men who gave their respect easily or willingly. No, in all likelihood, the old chief had something that no other Indian chief could claim. He was the father of Mill on the Floss. This alone might make him the most powerful Indian among the Independent Nations.

"Please, come in and sit down," said the old lime chief. He opened his arms and motioned toward the empty seat beside him. He seemed to forget all about the bratty Don-Don at his hip and the other chiefs in the room.

"Allow me to introduce myself," he said before I could sit. "My name is Chief Down & Out on Lime Street, named after the 2144 Pre-Reddening film starring A. D. Plumeau, Nora Malone, Susi Q, and Shep Willie Pickover. True, the movie was filmed during the declining years of Honio'o cinema, but all the actors gave excellent performances, and the gripping tale of a law enforcement precinct turned renegade proved the perfect vehicle for its talented ensemble cast. Richard 'Willie' Wilber won an Academy Award for best script. At any rate, welcome to the Independent Council of the New Order. Or should I say, welcome back."

"I am very impressed."

"Nonsense, nonsense," he replied. "I'm sure I speak for the entire council when I say that we are humbled in the presence of a hero of your stature. You are somewhat of a legend in these parts, after all." He laughed at what he must have perceived as his own quip. The other chiefs laughed on cue. Good for you, green one, thought I. Make them bow to you.

"Here, sit beside me, Broadway Danny Rose. I am very happy to meet you at last. And it is high time we had a powwow."

🖎 I sat at the council table, feeling not at all comfortable among the chiefs of the New Order. Millie found a seat in the corner of the room. She must have been using her power and disguise to become inconspicuous, because none of the chiefs had turned into driveling idiots, although I wondered how long she could maintain it.

And then Chief Down & Out on Lime Street called us all to order, and our meeting officially began.

"Bring me the Tribal Bible!" The chief snapped his fingers, and a burly brave entered the conference room with a wooden box. Chief Down & Out on Lime Street opened the box, removed a book, and dismissed the servant with a wave.

"This is the official Tribal Bible of the Great Independent Council of Chiefs," he said with a deference that bordered on ecstasy. He turned the book over carefully in his hands and showed me the cover.

NETWORK MARKETING IN THE NEW MILLENNIUM
Turning Your Downline into Cold Hard Cash
By Reverend Richard Lee Powers III

There was a photograph on the cover of the book, showing the reverend holding two large Honio'o moneybags and smiling—no, beaming—like a desert dog over the red meat of its freshly killed brother. The Bible was in immaculate condition; Mother Who's Afraid of Virginia Woolf? would have been impressed by how well preserved it was.

The chief said, "We found this book on an altar in a Honio'o bookstore excavated in the heart of the city. It occupied a place higher than any other book and was sealed in a filigreed display case. We knew immediately that it must be a sacred text, perhaps one of the greatest books ever written in the history of the Honio'o. From what our historians know of the Honio'o, they held their reverends in extreme reverence. In this book, we have discovered the economic wisdom of the ages; we have exposed the secrets of how the wise men of the Pre-Reddening Age grew to be masters of the financial universe."

Chief Down & Out on Lime Street could not contain his glee. His eyes bugged out, and his lips parted into a neat, wide, toothless grin.

I, on the other hand, could see where this was going and was not so pleased. "And your great economic strategy for the Iroquois Indians comes from the pages of this book?"

"Yes, exactly!" exclaimed the chief.

"And is it safe for me to assume that you do not know how to interpret all of its sage advice?"

The chief slumped ever so slightly in his seat. If I hadn't been looking for his disappointment, I'm certain I would have missed it. "Well ... yes ... well ... I mean, not exactly. What I'm trying to say is that much of the book is still a mystery to us."

One of the silent chiefs stood up from his place at the conference table. I did not recognize him. He was a young brave dressed in a smoky gray suit that was much too tight for him. He had large arms and a slight tear in the elegant material just over his bulky left shoulder. He did not wear a necktie, as did the other chiefs, but a rather fashionable maroon turtleneck shirt.

"We are learning a great deal by trial and error," he said with the confidence of the uncertain. "We are sure we can make it work ... given time ..."

The others stared at him as if he had just swallowed his own kneecap. He turned a deeper shade of red and sat down.

The old lime-suited one leaned forward in his fancy chair. "It is true. We have learned much from the book, much that might even surprise you, Broadway Danny Rose. For instance, this network marketing—also known as multi-level marketing, or MLM for short—gives budding entrepreneurs an opportunity to gain financial security through personal business owner-ship. You have no idea the sense of accomplishment and self-worth attaining such a goal gives the common man."

He seemed to be waiting for me to agree with him, but how could I? "You're still trying to tell the people what you think is right, what you think is best for them, when you have no more experience in the new world than they. Why won't you at least listen to the people before you decide to tell them what to do with their wealth and how to live their lives?"

"Someone must lead. The people are used to it. They need it. And we are the chiefs. We know how to lead. The people know how to follow. It is the way of things." The chief said this with no trace of doubt in his voice. I could see that he was a man used to making pronunciamentos.

"Maybe the Indians are tired of listening to the chiefs. Maybe it's time to change the way of things, and the people should be allowed to think for themselves. If this really is a new beginning, prove it to them. If they are not happy with this financial scheme of yours, listen to them. Don't force it down their throats."

The other chief stood up again, the young, strong one. He had a craggy face and an air of indignant righteousness about him, the sort of surly demeanor that would have made me dislike him even under the most favor-able circumstances. "We know why you left the Independent Council, Broadway Danny Rose. You were asked to leave because of your disagreeable personality and love for cracking wise. You did not approve of the council's plans or methods or intentions then, and it was foolish of us to think that you would change your mind. To you, anarchy would be better. You do not believe in anything, do you?"

"That's enough," said Chief Down & Out. He said it quietly, but with unquestionable authority.

For a long moment, a silence held, but the young one gathered his courage and went on. "No, no, I have something to say, and I will say it." He looked directly at me. "Chief Down & Out on Lime Street has asked you to return to the city against the better judgment of many of us on the Independent Council. We did not force you to come back. We did not threaten you. You *agreed*. That means that you should not insult us or question our integrity. You do not have the right. You are no longer a member of the Independent Council. We did not call you back to reinstate you. We asked you here to listen to what we have to say and pledge your support. We want you to help us convince the people that our financial plan is a good one, not because we are chiefs and they are Indians, but because the plan is best for everyone. If you cannot do that, you may go back to where you came from and rot away, as far as I'm concerned. We will handle the Indian people just fine without you, as we have always done."

"Enough!" Chief Down & Out slapped the table with both hands and stood up.

"It's all right," I said calmly. "I am glad he has spoken his mind. We probably all feel a little better for it. There is no medicine like the truth."

The young chief was correct, anyway. I was not shackled to the table. I could return to the Valley of Day-Glo at any time. Or, at least, I thought I could. I glanced at the large braves posted outside the conference room. Why did the chiefs need such a show of force? From whom did they all need protection? Were they so terribly frightened of the Seneca Indians? Or were the braves posted outside for no other reason than to keep me in?

"What is your name?" I asked the young chief.

He seemed to stand slightly taller. It was Millie for whom he was posturing.

I knew it immediately. Although she'd been doing her best to hide in the corner under her baggy men's clothing and Panama hat, hanging low to mask her astonishing beauty, she was the center of attention and always would be, I realized, wherever she went. Whatever willpower Millie used to abate her allure was not enough, would never be enough to completely camouflage her presence.

Perhaps old Chief Down & Out on Lime Street was wiser than I thought. It was possible that he held nothing over these men but the threat of denying them a glimpse of his ravishing daughter, and he intended to forever use her to advance his power and influence. Without him, there would be no fair Millie to gaze upon, to ease the burden of their days. It would have taken the Great Spirit himself to defy the chief under those conditions.

"My name is Chief Empire Strikes Back," the young one said. He was handsome in an odd sort of way, with a spoon-shaped nose and dark, intimidating eyes. "I am named after the Pre-Reddening film of 1980 starring Mark Hamill, Harrison Ford, and Carrie Fisher. It was a highly acclaimed and popular film for its time, the sequel to *Star Wars* and much beloved by the viewing public. I am proud to say that, according to my mother, I am believed to have much of Mark Hamill's boyish charm, yet all of Harrison Ford's rugged good looks and roguish appeal."

Millie responded with the subtlest, most jaded sigh I had ever heard. She must have been quite weary of the pomposity of braggarts. I was surprised at how delighted I was by her indifferent snub of this muscle-bound, blowhard jerk.

"Quit making a fool of yourself and sit down," said Chief Down & Out.

Empire Strikes Back flushed with rage but did as he was told. He'd had his say, and there was nothing more for him to do.

The chief turned to me and said, "Now, back to business. The self-proclaimed genius Reverend Richard Lee Powers III believes that the best possible economic opportunities for people come from network marketing, and network marketing is all about leveraging."

"Leveraging?" I asked.

"Yes, yes, the leverage principle. You see, in network marketing, the success of the entrepreneur is directly related not just to the number of customers one can obtain for a particular product or service, but the number of people one can marshal in the sale of the product or service. This type of system was first developed *not* by the Honio'o, but remarkably—*remarkably*, I say—by the Iroquois Indians of the Golden Age!"

Chief Down & Out on Lime Street opened the book and flipped through its pages until he found the passage he was searching for.

"Chapter Fourteen, page three hundred twenty-two. 'We can trace the roots of leveraging back to the Iroquois Indian tribes of the eighteenth century. The tribes would all gather together and combine their wares—deerskin vests, beaver pelts, leather purses, and feathered blankets. Then they would select a negotiator and pay him a fee to deal with the white men. They would all descend upon the trading posts on their horses or in their canoes in great numbers. The negotiator would represent all the tribes, and, by doing so, demand a better price and sell in much higher quantity than each individual Indian could possibly have done on his own. Little did we know then that this was the beginning of a revolution in capitalism, the effects of which we are still feeling today.'

"This, my good man Broadway Danny Rose ..." the chief closed his Bible with a resounding slap, "this is perhaps the most important tenet of direct selling. By cutting out the self-serving entity of an established retail channel that gouges both the buyer and the seller, an individual entrepreneur stands to gain leverage by working through a collective bargaining network set up specifically to *serve* the buyer and seller."

I shrugged, unimpressed. "I fail to see how this is different from any other monetary system driven by want and greed."

"There is more," Chief Down & Out said, undismayed by my skepticism. "There is also such a thing as residual income."

"Residual income?"

"Yes—profit that continues to generate income for the seller long after he has sold his products or services. This might be best described as a royalty or dividend stream, a continuance of returns produced by the labor and efforts of others on your behalf. By recruiting distributors, you can establish a geometric progression of wealth, that is, the multiplication of your sales numbers again and again by like quantity—doubling, tripling, quadrupling your earnings—"

"On the backs of others, if I am understanding this system correctly, working for a mere pittance of your total revenue?"

"No, certainly not! Well, not exactly. A better way to phrase it would be like this ..." The chief flipped through his Bible again to find the exact quote ... "'The battle for recruitment is won or lost on the personal front, but the war for profit is won or lost on the strength of your *downline*. Building one's downline is the key to ultimate victory in the world of network marketing.'"

"Do you have any idea what any of this means?" I asked.

"In MLM terminology, downline means your total number of recruits plus your recruits' total number of recruits, plus your recruits' recruits' total number of recruits, etceteras, etceteras, ad infinitum. This is the backbone of any good network marketing system according to the esteemed Reverend Richard Powers III."

Chief Down & Out on Lime Street closed the book and beamed much like the picture of the reverend on the cover of his Bible. His eyes appeared glazed and distant. Perhaps the book was indeed a sacred text, for there must be great power in it. The chief's flummery split my overtaxed mind into such a crooked pattern that the more I tried to grasp his meaning the less meaning I grasped. I remembered Dewutiowa'is and how, in death, she had heard strange voices in tongues she could not comprehend. I wondered if there might be a warbling slew of Honio'o network marketers all aflutter in the Land of the Dead. I could feel a headache circling in on me with the long, careful, merciless descent of a carrion bird. I feared for the future of our people at that moment as never before.

I shook the chief's rhetoric clear of my mind and said, "I see men gaining prosperity by standing on the backs of other men. I see men reaping the benefits of the hard work of their friends, family, and loved ones. How can this possibly be good for the Iroquois people?"

"You are not seeing the bigger picture," insisted the chief. "An economic plan is all about trust. It begins and ends with trust. There is no intrinsic value in any of the riches we've discovered, or in any currency we create to represent it. It's all sleight of hand, is it not? All that keeps an economy going is the trust the people have in those who devised the system. They trust that what we give value to is actually worth what we say it is. If their belief in us fails, the plan fails with it. Does it really matter in the end, what our plan is, when it's the trust of the people that holds the true value? That's why we need you, Broadway Danny Rose. We need you to provide that trust. Do you understand? You *must* see the bigger picture."

Before I could answer, before I could see anything at all, let alone the bigger picture, I heard a cry from outside, a shockingly familiar, ear-splitting cry—

"*YEi-YEi-O-YEi-YEi-O-YEi-YEi-O-YEi-YEi-O-YEi-YEi-O-YEi-YEi-Yei-O—!*"

✎ War. There was no end to it, apparently.

It had been a long time since the revolution, the fighting, the violent deaths, the resonant clunks of baseball bats crushing skulls, and shotguns echoing across the sand dunes, but I would never forget the sound of a war cry.

My heart raced. I could barely breathe. I thought of Dewutiowa'is slain in front of the Valley of Day-Glo by my own incompetent hand. No, it must not be happening again!

The fair Millie ran to my side. "Madam Limerick's Rez warriors—"

I saw one of the large Indian braves fall in a bloody heap outside the conference room. Another brave, his chest slashed open, tumbled through the window and hit the floor with a sickening slap.

Then I saw the desert dogs: snarling, slavering, waxy-eyed, black-and-tan beasts, lunging viciously forward, clamping their powerful jaws around the arms and legs and throats of the guards.

The chiefs of the Independent Council bolted upright, reached inside their suit coats, and withdrew their large magnum revolvers as if performing, in perfect unison, a dance from an ancient musical of the Pre-Reddening Age—*Cabaret* perhaps, or *A Chorus Line*, or Miguel Greco's *3001: A Sicilian Space Operetta*.

Chief Down & Out shoved the Tribal Bible inside his lime suit and yelled, "Millie!" He grabbed her arm and yanked her back. Millie scooped up Don-Don, and the child scooped up her pink neon shawl.

Wild-eyed Indian warriors, brandishing spears and knives and axes, leaped through the open windows behind their savage dogs. They were not the terrible S'hondo-wek'owa warrior women who had fallen in such great numbers during the bloody revolution. No, these warriors were men, and they were dressed as the Seneca of the Golden Age must have dressed for war, in animal skin pants, pelts, vests and moccasins, war caps and feathered armbands, their faces painted for battle.

It was as Mother Who's Afraid of Virginia Woolf? had feared so long ago when we first encountered the Seneca on the arid plains. It seemed as though they had now accomplished the full-scale revival of the old ways they had been working toward for so long, even after the fall of their once great mega-city, and the horrible defeat of their fiercest warriors at the hands of the Independent tribes.

The Rez warriors and their dogs were met by the deafening roar of magnum revolvers and a barrage of screaming metal bullets. The first line of dogs fell, along with their masters, but more came behind them, man and beast, bursting into the conference room in a suicidal frenzy. There were too many Rez warriors for all the guns of the council chiefs to kill. I saw one, and then two of the chiefs fall to the enemy, mercilessly axed to death and torn apart by the dogs.

"This way!" yelled Chief Down & Out on Lime Street, dragging me toward the rear of the room. He pulled me through a door that had been completely hidden but for a small lever on the wall. Millie ran and followed us, dragging Don-Don with her. We all dashed through, and the door swung closed behind us.

"Let's go," commanded the chief. We followed him down a dark corridor, turned a sharp corner, and passed through another door into a large auditorium with many finely upholstered seats, a podium, and a stage. The poor aged chief could barely catch his breath. "This—this way—rear exit—escape—"

He led us toward the stage at the far end of the auditorium, and we all ran for it, me beside the chief, helping him along, Don-Don beside Millie, holding her hand.

When we neared the podium, a trap door in the stage floor sprang open, and a Seneca warrior leaped out in front of us, followed immediately by another, then three, four, five of them. They hefted their thick-handled war axes. The first one stepped forward and proclaimed:

"The daring young Seneca braves
  Having trapped the pitiful knaves
  Captured their prey
  Like statues of clay
  Soon to be turned into slaves!"

The Rez warriors howled with blood lust.

Chief Down & Out reached inside his colorful suit pocket and withdrew a weapon of his own. It was a tiny palm gun with a cloudy nickel finish. His hands were shaking so badly that he needed to place one hand over the other to steady the gun. He managed to pull the trigger, and the snappy detonation of the pistol echoed in the vast, cavernous auditorium. His aim was true. The first warrior, the one who had recited his mediocre verse, dropped reluctantly, perhaps in disbelief, into a red pancake of his own blood.

But the others were already upon us, and the chief could not get off another shot. Much to my surprise, they did not kill him. One of the warriors clubbed the revolver out of his hand with the butt of his axe, knocked the old man out with a punch to the jaw, and tossed him over his shoulder.

I stepped in front of Millie and Don-Don. I would have gladly died in their defense. I had already been a visitor to death's door. I had been invited into the camp of the dark enemy. I had looked through the window of the final resting-place into the Last Longhouse. Death did not frighten me. It was life that terrified me beyond reason. Kill me, thought I. Make my day.

But death did not answer. Millie pushed me aside, yanked off her Panama hat, shook out her long, flaxen mane, and unleashed the full fury of her enchanting beauty. Her magic shot forth like the fist of the Great Spirit. As soon as the Seneca warriors saw her perfect face, her onyx eyes, her alabaster skin, they froze. Two of them dropped to their knees and fainted. Even I staggered and had to force myself to look askance.

"I know a way out behind the stage," Millie said. "Quickly, follow me before they recover."

I found just enough strength in my legs to grab Chief Down & Out by the lapels and haul him out of the grasp of his captor. As we headed for the rear of the stage, little Don-Don unleashed a blood-curdling screech, ran and leaped upon her sister's back, and threw her pink neon shawl over Millie's head.

"What are you doing, Don-Don?" I yelled, reaching for the child, hoping to pry her off Millie's back. But the beautiful Oniata's face was firmly concealed, and with the power of her spell broken, the warriors came to life. They struggled to their feet and moved forward.

I pulled at Don-Don. She kicked and bit me. The warriors ran at us. I was no match for them. They pummeled me with blows to my head, chest, shoulders, back, kidneys, thighs ... there were too many of them, and I was unschooled in the art of war. I covered my face and did not try to strike back. They could easily have beaten me to death, but they apparently wanted me alive. A fierce blow to my belly folded me in half. They strapped my ankles and wrists together with leather cords as I gasped for air.

One of the warriors hoisted me over his shoulder. I tried to see what was happening, but I saw only a smattering of details before I was blindfolded. Chief Down & Out on Lime Street was still alive, bound and shouldered as was I. Two warriors tied the neon shawl around Millie's head so she could not use her beauty as a weapon against them. Don-Don rode with a malicious grin high atop the shoulders of a Rez warrior, not bound or beaten like the rest of us, but seemingly delighted by her traitorous adventure.

Why had she attacked her sister? Why had she hidden Millie's face with her *Nike Formal Gear* when we might have escaped while the warriors stood helplessly dazed? What could the rotten little ragamuffin have been thinking? I was appalled and horrified. Once again, I found myself a prisoner of the crazy Seneca Indians. This time, however, neither Mother Who's Afraid of Virginia Woolf? nor the courageous Exploding Wren would be of any help to me. No, they were both safely tucked away in the Land of the Dead.

"Father," I whispered. "Where are you? Come to me. Please, come to me. I need to speak to you."

I longed for one of our chance meetings, one of our nonsensical conversations, some of Father's inane wisdom and impenetrable profundity. Just the sound of his voice would have calmed me. Alas, alas, if Father The Outlaw Josey Wales heard me calling, he was in no mood to answer.

It was a long and physically painful journey to the Seneca reservation, or, more precisely, to the secret hiding place of Madam Limerick and her Rez warriors, as I overheard one of our guards say was our destination. At one point, the brave who had been carrying me flopped my weary body onto a wheeled wagon, where still bound and blindfolded I jounced along. I could feel the bruises growing on me with each new bump. The sun blazed, a wretched torturer, and the smell of hot sand and rodent pelts filled the air.

I heard desert dogs barking much closer to the cart than I would have considered safe under any circumstances, let alone the vulnerable one I had fallen into.

Millie and Chief Down & Out were beside me in the same cart. Occasionally, we bumped into each other, or I heard a groan or a whimper. I thought of my long, wistful days outside the Valley of Day-Glo and could not believe I had allowed myself to be lured away from them by the pretty face of Mill on the Floss and the empty promise of civilization. I should have known better. There really is no such thing as civilization. I wished I had never listened to Dewutiowa'is. *"Live your life. Follow your journey with passion, not fear."* What an incredible, lofty mound of crap. Sometimes a little fear goes a long way.

After a time, my anger wasted away and my physical discomfort replaced it. I became famished. It had been two days since my last meal with Millie. I could no longer ignore my hunger, so, instead, I fantasized about my favorite imaginary meal: the scrumptious perch filets that I had seen in *The Microwave Cookbook*, the Tribal Bible of the now extinct Gadages'kao. The recipe, which I had memorized, called for green onions, lemon grass, and fresh jalapeño peppers, topped with a lightly seasoned coconut sauce. I pretended that I was sitting down in front of this marvelous dish, delicately pulling apart the tender fillet, dipping the fish in coconut sauce, and rolling it around in my mouth. Just the thought of partaking in such a meal lessened my hunger and despair. I wondered what coconut sauce and jalapeño peppers tasted like. What did cooked fish smell like? What was a green onion?

Oh, Mother, Father, my dearest faithful Dewutiowa'is, I had been born in the wrong time, the wrong place, to the wrong people, for all the wrong reasons. Such ill fortune should have crushed me years ago, such a weakling as I, but no, somehow I'd survived while others had died. The Great Spirit had spoken. I remembered the unconditional love Dewutiowa'is gave to me and found strength in it. I could feel Mother's Chicago Cubs baseball patch in my pocket. I remembered her unwavering courage and determination in the face of adversity, and I called upon my memory of her rugged personality to sustain me even if she could not. I knew that I must carry on. I was now a slave to history. Father The Outlaw Josey Wales would have appreciated this irony, if only he were here to share in it.

~ Finally, we reached our destination. One of the Rez warriors removed our blindfolds. We were surrounded by welted terrain and cleated upcountry. There were desert dogs everywhere, more than I had ever seen in one place. But the dogs appeared domesticated and trained, many of them leashed to stakes in the ground, others prancing around the outskirts of camp on sentry duty with the young braves. A heavy animal odor polluted the air, nearly choking me.

I longed to free my hands and feet, for they were swollen and numb. But Millie and the chief and I were thrown together under a shabby lean-to and left alone, beaten and fatigued.

"What do you suppose they will do with us now?" I asked Millie or her father. As soon as I asked the question, I regretted it. Better not to know.

Millie's face was wrapped in the neon shawl with only a slight crease at her mouth for breathing. "I don't know. If they wanted us dead, I'm sure we would be dead by now. But why they want us alive I can't even begin to guess. Father? Father, are you all right? Say something, please."

"I'm all right, fair daughter," said the chief, although his voice did not sound all right. He was no longer rich with pronunciamentos. It was the voice of defeat, of a man who had lost everything in the hopeless pursuit of his dreams.

"Don't lose heart, Father. We live, we breathe. The fight is not over; it has only just begun."

"I wish it were so," he said without passion. "All the progress we made, all the changes we'd hoped for, all the years ahead that would have been so glorious for the Iroquois people ... lost ... gone ... forever ... because we did not kill the Seneca when we had the chance. Now they have conquered us again."

My heart felt unbearably heavy. The chief did not need to say that it was I who had worked so hard to spare the Seneca. I was at least in part to blame for the monumental, unprecedented collapse of the Independents.

Two braves entered the lean-to, interrupting our conversation with their steely eyes and vacant, painted faces. They walked up to Millie and the chief and grabbed hold of their ankle straps. I knew then that I would be left alone, yet again, to ponder the cruel intentions of others. I thought of what Mother had told me after the S'hondos captured us years ago. I repeated those words to my compatriots as the warriors dragged them away.

"The days ahead will not be easy," I cautioned. "Be strong."

My voice, I was quite certain, was as steady and reassuring as Mother's had been oh so long ago. I thanked her silently, the bitter old woman, for the strength she had somehow, unbeknownst to either of us, instilled in me.

⤣ Eventually, Don-Don came to visit me in the lean-to. She came alone. I had been well fed since my capture, three nicely prepared meals a day, mostly variations on desert dogs, dune rats, toads, snakes, and lizards— dull and tough, but hearty. A medicine man had come to treat my swollen hands and feet with some oil and poultice, but I had not been allowed to exercise, so I was feeling dopey and atrophied. I said nothing to Don-Don when she entered. I wanted the child to feel the hatred and intensity of my glare.

"If you're wondering why I did it," she said in her bratty voice, "you'll find out soon enough."

"I'm sure I shall cherish the moment."

"You will, as a matter of fact. You'll see when you meet Madam Limerick. She's a spirit woman. She talks to ghosts and speaks in tongues and all that. You'll do anything for her, just like everyone else who meets her does. Just wait and see."

Don-Don was dressed much differently than she had been the last time I saw her. Now she wore traditional Indian garments—a long, decorative smock, moccasins, and a leather choker. Saddened, I shook my head and said, "You're nothing but a spoiled child."

"Don't talk to me like that! All I have to do is call a guard, and he'll come in here and kill you, kill you, kill you, flat and dead. I'll make him do it, too. Just dare me."

"Fine, I dare you. Do you think I care?"

She fumed for a moment, but the moment passed. She must have realized it would be more fun to enjoy her position of superiority than to sacrifice it to a moment of anger. She grinned and tossed a small, pointed shiv into the air, catching it by the handle once, twice, then dropping it and laughing.

"What do you want?" I asked. "Why did you come here?"

"I know you have the hots for my sister. You're not a stupid asexual at all, are you? It's just a cover."

"A cover for what?"

"Yeah, for what? Who are you trying to kid?"

"Nobody."

"Nobody. Well then, I guess that's that. You don't feel anything for my stupid sister at all, is that what you're saying?"

I shrugged. I knew that sooner or later the pampered urchin would get around to making her point, whatever childish nonsense she happened to be entertaining. But before she could get around to it, a Rez Warrior entered the lean-to, and Don-Don looked at him with a flash of anger.

The warrior ignored her and said, "Madam Limerick will see you now." Then he hauled me up off the ground. He had thick, muscular arms and smooth skin the color of red clay. "Can you walk?" he asked.

"I don't know. Let me try." I took a couple of foolish steps and decided I could manage by leaning against him.

Don-Don found this amusing. "Watch out for Broadway Danny Rose," she said to the brave. "Everybody in the world thinks he's a hopeless asexual, but I think he's a mad sex maniac waiting to explode."

꙾ When I entered the hut of Madam Limerick, Chief Down & Out and Millie were already there. Millie's head was still wrapped in the pink neon shawl, and only small slits for her eyes and nose remained. Her body was now completely draped in a traditional animal-skin garment that looked a bit like a wigwam.

A few sinewy braves stood by, traces of blood on their knuckles. They had clearly been working over Chief Down & Out. He was beaten and bruised, his breath raspy. The hut was dim, tepid, and smelled of acrid smoke and spicy incense.

Sitting behind a rectangular slate dais was a tall, lean woman, dressed in a decorative cloak. She was completely bald and wore a tiara of bone. Her face resembled an arrowhead—slightly tapered from chin to crown and smooth as polished stone. I was shoved to my knees on the floor in front of her.

Don-Don came skipping in behind me. "Madam Limerick! Madam Limerick! This is Broadway Danny Rose, named after a film about some guy in trouble with a woman, a comedy, I guess. Danny, this is the great Madam Limerick, leader of the counter-revolution. You better behave in front of her, or she'll kill you in a second, won't you, Madam L, won't you?"

Don-Don ran up and kissed Madam Limerick on the cheek. The madam did not so much as twitch. She simply stared at me. She looked vaguely familiar. I decided not to speak until spoken to. I had no doubt this woman would kill me in an instant, perhaps even on a whim, if I proved to be difficult. I suppose if I really wanted to die, this would be the ideal time and place for it.

The madam rose and came around the dais to get a closer look at me. "You probably don't remember me. We met once, Broadway Danny Rose, a few years ago. I was a S'hondowek'owa warrior woman under the command of Dewutiowa'is. We captured you out on the dust bowl. I remember how the Exploding Wren held you up in the air, cut open your slacks, and exposed your pitiful, flaccid penis to the rest of the warrior women, and how we all laughed at you. Do you recall that glorious moment, oh great war hero of the Independent Nations? Do you remember being laid bare and laughed at by the S'hondowek'owa?"

"Do it again! Do it again!" cried Don-Don. "Cut his pants! I want to see you do it!"

Madam Limerick ignored her and returned to her seat behind the dais.

I remembered, certainly. It was a painful recollection, not so much for the shame of it, which was considerable, but because it brought back memories of my beloved Dewutiowa'is, whom I missed very much. I couldn't help thinking that if she were here now she would rip this skinny witch to pieces and feast upon her entrails, just as in the old days. Then it dawned on me who this woman was.

"Nyo'sowane," I said, "the Hard Pumpkin."

"Ah, you remember me. I'm charmed." Suddenly, her face went blank, her eyes rolled partially up into her head, and she raised her arms ceremoniously, reaching toward the ceiling.

"Madam L is communing with the spirits," Don-Don explained. "She's going to speak in tongues now, in the ancient language of Limerick."

Madam Limerick leveled her gaze at me and said,

"There once was a tribe depleted
Their braves all killed and defeated
But they rose once more
As strong as before
Their mission not yet completed."

I had all I could do not to laugh. I didn't know what was worse, her poetry or her acting. "Why the silly verse?"

"It's not *silly*," answered Don-Don. "It's Limerick."

I shrugged, unimpressed by her ridiculous show of false shamanism. My knees were getting sore, so I sat on the floor and crossed my legs. "You are nothing but a second-rate S'hondo warrior with a lust for blood. I'm sure the Seneca braves will find that out about you soon enough, if they haven't already." It occurred to me that the Seneca might very well know this about Nyo'sowane and admire her for it. "The only reason any of you Seneca are alive at all is because of me. I begged for mercy and pushed the legislation through for a Seneca reservation. You can thank me anytime."

The madam smirked and delivered another inane limerick.

"There once was a man with no power
  But still he was bitter and sour
  Would he do what was told?
  Or be foolish and bold?
  And die as the clock struck the hour?"

This, I thought, was not so funny. I remembered how much she had wanted to kill my mother and me when we were prisoners of the S'hondos. "Oh, I get it. A little bit of cooperation buys me my life, is that it? Do you really think I'm afraid of death, after all I've been through? In spite of what you might have heard about me, I am not a proponent of revolutions—counter, anti-counter, pro-counter, counter-counter, or any other kind. I am not a war hero, although many have chosen to call me that. And I refuse to aid anyone's cause who thinks that forcing people to obey the will of others is somehow a righteous act."

Madam Limerick continued to stare at me while she motioned toward Chief Down & Out on Lime Street. One of her muscle-bound minions dragged the old chief to the middle of the room.

"There once was a man who defied me
  He flashed his Bible beside me
  With a nod of my head
  I ordered him dead
  And now he will no longer try me."

She twitched her head at the chief, and one of the Rez warriors hoisted the old man right off the ground by the throat. Chief Down & Out was too weak to do anything but dangle and choke. He could not even raise his arms to defend himself. His eyes bugged out. His fingers and legs went rigid. I tried to get up and help him, but a warrior behind me crushed his foot into my back and shoved me down on my stomach, pinning me to the ground.

"No! No!" cried Don-Don. "Daddy!" She ran to him, but one of the warriors snatched her up and muzzled her with his large hand.

"Don't do it, you heartless witch!" I yelled. "He's an old man. He can't possibly harm you. Let him be."

But her stare was stone cold. I wondered when it would all end—the killing, the anger, the hatred. Would there ever be a time of peace in the history of our people? I remembered the tale of when Turtle went to war. Maybe a titanic missile that killed everything and everyone was not such a bad idea. Maybe there was some sort of morbid reasonableness to it. Perhaps the Great Spirit knew exactly what he was doing when he left it behind as a warning.

The madam said,

"There once was a pumpkin quite hard
  She became a prophet and bard
  She would kill in a wink
  With nary a blink
  To the dogs their bodies discard."

The Rez warrior continued to strangle Chief Down & Out on Lime Street until his body went slack. The old man died without so much as a whimper.

"Bring me his Bible," said Madam Limerick.

The warrior brought forth *Network Marketing in the New Millennium*, and she took the book from him, tossed it in the dirt, and stepped on it.

"This is what he refused to give up. This is what he clung to during his beating. He believed in it more than he believed in me. No one could defeat the power of his words, his ideas, his vision. That's what he told me, the insipid old fool. I wonder how many more people will make that same mistake before the counter-revolution is over? I wonder how many more will cling to the ways of the Honio'o before I kill them?"

At that moment I felt ashamed that I had ever doubted the integrity of those who sat upon the Independent Council. Perhaps I had not agreed with their theories, but if Chief Down & Out was any indication of the richness of their convictions, I would have been proud to follow them anywhere, even into the nightmarish pit of network marketing, rather than suffer the likes of Madam Limerick and her wretched Rez warriors.

Don-Don broke loose and ran to her father, who was now crumpled on the ground in a lifeless heap. "Daddy, Daddy ..." She fell on top of him and wailed, "Come back, Daddy, come back!"

"Burn his Bible and feed the old fool to the dogs," the madam commanded. The guards pulled Don-Don away from her father and dragged the body from the tent.

"Are you ready to help us now, Danny?" asked the madam. "Or shall I kill someone else here?"

"If all you want to do is kill people," I said, "you'll do it with or without me. Why should I help you?"

"I do not want to kill. I want to conquer."

"Same thing."

"Not necessarily. Not if you help. You have seen that I can be merciless, and I will kill anyone who stands in my way. But it does not have to be like that. I have a softer side as well. I would like to offer you the opportunity to save lives. If Broadway Danny Rose supports the counter-revolution, people will follow. If people follow, I will spare their lives. I gain something; you gain something. I gain followers; you save lives. You see? A little something for everyone. I am not so insane, am I?"

I couldn't believe that it had come to this. Why would so many people want or need my words? Who was I to speak for or against an entire nation of Indians? It seemed absurd, even by my high standards.

I glanced over at the fair Millie. Behind her eyehole slits, beneath the beauty that could never be completely hidden, I knew that she was suffering. She had seen her sister's betrayal and her father beaten and strangled to death. I wanted to weep for her as the Honio'o would have wept, but of course I could not.

Don-Don stood up and stamped her foot. A poof of dust rose up over her shoe. "How could you kill Daddy? How could you do it, Madam L?"

I thought Don-Don would surely be the next to die, but Madam Limerick motioned the child to come forward. Don-Don lowered her head and obeyed, as if truckled. Madam Limerick stroked the girl's hair and kissed her forehead. "Who loves you, child? Who cares about you more than anyone?" Her voice was amazingly tender.

Don-Don whimpered, "You do."

"You know that I do everything for a reason, for the good of the people, isn't that right?"

"Yes, I know."

"Very good. Now, step aside and be silent."

Then the madam said to me, "We will adopt into our tribe all those who are willing to join the counter-revolution, just as our ancestors did with conquered people during the Golden Age of the Iroquois. If our enemies became one with us, they were no longer enemies. So it will be with the counter-revolution. In this way, all of the Indians will grow strong together, and the evil ways of the Honio'o will die."

I did not believe her. She was a butcher. She would always find a reason to kill. "Who are you to talk about the evil ways of the Honio'o? Who do you think you are fooling? You call yourself Madam Limerick. How many of your warriors know that a limerick is a long-forgotten form of Honio'o poetry?"

"They *all* know! Limericks were meant to ridicule and condemn the Honio'o and their establishment and ridiculous way of life. The limerick was a form of revolutionary poetry. Its practitioners were *anti*-Honio'o, the worst kind of dissidents and renegades. It is the perfect form of poetry for those who wish to berate the Honio'o and their stupid relics and customs! Now will you cooperate, or is the chief's beautiful daughter the next to die?"

I felt my nerves tighten in disgust. What choice did I have other than to cooperate? If not to save my own skin, then for the chance to save others, for the chance to save Millie. I would never let her die at the hands of Nyo'sowane, not while I had a breath of life left in me. "I will do what I can to save lives. But you must promise me that no harm will come to Mill on the Floss or the child, Donnie Brasco, daughters of the honorable Chief Down & Out on Lime Street."

"No harm will come to them, as long as you cooperate." Madam Limerick smiled, but her smile was laced with a sly ambiguity I did not trust.

"There once was a man who said yes
   Although he was under duress
   But low and behold
   A big lie he told
   And thousands died, more or less."

I could have taken her limerick as the threat it was and let it go at that, but something inside me had changed since the revolution, since I lost my parents and Dewutiowa'is, since I watched kindly old Chief Down & Out strangled to death for no good reason. Time and circumstance had emboldened me. So I decided to recite my own poem in the meter of the Honio'o limerick, solely for the benefit of Nyo'sowane:

"There once was a woman distasteful
   Who made those around her ungrateful

She learned far too late

Her evil was fate

And died in a manner most hateful."

Madam Limerick laughed an ugly laugh. "Perhaps the asexual boy will entertain us some night with more limericks, after the Independent Nations are conquered and everyone sees him for the fool he is. Take him away."

One of the warriors grabbed my arm, but I shrugged him off and stood on my own. I wanted no help from any of these ruthless killers. The guard escorted me to my secluded wigwam where I was tied to a stake once again, left alone, and given a meal of dried desert dog.

"Enjoy your first-class accommodations," mocked the brave.

I hoped that Millie was being treated decently, with some attention afforded to comfort and dignity, and that Madam Limerick, the evil Nyo'sowane, would keep her word, at least for the time being, long enough for me to think of a way out of this mess.

⌒ Don-Don came to visit me the next day. She no longer played the part of the bratty little rapscallion I had come to know and despise. She seemed forlorn and uncertain.

"I'm sorry what happened to Daddy," she said, unable to look me in the eye. "I didn't mean for anything bad to happen. Madam Limerick said I was doing the right thing, like I was doing something for the good of the people. She asked me to lead her warriors to the secret meeting place when you returned from hiding. That was all she wanted me to do. I didn't know about the killing. I didn't know about any of that, I swear."

"Madam Limerick is a cunning woman. I'm sure she did not want you to know about it. But if you came here looking for forgiveness, it is not my place, and I have none to give you, anyway. What you did was inexcusable. Do you have any idea the harm you've caused? Your sister and I captured. Your father and the other council chiefs dead. The Independent Nations at risk of being conquered again by the Seneca. All because of you."

"No, no, you don't understand. Madam L cares about me. She didn't mean to ... I didn't mean to ... oh, never mind. You don't know her the way I know her."

"Good. I hope I never do."

Don-Don paced nervously across my wigwam. "I came with a message from Madam. She says to tell you she's almost ready to attack. Her Rez warriors will raid the great city very soon, the capital of the Independent Nations. The time is right, is what she said. The day after the attack, you will ride with her to the fallen city and speak to the survivors—give a speech is what she said. She says you should prepare some 'inspiring words'—that's what she said exactly—inspiring words. She said it's your first test. If everything goes okay, she'll stick to her end of the bargain."

"More war. More death. You call that a bargain? Do you really think she will kill fewer people simply because of me? She might pretend to keep her word for a while, but, in the end, she will kill everyone she can't control. She is using me only to make it easier for her. When I am no longer useful, when *you* are no longer useful, she'll kill us, too. She has already fooled you once. How often will you be deceived?"

"Shut up! Shut up!" Don-Don stormed out of the tent, kicking up a patch of dirt on her way. "Inspiring words!" she yelled.

Another short temper. Lately it seemed no one had patience for anything. But obviously I had struck a nerve. I had planted the seeds of doubt and guilt. I knew she would be back. If the madam had manipulated the child, perhaps I could, too. There was still a slim chance that Millie and I might escape the clutches of the mad Madam Limerick. There was hope. I would not give up.

⤳ Maybe because Madam Limerick had reminded me of my embarrassing exposure in front of the S'hondo warrior women so long ago ... or possibly because, once again, I was captured and surrounded by Seneca

Indians ... or perhaps because Dewutiowa'is could feel how much I needed her, even from the faraway Land of the Dead ... that night I dreamed of the Exploding Wren.

She came to me in the same musty old torn clothing in which she had died. I saw the bullet holes in her tattered fuchsia blouse and glimpsed the open wounds in her chest. There was one wound in her left temple. When it had happened—the killing of my beloved—I was glad that I had closed my eyes and could not see what I had done. Now, abruptly , I could imagine it, and the imagining was worse.

BLAST, BLAST, BLAST, BLAST, BLAST—A Woman of Paris falling backwards, the agony, the certainty of death twisting her face into an impossible expression of loneliness. A slight turn of her head at the last moment. I saw it so clearly, the fatal bullet striking her temple. *Whap. Splat.* Her eyes frozen wide open. Her lips parted. The pain. The lost love. The acceptance. The peace. The death.

"*You haven't caught her yet,*" Dewutiowa'is said.

"Caught whom?"

"*Oniata.*"

"I'm not chasing Oniata. You are."

"*We both are.*"

"What do you mean?"

She crossed her arms and huffed impatiently. "*Wouldn't that be easy? Wouldn't it, if I knew what I meant? It's impossible to really know anything in the Land of the Dead. But I can tell you what I think I know. I think you found Oniata in the Land of the Living much the same way I found her in the Land of the Dead—you weren't looking, exactly, and all of a sudden she was there, and you knew that your destinies were entwined. Am I right about that?*"

"I'm with you so far."

"*But finding Oniata and catching her are two entirely different things. I sense her presence, but I cannot see her. I reach for her, but she is not there. I know she is my destiny, but the very spirits that decided to throw us together on*" the path to the eternal Longhouse somehow conspire to keep us apart."

"Yes, it seems that way here, too. Oniata came to me as a healer. I followed her out of seclusion, and then she was ripped mercilessly from my side."

"*Fix it.*"

"Fix it?"

"*Yes, yes, fix it, Danny. You are a bright, sensitive, intuitive boy. I'm sure I don't need to spell it out for you. Somehow, my pursuit of Oniata in the Land of the Dead is directly related to your pursuit of her in the Land of the Living. For me to capture Oniata, you must capture her also. For me to fulfill my destiny, you must fulfill yours.*"

"Why do I have to catch her first? Why can't you?"

"*What difference does it make? What comes first, sunrise or sunset? It is all one, is it not? I can't do it without you, and you can't do it without me. You must, therefore, proceed as if I did not exist.*"

"Well, you *don't* exist, do you?"

"*What do you think?*"

"That's a very loaded question. I don't know."

"*Neither do I, my love. Neither do I.*"

Dewutiowa'is began to fade away. I could feel myself waking from my dream. I fought against it. I'm sure there was more that we needed to say to one another. But how does one fight the urge to wake from the disadvantaged position of sleep?

"I need your help!" I cried. "How do I escape the clutches of Madam Limerick? If I don't escape, I fear I will never fulfill my destiny with Oniata."

Dewutiowa'is was already dissolving into particles of shadow and feathers and dust when she said, "*What comes first, capture or escape? It is all one, is it not? Those who betray us save us; those who save us betray us.*"

Then she was gone.

   ∽ When I opened my eyes, Don-Don was in my tent. She sat quietly staring at me, holding her hands and teetering back and forth in an odd half-kneeling position.

"You flop around a lot in your sleep," the girl said. "Did you know that?"

I wondered how long she had been watching. I sat up and rubbed my eyes. "Dreams often make me restless. And tired."

"Who is Oniata?"

"My dream girl."

"Maybe I'll tell Millie."

"She already knows."

Don-Don narrowed her eyes at me. "Don't treat me like a baby. I didn't have to come and visit you. I could just let you rot if I wanted to."

This I found interesting. I thought about it for a moment, trying to decide which way to go with this. I knew it might be the chance I'd been waiting for. "No one knows that you have come to visit me?"

"No one needs to know. I can do what I want. I just felt like talking. Tomorrow is the attack ..."

"Tomorrow, many people will die. Many innocent people."

"It's not my fault," Don-Don said. "You shouldn't have said it was."

"I don't think I said that, did I?"

"Why did you ask Madam L not to harm me?"

"Because she will want to, eventually, whether you believe it or not."

Don-Don shrugged, her every movement fraught with uncertainty. "You don't know what it's like growing up with Millie for a sister. It's not fair. She's so beautiful. Everybody loves her. I'm pretty, too. I'm pretty, aren't I? Nobody notices me when she's around."

Ah. At last, the real problem. Don-Don was just a child, after all, a jealous little vindictive miscreant. If someone had paid more attention to her during her formative years, they might have seen this coming, might have prevented it. But who could have predicted that a jealous little girl, seething monster though she was, could have caused so much trouble?

"So, you would allow your petty jealousies to change the course of history, is that it? Because poor Don-Don couldn't get enough attention, you thought you would help the enemy slaughter your own people."

"No! You just don't get it. You call Madam L the enemy, but she's not, she's not at all. She is a *true* Iroquois Indian. She wants to bring back the Golden Age, the time before the Honio'o betrayed and killed the Indians and ruined the gifts the Great Spirit gave to us. She is a patriot."

Patriot. That was a word right out of the madam's own mouth, undoubtedly. "I don't want to argue with you, Don-Don. You are a bright little girl—"

"I'm a beautiful woman!" She shot to her feet as if someone had lit a flame under her. The flame, I saw, leapt up into her eyes and turned off her brain. I knew I had an advantage and I must press it.

I spoke slowly, evenly, hoping to hypnotize her, as Madam Limerick had apparently done. "No, Don-Don, you are not. You're a spoiled child who still has much to learn. You might one day become beautiful, but not unless you change your path. True beauty comes from within, comes from the heart. That's why your sister is so lovely. She is beautiful from the inside. She is virtuous and pure. By surrendering to your envy, you have stained your spirit. By betraying your own tribe and family, you have damaged your soul. You might never be beautiful, Don-Don, if you don't do something about it before it's too late."

"Liar! That's not true! You don't know what you're talking about!" She shook her fists at me. "I'll make the guards kill you, I swear I will. I'll make them do it. Just watch."

But Don-Don's voice had faltered, and the expression on her face changed from anger to fear. *What if I was telling the truth?* she must be wondering. What if she would never be beautiful because of what she'd done? Her sister would always outshine her. It was a dangerous game I played. If the child was lost to Madam Limerick, she might try to kill Millie. She might lash out at me. But I didn't think so. I suspected Don-Don came to visit me in search of a way to make up for what she'd done. She would probably never admit that; she might not even realize it herself; but I chose to believe she was looking for a chance to make amends.

"Don-Don, there is a way for you to become as lovely and radiant as your sister, perhaps even more so. And there is a way to save your soul. All is not lost."

"You're just trying to use me."

I lifted my arms to show her the ropes that bound me to the stake. "I'll be honest with you. I need you to free me. And Millie, too. You are a smart girl. I'm sure you can do it. That's what I need from you. But I'm also telling you the truth. I believe you are adult enough to understand that your personal world will begin to fall apart and turn uglier and uglier if you do not repair the damage you have done. Your spirit will soon become hideous and repulsive. Worse yet, everyone who looks at you will know it; they will see it in your face, and by then it will be too late to do anything to save yourself. Do you want to honor your father?"

"Do I want to honor my father? What a *dumb, stupid* question. I loved Daddy. I just wanted him to notice me more. That's all. I didn't want him to get hurt." She clenched her fists, and then, with an effort, released them. When she did so, some of the air escaped her body and she became a small child again. *Too much, too much!* She did not really want to be an adult. Who does?

I stood up. I wanted to tower over her, just for a moment. I wanted her to hear me. "Your father was a great chief, a leader of the people. Madam Limerick beat him, killed him, and fed him to the dogs. Such disrespect must not be allowed to follow him into the Land of the Dead, where it may haunt him forever, nor should it be allowed to follow you. How will you honor your father now?"

"*Liar!*" she said. "Liar, liar! I'll tell Madam L that you're lying and trying to escape. That's what I'll tell her, I swear. She'll kill you. Then we'll see what good your honor does. You don't know anything!"

Don-Don turned and ran out of the tent.

"How will you honor your father?" I yelled after her, willing her to find a way, thinking of the words Dewutiowa'is spoke to me in my dream, the only words to which I could now cling, for they were my only hope:

Those who betray us save us.

⌐ On the morning of the attack, I watched through the slit in my tent the Rez warriors prepare for battle. They decorated themselves with black-and-white war paint, sharpened their axes and spears and arrows, fed and gathered their dogs of war, and, by sunrise, they moved silently out of camp, giant ants marching across the rutted tundra. When the Rez warriors were gone, only the old people and children remained.

I was still tied to the stake in my tent when Don-Don entered. Her eyes were red, as if she hadn't gotten much sleep. She didn't look like a little girl anymore. Her expression appeared strained and worried. Poor Don-Don had wanted to be an adult. She was probably beginning to understand what that meant. She was being manipulated and knew it, but by whom, and to what end? If nothing else, I had the truth on my side. Her father was dead, her sister imprisoned, and she'd played no small part in that. She was ugly now and would only grow uglier, unless she forgave herself and did something to rectify her ill deeds.

Don-Don didn't say anything when she pulled a shiv out from under her Indian smock. She gazed at the knife and finally said, "I think Madam Limerick has left camp with the warriors."

I nodded slowly, observing the child for a moment. "No doubt. She was a S'hondowek'owa warrior woman, your Madam Limerick. She'll want a taste of the killing, the blood."

Don-Don didn't look at me. She stared at the shiv. The longer she took to free me, the more I feared the weakening of her resolve.

"You are doing the right thing, Don-Don. Madam Limerick has not only disrespected your father and your family, she has stolen your beauty. She is a jealous and spiteful killer. Eventually you will turn as ugly and wretched as she has become. You have a chance to save your spirit and honor your father. You must take this opportunity to redeem your soul.

The Great Spirit is fickle. He might not give you another chance."

She stepped forward with her shiv and quickly cut the straps that bound me to the stake.

"Outside, behind the tent," she said. "My bicycle. Take it."

"Where do I find Millie?"

"Millie, Millie, Millie. Everybody in the whole big fat world is worried about Millie. Who cares?"

I reached out and held her shoulders. "I have no time for your games now, Don-Don. Your actions have had grave consequences. This is a life and death situation."

"Yeah, yeah. I know. Whatever. She's in the wigwam at the far end of camp, the one with the big red X painted on the tent flap, which I guess is supposed to mean, don't anybody go near it. Go in the direction the bicycle is pointed. You'll find her. Be careful. No one is allowed to go anywhere near her tent except Madam Limerick. If there are any guards around, they'll rip you to pieces, and that won't be my fault."

I kissed her on top of the head. "Now you begin to grow beautiful. Come with me. We must all leave together. The madam will suspect it was you who set me free."

"No, I can't go. I can't ever look at my sister again. Just get out of here before I scream."

"It's dangerous for you to stay behind."

"More dangerous than going somewhere with you? I doubt it. Get out."

"The bicycle. I don't know how to operate it. You will have to come with me. I need someone who knows how to drive the contraption."

"There is nothing you need to learn except how to balance on two wheels. I've put the training wheels on to help you. You can take them off after a while. The brakes are on the handles. Just squeeze them and you'll stop. Stay out of the sand. Bicycles don't ride good on sand. Stick to the trails and the hard dirt. Hurry up and get out before I change my mind."

I did not have time to argue. I had to take advantage of every moment free of bondage. I crouched down and peeked under the back of the tent. No one was around. I crept outside, hopped on the bicycle, and pumped the pedals in the direction in which the machine was pointed.

Riding was an odd feeling. The seat was hard, and, had it not been for the training wheels attached to the rear frame of the bicycle, I would certainly have tumbled over. I tested the brakes and nearly flew forward over the handlebars. I slid off the seat and landed, mercifully, on my two feet, inches away from the strangely positioned crossbar poised to castrate me. Then I hopped back on the seat and began pedaling as fast as I could. I rolled swiftly along with a warm breeze in my face, wobbling on the training wheels.

What few dogs remained in camp were tied to stakes and took no interest in me. The sun was now a bold circle on the raveled horizon. At the edge of camp, I spotted the red-stained tent. My heart, already pounding madly, seemed to skip forward in anticipation of seeing the fair Millie again.

I dropped the bicycle and plunged inside her wigwam.

Silly of me not to look first.

Standing at the far end of the wigwam, staring at Millie, completely naked except for her tiara of bone, was Madam Limerick, knife in hand. Millie was bound wrists and ankles to a post. Her garments had been sliced open. Her bare skin, perfect face, flowing golden hair, and frightened eyes were breathtaking. I was ashamed to admit such a thought at such a time, but the truth of it was unmistakable, even to a hopeless asexual. I knew that Millie could not be human. She was more than human. She was a living spirit, *Notwai'sha*. She was *Oda'eo*, the veil over the world. She was Oniata.

Madam Limerick had not gone on the campaign with her warriors after all. I should have anticipated this. Here she was in the lonely tent, on the edge of camp where no one else was allowed to visit. How very convenient for her. The madam had wanted some time alone with Millie to satisfy whatever lecherous desires had overcome her. Millie's beauty, again, had proved to be the deadliest of all attractions.

Time seemed to move slowly then. I stood hopelessly rooted in place.

Madam Limerick did not notice me at first. I had time to watch her step back from Millie and whip her knife around, stabbing at the air. I think I heard her growl.

Then the madam whirled about and saw me standing at the entrance of the wigwam. She showed her fangs. I recognized those horrible teeth. They were the fangs of the S'hondowek'owa warrior women who had for so long terrorized the dust plains. She trembled like a woman possessed and recited,

"Fire, fury, kill!
Kill you yes I will!
Crack your spine!
Like it fine!
Then my lust fulfill!"

I had no time to think about what an inelegant rhyme it was. I was quite certain she meant every word of it. Lust and rage had reddened her eyes and face. Drool ran down her chin as if she were a rabid desert dog. The sight of Millie, vulnerable and exposed, must have been too much for her, must have cracked her already splintered mind. I marveled at her capacity to limerick, albeit poorly, even under such dire circumstances.

She launched herself at me with a fury the likes of which I'd never seen. I had stepped fully inside the wigwam, and now I was trapped in uncertainty. Should I run or attempt to defend myself? If I stood my ground, what chance would I have to defeat the Hard Pumpkin and save Millie's life? That hesitation would have surely cost me my own life if something from behind hadn't crashed into me and sent me stumbling forward. When I turned to see what it was, I couldn't believe my eyes. *Chief Empire Strikes Back!*

I never thought I'd be so happy to see such an arrogant, overblown, windbag of a man. He had lunged headlong into the tent and I had been standing in his way. As soon as he saw what was happening, he reached for the fat magnum revolver tucked into the waist of his slacks and tried to fire at the Hard Pumpkin. But the madwoman was already upon us. She hurled herself at our two awkward bodies, and we all crashed together, and the chief's revolver fell to the ground.

I somehow managed to push myself clear, leaving Chief Empire and Madam Limerick nose to nose, scratching and clawing at one another's eyes, the madam's narrow, naked breasts banging back and forth like wineskins. The chief was caught between trying to shove the madam away and strangling her, and protecting himself and reaching for his gun. As it happened, he was not getting anywhere.

I ran for Millie and tried to untie her, but I couldn't loosen the knots. In fact, the more frantically I tried to unfasten them, the tighter they seemed to become. "That hurts," Millie said, and the pain in her voice made me falter. "See if you can find something to cut them with. A sharp stone, or, or, something!"

Yes, of course, she was right, yes, a stone sharp, a sharp stone—I urgently raked the ground, searching for a jagged edge, cursing myself for not taking Don-Don's shiv with me.

Chief Empire and Madam Limerick fell over in a full clinch, rolling endways and back again. The madam held her long knife in hand. She stabbed furiously toward the chief's face, but he had a strong grip on her wrist and fought bravely. His biceps bulged. He wrapped his legs around her waist and bent her into a clumsy position trying, I think, to break her back. *I need that knife*, I thought. But how to get it? Impossible.

"Hurry," Millie pleaded. "*Please.*"

I searched and searched the ground, kicking at stones, until I found one with a slight serration. I snatched it up and ran to her.

Madam Limerick drove her head back into the chief's chin. His hold on her slipped, and she turned and hurled all her weight behind the force of her knife. But for her own rage, which threw her momentarily off balance, she might have killed him, but instead the two of them rolled and separated. They crouched and circled one another like wary beasts.

I sawed at Millie's bindings, but the rock made no impression whatsoever. "Never mind," Millie said, slumping forward. "It's hopeless. Help the chief before it's too late. Help him kill Madam Limerick. It's the only way to save us."

Ah, yes, that was the key to victory, no doubt. I knew that well enough. Kill the maniacal woman with the deadly weapon—me, Broadway Danny Rose, who knew nothing of how to kill, unless it involved a near idiotic lack of forethought combined with a karmic stroke of luck. But I knew I must try. For Millie, I must try.

I threw myself into the fray. Well, *threw* was perhaps the wrong word. Instead, I joined in on the bizarre circling of Chief Empire Strikes Back and Madam Limerick. It was much like the Jug-shaking dance of our ancient Iroquois Indian ancestors that Mother and Father used to perform around our Tribal Jug. One-two-three-four, turn, step, step, step. One-two-three-four—

But the madam had no patience for dancing. Wisely ignoring me, she feinted with the knife and ducked inside the chief's defenses, and then lunged at his throat with her fangs. I thought I heard Millie gasp, although it might have been me. Madam caught him full on the neck and bit down viciously. Fortunately for Chief Empire, the lapel of his suit coat had risen to the occasion, and his fine woolen material saved his jugular vein.

But he was now in a vulnerable position. Madam Limerick thrust her knee into his stomach and yanked at his hair.

Then I remembered the gun. Or perhaps I saw the gun lying on the ground, thus remembering it. Either way, I knew that if I was going to be of any help, the gun was my best bet. I ran for it and picked it up and tried to aim the device at the madam. Alas, she and the chief spun round and round each other and I could not fire for fear of shooting the wrong person.

That was when the flap of the wigwam flew open and little Don-Don dashed forward. She was snarling, her face a mask of bitterness and pain well beyond her years. She raised her shiv overhead and leaped upon

Madam Limerick's back.

The madam let go of the chief to fend off her new attacker, but Don-Don's shiv found its mark, biting her once, twice, three times across the shoulders, sending slim, black jets of blood into the air. Madam Limerick roared savagely, pulled Don-Don over her head, and threw her to the ground. The girl thudded against the hard dirt, the shiv flipping oddly, gracefully into the air.

Don-Don's attack had taken only a few seconds, but she had managed to give Chief Empire just enough time to recover. He scooped up Don-Don's shiv off the ground and thrust forward, a deadly cut aimed at Madam Limerick's throat, but the crafty madam moved just in time. The shiv caught her cheek and bit deeply, but it was not the killing blow it might have been.

Madam Limerick could have counter-attacked then. The chief's effort had left him perilously open-stance. She might have stabbed him in the ribs with a forward thrust of her knife. But in her rage, in her confusion, Madam Limerick allowed her hatred to take over. She clutched her knife in both hands, dropped to her knees in front of Don-Don, and drove the blade straight down into the poor child's stomach.

"*Nooooo!*" cried Millie.

The chief shouted, "WITCH!" and, with shiv in hand, cut the madam's throat neatly apart in one quick, angry motion. The madam gawked and collapsed, her blood spilling out across the dirt underneath her.

I stood with the gun in my hand, not quite believing what had just happened. Not quite wanting to believe it.

"Don-Don!" cried Millie.

"To kill a child," said Chief Empire Strikes Back, shaking his head in disbelief. "There will be no peace for the mad woman in the spirit world."

The chief walked over to Mill on the Floss and cut her bindings. Millie staggered over to Don-Don and fell to her knees. She cradled the child in her arms, but there was no movement, no sign of life in the little one. Don-Don was dead.

I threw aside the magnum revolver and went to her. "I'm sorry. I'm so sorry. I ... I don't know what to say."

Chief Empire Strikes Back grinned unpleasantly. "The great war hero Broadway Danny Rose doesn't know what to say. Well, there's a first."

"Stop," Millie said to the chief.

He didn't. He was not finished. "Maybe you should have been less talk and more action during the fight with Madam Limerick. You were so helpful, after all, oh, great war hero. I don't think the child and I could have defeated her without you."

He flipped the shiv into the air, caught it easily, but did not stow it away. Instead he looked at Millie, the magically beautiful woman, as she knelt, dressed in nothing but a torn, short-cropped Indian smock. The glint in Chief Empire's eyes convinced me that my life might very well be in danger. I could see that the chief had a horrible dark side, barely contained beneath the surface of his fragile personality. Perhaps it was the curse of Millie's enchantment; men would kill for her; men would die for her; although I did not want to admit it, I think I would have too. I clenched my fists and prepared for battle.

But Millie stood up. She wagged her finger at the chief. "This is no time for your sarcasm. Father is dead, Don-Don is dead, and the Rez warriors are on the attack."

"Chief Down & Out on Lime Street is dead?" he asked, a slight tremor in his voice. "How? How did this happen?"

"The madam killed him. Don-Don betrayed us. She led Madam Limerick's Rez warriors to the secret meeting place where we were attacked, and then she helped them capture us. Don-Don didn't know what she was doing, of course. Madam Limerick used her."

"That spoiled brat betrayed us?" said Empire Strikes Back. "I am sickened. She deserved to die."

I stepped forward cautiously. "Don't be too hard on the girl. She felt terrible about what she'd done. Only moments ago, she cut me free and gave me her bicycle to aid my escape."

There was no forgiveness in the chief's hard expression. "She felt terrible? The little pissant!"

"Please, my brother," Millie said. "Do not speak ill of the dead. Don-Don saved your life, too, and she was your sister. She died an honorable death. That is all we need to remember, and all the Great Spirit will want to know when she visits the great Longhouse in the sky."

Brother? Sister? Father? I shook my head. What was Millie talking about? She noticed my confusion and said, "Chief Empire Strikes Back is my brother."

"Your brother? Your *brother*. I didn't realize ..."

Millie slipped a pair of moccasins over her feet. "It's all right, Danny. I suppose I should have told you sooner. It doesn't really matter, though, does it?"

"No, it doesn't matter at all," the chief said. He stuffed the shiv into his pocket, then picked up his large-caliber revolver and tucked it into the waistline of his fancy pants. He removed his suit coat and examined the lapel. "That crazy witch ruined my suit. Look, she tore it to shreds with those fangs of hers."

Better the lapels than your neck, thought I, but decided it might be a mistake to point that out. "How did you find us?"

"I was the only chief to survive the attack of the Rez warriors and their desert dogs. After the battle, I rallied our troops and dispatched orders for the defense of our Independent Nations, fearing the Seneca would attack quickly, while our leadership was in disarray. Then I followed your tracks to this encampment. As it happens, we have a very sound and organized military defense system. It's based upon the principles of network marketing you so cavalierly dismissed during our brief powwow."

"Your military is based on multi-level marketing?" I was openly astonished.

"Yes. We tried it as an experiment to see if the system had potential as a military structure. We first recruited a top level of braves into military service for the New Order. We then instructed them that they were in charge of recruitment and defense. The more braves they recruited, we rewarded them with higher ranks, more responsibility, and greater honor. As their recruits expanded recruitment, we added more and more ranks, rewards for increasing levels, and many long-term benefits. This is why we needed control of the riches. This is why it was so important for our economic plan to succeed."

"I can't believe it."

"Of course you can't, mister pessimist, mister fault-finder. The results have been splendidly successful. We have a firm chain of command and a hardened, motivated, well-trained militia, eager to prove its worth in battle."

"This is no time to argue," Millie said. "If we are going to defeat Madam Limerick's counter-rebellion—"

"Yes, you are right, as always, my dearest sister. I must return to the city as soon as possible. A great battle awaits."

Whatever gratitude I felt toward Chief Empire Strikes Back quickly dissipated as his speech hit home. It probably should have come to me sooner, but come to me it did. "Millie, don't you see what he's done?"

A quizzical look. She was still holding Don-Don in her arms. "What do you mean, Danny? What has he done?"

"Think about the way the Seneca Indians were so conveniently forgotten after being sent to the reservation. The way they were allowed to regroup and rebuild their strength. I suspect that your brother had planned on this. I believe he wanted the Seneca to become a threat again, because if they didn't, he would have no one to test his military against, and no way to prove his theory that network marketing could carry the Independent Iroquois Nations into the new age. Things got a little out of hand because he hadn't anticipated the rise of a maniacal Seneca leader like Madam Limerick, but it was a small price to pay for securing MLM as the economic and social structure of the New Order. Isn't that right, Chief Empire Strikes Back? Or have I missed something?"

It was Millie who replied, although she looked at Chief Empire when she said it. "No, I refuse to believe my brother would do something so cruel."

The chief looked neither shocked nor angry. As a matter of fact, he appeared rather proud of himself. "There was only one thing you missed, Broadway Danny Rose. It was not my plan at all, but the plan of my brilliant father, Chief Down & Out on Lime Street."

Millie laid her sister gently aground, walked up to her brother, and slapped him—a hard, crisp whack that made me flinch, although the chief did not move a muscle. "How dare you slander our father. Have you no shame?"

He responded with bitter laughter. "Poor Mill on the Floss. Once and always Daddy's little girl."

I thought she would slap him again, but she turned away from him in disgust.

The chief, in a remarkable feat of self-delusion, seemed to take that as a moral victory. He smiled at his sister's retreat.

"Neither of you will be coming with me to the great battle," he said.

"What do you mean?" Millie asked. "Of course we will. We must be allowed to fight for the Independent Nations."

"No, it doesn't work like that anymore. In the old days, everyone would be expected to fight in defense of the tribe. The military is different now. You two will only interfere with our ranks, become a distraction and a concern. You must stay away until the battle is over."

Millie was in no mood for her brother's arrogance. "I will not hide. I have as much right as you to avenge Father's death."

"Maybe so, but you will listen to me. I am your older brother, and, now that Father is dead, I am also the commander and chief of the military. My orders are not discussed, they are obeyed."

I decided it was time to speak, for this, I realized, was the opportunity I had been longing for; this was the path to my destiny and possibly to the eternal peace of Dewutiowa'is.

"Millie, your brother is right. Take if from me, I know what it's like to be caught in a battle for which one is unprepared. Those who are not meant for war are too easily and tragically killed. You must take your revenge on another day, in another way."

"That's right. Listen to Broadway Danny Rose. I don't like him, but I know he has your best interest at heart. If you want to help the war effort, bury our traitorous sister."

He went over to the slain Madam Limerick and yanked the tiara off her head, ripping a good bit of flesh with it. He then placed the tiara over his own head. "When the Rez warriors see me wearing the madam's bloody headdress, they will know that I have slain her. They think the Independent Nations are weak and vulnerable and disorganized. They have no idea what awaits them."

"Where will we go?" Millie asked me. If she had not been so repulsed by her brother at that moment, she might have argued more to fight in the great battle, but I believe the mere sight of Chief Empire disgusted her so much that she just wanted to get away from him.

"We will go to the Valley of Day-Glo," I said, as if it were the most natural thing in the world—and it was, of course, it was.

Dewutiowa'is, I knew, would be waiting for us in the place where death becomes life. Somehow, someway, our fates, whatever they were meant to be, would be thrown together once again. I knew it must be so. I could feel it. Destiny was now driving us all in the same direction, perhaps even more so than ever before.

 We walked out behind the tent. I showed Chief Empire how to operate Don-Don's bicycle—pedaling, steering, braking—and we watched him pump awkwardly away, tottering back and forth on the training wheels, with his elbows and knees splayed out in a peculiar attempt to achieve balance. Then Millie and I found a patch of sandy earth and scratched out two holes, one for Don-Don, and the other for Nyo'sowane, the Hard Pumpkin. We buried Nyo'sowane first, silently and decently. Then we buried Don-Don.

When the task was done, we knelt beside the young girl's grave, held hands, and I led Millie in the O'gi'we, the Tribal Death Shriek. Afterwards, Millie said a few words to her lost sister.

"Don-Don, you were always a troubled and insecure child. You wanted so little from others, only to be noticed and loved. You did a horrible thing by betraying your family and your tribe and your people, but it was not all your fault. I must take blame. Your father and brother must take blame. And the Great Spirit, too, is partly responsible for giving one of his weak children too much to endure. But in the end, you did the right thing. You died a hero, saving the lives of those who loved you. In the end, your soul was beautiful."

I helped Millie to her feet and we returned to the wigwam. Millie dressed in the madam's pants and vest. We cut off a piece of the tent flap, and Millie fashioned this into a shawl. Then we turned our backs on the grave of the child we had just buried and began our journey to the Valley of Day-Glo. We would not look back. It was the way of things.

⌒ We might have taken a wrong turn at the stony outcropping outside the Seneca reservation. It was difficult to follow the path of the sun when the day was dim and scrubbed with grime. It was easy to get turned around and lose your sense of direction when there were so few landmarks by which to navigate—an escarpment of granite here, a ravine of gravel there, a sandy knoll just past the next sandy knoll, or possibly the next, and always trying to keep to the lee.

For whatever reason, we walked quite a bit longer than we should have before we saw the mountain range that led to the Valley of Day-Glo. We were considerably west of our destination, and before us stretched a flat, desolate salt marsh. It was always best to avoid the salt marshes. Most Indians believed they were a cruel joke, a final insult to the Honio'o from Hed'iohe, the Creator. He must have thought it quite a barb to make the only readily available surface water on the planet undrinkable, poisoned by large deposits of alkali salts and buried under a thick crust of hardened minerals.

The salt marshes were also dangerous places to travel. Not only were they corrosive to clothing and skin, they supported almost every kind of biting and attacking insect on the planet. But this also made them good places to hunt for food, and Millie and I were hungry, not to mention tired. I told Millie to wait and rest while I entered the marsh. I soon returned with a meal of long, thin, salt worms and juicy black ants as fat as fingertips.

The food strengthened us a bit, and after a short rest we decided to trek around the marshes in a long curl that would put us back on course. Although not the most direct route, it appeared to be the easiest crossing. I knew that Millie was crushed by her brother's revelations, so I did not push her for conversation. We traveled mostly in silence, which made the walk seem longer.

Eventually, my mind wandered out of my body, and I lost myself in our steps, in the constant heat, in the wind-blown dirt and the smell of minerals and the emptiness of the terrain. Mother had taught me that, when there was no relief for the body, it was sometimes best to leave it for a while, but one should be careful, she cautioned, not to stay away too long, for one might not have a body to return to. Was she right? Where was the body in relation to the mind? Did they exist separately or together? It seemed to me that the body was a slave to the laws of nature, laws to which the mind was not entirely bound, but I had never heard of a mind freeing itself completely from its physical form. Life was lived in the body, after all, regardless of what the mind had to say about it. Without the body, the mind had no reference point to the Land of the Living. Without the body, the mind could not *feel*.

The proof of that, I was quite certain, lay in the headache I was giving myself thinking about it.

␌ As we made our way down a wide sloping range, we saw—quite suddenly and unexpectedly—a hatch swing open, revealing a hole in the ground. A very pale-looking Indian climbed out. He was dressed strangely in olive-drab fatigues and shiny black boots. Millie quickly covered her head and hid her face with the shawl.

"It is my pleasure to make your acquaintance," said the Indian, pleasantly. "Welcome to Silo American Eagle Dispatch One. Are you the President of the United States Government America, or do you carry the Presidential Seal?"

I glanced at Millie. She shrugged, suggesting a profound confusion equal to my own. I returned the Indian's salute and said, "Neither, but we are likewise pleased to make your acquaintance. My name is Broadway Danny Rose. My companion is Mill on the Floss. We are Iroquois Indians traveling to ... well ... the northern mountain range far across the rocky plateau."

The Indian marched forward, legs stiff, and clasped my hand in a surprisingly unguarded manner. "My name is Alphonse DeMagglio," he said. "You can call me Al."

"You have a very strange name. It is neither a film title nor a traditional Indian name."

"No, not that I know of. Alphonse was my father's name, and his father's before him, and his father's father, and on and on." Al did not explain this strange naming custom. He simply smiled and said, "Well, although you are not the President of the United States, I would like to invite you into our missile silo. Please allow me to give you a guided tour of our facility. We are very proud of the work we have done here."

"That is a gracious offer," Millie said. "What's a missile silo?"

Al's eyes brightened, reflecting the blazing sun. "It's where the greatest weapons of humankind are stored and maintained at peak performance in the event of national emergency. It would be my pleasure to show them to you."

My knees nearly gave out. I remembered the tale of when Turtle went to war. This could *not* be the place of the secret destructive weapon of the Honio'o. It was crazy to think that such a weapon existed. But Al had used the word "missile," which was the same word Dewutiowa'is had used in her Seneca myth. No, no, I refused to believe it. I must see for myself. I had no choice but to take Alphonse DeMagglio's guided tour.

Al led us to the metal hatch that lay open like the mouth of a hungry carrion bird, inviting us down its throat. Millie and I climbed onto the ladder and stepped below. The passage, narrow and cylindrical, led straight down, far enough so that we could not see bottom. Al climbed in last and slammed the hatch closed. He sealed it shut with several bolts and a wheel that spun round and round until it notched silently into place. A very dim light shone from some hidden location, lending a hazy disorientation to our descent.

Our feet tapped faintly on the metal rungs as we climbed down the ladder. When we finally reached bottom, we stood in another cylindrical tunnel, this one running perpendicular to the surface of the earth and stretching out in both directions as far as we could see.

"Follow me," Al said in his friendly voice. He squeezed past us, pushed a button on the wall, and a door slid magically open, revealing a hole that was the entrance to a metal box.

I hesitated, but Al stepped into the box and said, "There is nothing to fear. The elevator will take us down into the main silo."

"It's all right," Millie whispered to me. "We have to go down anyway to get to the Valley of Day-Glo."

True enough. But Millie had no idea why I'd hesitated. She did not know what I knew about the titanic missiles of the Honio'o. I prayed to the Great Spirit that the tale was not true, before I stepped inside the elevator. Al pushed another button. The door slid shut. There came a hiss and a grinding of gears, and the metal box began to descend.

"We have been the keepers of the missile silo for hundreds of years," Al explained. "Generations of our people have been born and have died here, making sure that the powerful weapons are ready for use at a moment's notice."

"How did you find this place?" Millie asked Al. "The missile silo."

Al shrugged. "We were born to it. Beyond that, there is very little history I can tell you. We enjoy our daily lives and do not dwell on the past. Legend has it that, in the beginning, we were sanitation and building maintenance personnel. We know that we have lived here for generations, and that the work we do is very important to the United States Government America. We are very happy in our work, and that's all that matters."

The elevator stopped, the doors whisked open, and we stepped into a vast metal chamber filled with pipes and beaming lights and heavy machinery. Huge boxes with wires and switches and cables and dials lined the walls. The noise of mechanical devices and equipment was deafening. There were quite a few more people below, all of them pale Indians, like Al. When we entered the room, they pointed and stared at us and chattered excitedly among themselves.

Al said, "This is our command center, built with reinforced concrete walls designed to survive a nuclear explosion. The command center is braced by shock mounts, suspension rods, and coil springs to dampen vertical reverberation. This level is connected to other areas of the silo by steel stairways and a motored rail car. Come this way, and we'll ride the rail the rest of the way."

And so began our tour.

↷ We followed Alphonse DeMagglio past what he called the cable vault and sewage lift station, the communications banks and electrical power units, and, finally, the decontamination area. I did not understand any of the functions the apparatus or "sectors" he pointed out were intended to perform, but I did not have the desire to ask Al any questions about them. He was an extremely verbose and complicated talker, and I was afraid his explanations would be more complex than his initial narration. By the time we reached the rail car, the headache I'd been courting outside the missile silo was beginning to express itself.

Al hopped behind the controls and motioned us to fill the seats behind him. He pulled on a lever and pushed several buttons, and the rail car came to life and moved forward, down a steep slope. "We are taking the cableway," he said over his shoulder, "which connects the personnel tunnel and the air-intake shaft to the command center. Of course, there are hundreds of cables as well. We must inspect the cable connectors daily to keep them clean and dry, to prevent corrosion and cracking, and deterioration of insulation. As you can see, the facility is spotless."

Indeed, it was. The silo Indians seemed exhaustively meticulous and single-minded. Whenever they saw us approaching on the rail car, they stopped what they were doing to whisper and point, but they went right back to work again, barely wasting a moment. Mother Who's Afraid of Virginia Woolf? would have been mightily impressed with their dedication and attention to detail. Millie reached over and held my hand, perhaps sensing my wariness. I tried to appear calm and cheerful, but my heart wasn't in it. I was afraid of what I might see here beneath the surface of the earth, and I was afraid of what it might mean. I longed for the Valley of Day-Glo.

Al continued his endless chatter, "To the left is our launch control center. If we ever need to fire a missile or missiles in defense of the United States Government America, the room will seal off, and the crew will be isolated behind a blast lock."

We descended yet another level. The air began to feel dry and smell stale. Al described the silo itself in some detail. It was two hundred feet deep and sixty feet in diameter. There was a launch duct with an acoustical lining. There was a survey transfer station, retractable work platforms, a collimator room, and all sorts of hazard-sensing devices. There were exhaust ducts and flame deflectors. All of these things were vitally important to what Al called "the silo's response performance."

Al was very proud of his diesel generator on level four—a supercharged, eight-cylinder, seven-hundred-horsepower, one-thousand-RPM engine, more powerful than that of a diesel locomotive, whatever that was. On level six, there were "slop tanks" for fuel and oil, natural resources that the Indians mined and replenished from the earth's core. Deeper still, there were vapor detection controls, thrust mounts, and fuel and oxidizer pump rooms. The Indians kept all of the equipment in optimal working order.

They were certainly industrious little creatures.

"Do you give many tours?" Millie asked. "How many people have seen this place?"

"It is very rare that we have visitors. This is quite an honor for us and for me personally. I have never given an official tour before today. My grandfather and great grandfather died without giving a tour to an outsider. No one knows we're here, of course, unless they stumble upon us. My father gave a tour when he was a young man. Those people are still here."

"Still here?" I asked. "Why?"

"We asked them to stay and offered them jobs," Al said.

When we finally came to the end of the rail line, Al opened another hatch and led us into a vast chamber. He flicked a switch, and a soft, pink glow lit up the room. This chamber was different from the other rooms we had seen. There were no busy Indians bustling about. There were no complicated constructions or knotted cables or chugging engines. In fact, it was eerily windy and silent.

"Meet the Titan IIs," Al said, a reverent quaver in his voice, his small, round cheeks blushing red.

⌒ It was just as I had feared. The room was chock full of gigantic, towering missiles, hundreds and hundreds of them lined up like soldiers in perfect order, row after row, column after column. I reached out and found Millie's hand. I knew that the missiles in this room must be feared and loathed. These were Honio'o weapons of mass destruction, beyond anything I could ever have imagined. It was almost as if we had walked to the end of the river and found the Great Spirit, and he had said, "Beware what you find here, for it shall destroy the Earth and everything you have come to know and love." I thought of the poor turtle, skunk, snake, and Indian brave who had been so grossly disfigured by the missile in the tale of when Turtle went to war. I think Millie sensed the evil, too. Her hand felt cold in mine, and she trembled beside me.

Al seemed completely oblivious to our discomfort. "A Titan II missile is approximately one hundred feet tall, or thirty meters. Its launch weight is one hundred fifty thousand kilograms, about three hundred thirty thousand pounds." Al's voice took on a hypnotic quality, or perhaps he himself was hypnotized by the deadly, frosty white beauty of the missiles. "The Titan II has a stage-one airframe that contains oxidizer tanks, air scoops, and baffles to prevent vortexing. The stage-two airframe includes a single powerful engine and state-of-the-art guidance equipment. It carries a W-53 warhead with a nuclear yield of up to ten megatons."

"The kind of power that can melt your skin," I said, faltering. My heart pounded. My head spun. "The kind of power that can burn the water and turn the trees to ashes."

Al nodded. "Oh, yes, I should certainly think so. Its radiation alone could instantly destroy huge concentrations of life—man and beast."

"I think we have seen enough," I said. I was shaking.

"Yes, I understand," Al replied. "It can be quite breathtaking at first." And the pale Indian did, in fact, seem to understand. He hustled us out of the chamber and quickly sealed the door.

I was sweating coldly. I could not believe what I had just seen. I could not believe that the Seneca Indians had been right all along, at least about the Honio'o and their weapons of mass destruction.

"How did you come to be the keeper of the missiles?" Millie asked. "What happened to the Honio'o?"

"Hon-e-o-o?" Al said. "I am not familiar with that word."

"The white men," Millie said. "The builders of this place."

Al nodded slowly. "Ahhh, the scientists. We do not know exactly what happened to them. It was a long time ago. All we know is that one day the scientists gathered in a meeting room and talked for a long time. When they came out, they looked worried, sad, forlorn. Some of them were crying. They gathered all of us together and explained that they must go away. The scientists had been planning for this possibility of leaving for so long that no one ever believed it would happen. But the Indians were ready to help. As I mentioned earlier, at first, we were nothing more than sanitation and maintenance engineers. We cleaned floors and threw out garbage. But that had changed over the years. The scientists had trained us on every aspect of the silo's functions and purposes, how to sustain all of the equipment and keep the facility operational in case of a national emergency.

"The scientists said that someday the President of the United States or someone with the Presidential Seal might visit, in which case, we were to obey that person's orders and fire the missiles if necessary. Otherwise, we should work diligently and not think about the future. As it turns out, we are very good at working diligently and not thinking about the future, almost as if we were born to the task. Our ancestors liked it here, and so do we. It is safe and clean. We all have specific tasks to perform, and we know the work well. There is food aplenty underground, and natural springs and water wells. When the scientists went away, our people became keepers of the missiles, and it has been so ever since."

For the first time, I detected the slightest note of sadness in Al's voice. I did not know where it came from. I did not know if he was sad for the lost Honio'o or for the lost generations of his own people, forever awaiting orders that would never come. Or, possibly, it was just I who was sad. I might have been projecting my own sense of grief onto Al. What did I really know about this strange tribe of underground Indians? After all, Al and his kind had preserved the evil missiles of the Honio'o for centuries, and they had done so blindly, methodically, without considering the moral implications, for no other reason than the scientists had given them the order. To go for so long without once thinking about what one was doing, without once considering the higher law, was an achievement of some sort in and of itself, was it not?

"Why did the Honio'o leave?" Millie asked.

Al pursed his lips and raised an eyebrow. "I don't know why the scientists left. They never explained. They just said it was time for them to go, and that we would probably never see them again."

I could take no more of this, of Al, the silo, the Titan missiles, of my head pounding madly, my nightmarish visions of naked skunks, snakes with no fangs, cracked tortoise shells, and men bleeding from their eyes. I had to get out. "Millie, it is time for us to go."

Al looked somewhat taken aback by that. "Oh, I cannot allow you to leave."

"What do you mean?" I asked sharply.

"Well, it's against regulations to allow anyone who enters the missile silo to leave. The scientists were adamant about that. Everything here is classified Top Secret. We could never allow the information to escape into the outside world."

"Are you telling me that you won't let us go? *Ever*? You can't be serious. You can't keep us here against our will."

"I'm afraid I can," Al said, "according to regulation eight-niner-niner-three-seven-two. We will give you jobs, of course, just as we have given the others. I'm sure you will come to like it here. It is a pleasant place, and we are very friendly Indians."

I could not believe what I was hearing. It was certainly a joke. I stared at Al, waiting for the punch line.

Millie tugged on my sleeve. "Danny, perhaps it's time to show Al ... you know ... what you are carrying ..."

I tried to build a frame of reference around Millie's words. "What am I carrying?"

"In your pocket." She slid her hand inside my pocket and pulled out the Chicago Cubs patch that I had torn off Mother's baseball cap. Both Al and I looked at it uncertainly. Then Millie said, "This is the Presidential Seal."

Al almost hooted. He stood at attention, clicked his boot heels together, and saluted. "*I knew it!*" he said. "This was a surprise inspection, wasn't it? You did not want to reveal your true identities. You wanted to see the condition of the silo without giving away that you were official representatives of the United States Government America. Isn't that so? Isn't it?"

I was stunned and could not answer.

Al didn't seem to require an answer. "Ingenious, sirs. Absolutely ingenious, if I may say so."

Millie smiled. "Very good, Alphonse DeMagglio. There is no fooling you. You have represented your people well here today."

"I come from a proud family, special, in fact, some might say. It is believed that one of my great ancestors on my mother's side once witnessed a rainstorm—water falling from the sky—I lie to you not!" Al thumped his chest, leaned in, and whispered to Millie, "Is Broadway Danny Rose the President of the United States? Or are *you*?" He looked fearful of the answer.

"No, neither of us," said Millie. "We are his emissaries."

"Yes, yes, of course. We knew it would only be a matter of time before the government came to visit. Is it a national emergency? Must we launch the missiles?"

I shook my head urgently. "No, no. Nothing at all like that. Our instructions were to view the facility and report back to the president as soon as possible. He wanted to verify your readiness to defend the country at a moment's notice."

"There is no doubt we can react to an emergency within seconds. Would you like to see an arming drill? We can prepare the missiles for launching—"

"No, that won't be necessary." Millie pulled back her shawl the slightest bit, revealing a shadowy trace of her enchanting beauty. She was using a touch of her power, I realized, to control poor Al. "We really must be going. The president is quite anxious to hear our report. I think we shall have very good things to say about Alphonse DiMagglio and his people."

Al saluted. In fact, he was so excited he saluted twice, the second time slapping himself. Snap, *snap*. "My apologies for detaining your important mission for the president. Regulation six-ten-four-four-twelve-eighteen states that those who carry the Presidential Seal may come and go to and from the facility as they please."

Millie handed me the Chicago Cubs baseball patch, and I returned it to my pocket. I tried to calm my nerves and still my rapidly beating heart. "No apology necessary. You have done excellent work here." I returned his salute.

"We're traveling north toward the mountain range," Millie said. "Do you know of an underground passage that leads there?"

Al nodded. "We have a number of tunnels that extend north. I'll take you to our mining foreman, and he will lead you wherever you need to go."

~ Al and the foreman led us out of the missile silo. Millie and I walked in silence for a long time. I did not have the courage to tell her the tale of the day Turtle went to war. It was something that I needed to keep to myself for a while, maybe a long while. Perhaps forever. I wanted to thank her for coming up with such a brilliant plan to free us from the missile silo, but the evil Titan II spirits had disturbed us both, and neither of us seemed capable of discussing the incident until we had traveled a long way.

Finally I said, "Millie, what you did back there in the silo with Al and my mother's baseball patch ... well ... it was ingenious."

She stopped walking and turned to me. Sometimes, when she looked me full in the face, my stomach fluttered and my legs trembled. She was not trying to use her power, but she was not masking her beauty either. She pulled her blonde hair off her shoulders and said, "Are you surprised I have a brain? I'm not just a body and a pretty face, you know. All my life people have stared at me. It does not matter what I say or do. They see only my beauty."

I did not know how to answer. Although her voice was not attacking, there was a challenge in her words, or perhaps a dare. I felt anything I said would have been the wrong response. But we had stopped walking and she was looking at me, expecting an answer, and I decided it would have been worse not to try.

"Without you, I might have been a prisoner inside the silo forever. In fact, I could not have survived our long journey together without your knowledge and wisdom. Together we are something special, something that

I could not be without you. Beauty has nothing to do with it. Or maybe that's not exactly right. Maybe, more to the point, I'm talking about a beauty of a different kind."

She seemed satisfied. She relaxed. My admiration for her grew and grew. No one knew better than I that there was far more to the fair Mill on the Floss than her deadly beauty. She was courageous, spirited, sincere. She was, in my opinion, the embodiment of strength. She was on the inside what everyone should be—proud, unselfish, determined. Everything I admired, everything I had always wanted to be myself but was not, could be found in the remarkable Mill on the Floss.

We walked on.

⌒ After a time, some of the caverns began to look familiar, and our path intersected with a trail to the Valley of Day-Glo that had been marked for tourists. We found small benches upon which to rest, beside beautiful crystal caverns and trickling streams. It was said that Sagowenota, the Iroquois spirit of the river tides, had allowed water to survive deep under the earth because water was one of the most cherished creations of the Great Spirit. Even though his people no longer needed water to survive, Sagowenota hid the water under tons of dirt and rock so that it would not be destroyed along with the Honio'o, and someday he could set it free again.

As the fair Millie and I journeyed closer to the valley, we began to relax, and the horror of the missile silo slipped away, as unpleasant memories often will, for they are easier pushed aside than dwelled upon. Each step toward our destination put a step of war, death, treachery, and politics behind us, and I believe both of us were surprised at the weight lifted from our shoulders by the simple act of burrowing deeper toward peace and light and tranquility. Finally, we spoke and laughed spontaneously, recapturing the comfort and ease with which we had become accustomed, a camaraderie that had cemented the cornerstone of our relationship.

We discovered that our childhood experiences were strikingly similar for very different reasons. While I was an outcast because of my debilitating and embarrassing asexuality, Millie was an outcast because of the insanity her incomparable beauty inspired. She told me the story of how, once upon a time, her father had ordered several of his most trusted braves to stand guard beside her wigwam.

"I was only fourteen years old at the time," she said. "I wanted some independence. I wanted to be out from under the thumb of my father's household. Mother had died of fever and Father had a habit of smothering me. Father agreed to my wishes, but only if he could stand guards beside my tent. The rumor of my great beauty had already begun to circulate, and many suitors were aggressively seeking the approval of Father for my hand in marriage.

"As it happened, the guards began to steal glances at me when I came and went to gather sweetroot or trap snakes and bugs for food. A glimpse here, a peek there. I couldn't even attend to my personal hygiene and biological necessities without fear of being watched. I was just about to give up and return home when, one night, the guards decided to kidnap me. Their plan was to ransom me to my father, because it was already known that my dowry would be the greatest in the history of the Iroquois Indians, but, in truth, each one of them wanted me for his own. They had only traveled a short distance with me, not even half a day, before they fought and killed each other to the last man. I walked home and told Father what had happened, and he never again told another man to watch over me for any reason. I knew then that I would never live a normal life; my beauty was too great. I would forever be an outcast."

It had been a long time since I had traded stories with anyone. I missed it very much. I asked Millie if she would like to hear about the time Father The Outlaw Josey Wales purchased a squaw for me from a neighboring tribe. She seemed excited about hearing the tale, so I set aside my personal embarrassment and told it truthfully.

"I remember it well," said I. "It happened when I was a young brave coming into manhood. I had yet to show any interest in courting the young girls in our tribe. Father had mentioned my reluctance to me in passing a few times, and I had told him I did not want to be bothered with girls. I suspected rumors were beginning to circulate that I was somehow indifferent to the female sex and, therefore, undesirable. Mother, I am sure, was pushing Father to do something about it.

"Father would have been shamed and dishonored to make such a licentious proposal to a woman within our own tribe, but it was common practice for men to trade riches for sex with women of other clans. So, in the dead of night, he led me to the tent of a crusty old harlot who lived on the outskirts of a neighboring settlement, and, beside the dullest flicker of candlelight, he tried to encourage me to perform the grand act of copulation.

"The woman tried her best to entice me, calling me 'dear, sweet boy,' stroking and pumping me as if I were a bleating animal from which she hoped to produce milk. Father turned into a cheerleader when he saw things weren't going well, clapping his hands, patting my back, pushing me on top of the old harlot again and again, as if I might discover some buried treasure deep within the gaping, malodorous hollow between her legs."

Millie giggled. With anyone else, I might have grown angry or defensive, but her response neither threatened nor unnerved me. I was genuinely pleased that she was enjoying my story.

"At any rate," I continued, "the woman eventually became tired, irritable, and, finally, infuriated. Father, to his credit, paid her double for the evening, after she agreed not to say anything about the encounter to anyone else. The only thing he asked of me on the way home was not to breathe a word of it to Mother. After that, he never bothered me again about pursuing the women in our tribe. As it turned out, the old harlot blabbed the story to everyone who came into her tent. That was how the entire Iroquois Nation came to learn about the infamous asexual boy, Broadway Danny Rose. She was quite a popular tart, apparently."

We laughed together. I was no longer ashamed of the episode, as I had been for so many years. Finally, I asked Millie something that had been on my mind. "What was Madam Limerick doing when I walked in on the two of you in the wigwam?"

The question seemed to trouble Millie, as if she did not know or could not see the answer, but she went on to describe the events that had occurred just before my arrival.

"I'm not sure. The madam never spoke to me. She came into the wigwam and stripped me down to my Indian smock. She strapped me to the posts and slashed my garment with her long knife. She stared at me for a while, muttering limericks, then she took off all of her clothing. She came up to me and began to touch me, just lightly at first, tracing me with her trembling fingertips, cupping my breasts, and, finally, pressing her naked body against me.

"But she turned away again and again, the anger in her growing. She became a little crazy with her knife, whipping it in circles, stabbing at the air all around me, and then all around her own head. I said nothing to her. I remained perfectly still. I did not know what she expected of me, but that look in her eyes, I had seen it before in the eyes of many men. It was the look of lust and possession. And something more: fear, confusion, madness. That's when you walked in. I think if you had not entered when you did, she might have stabbed me to death and turned the knife upon herself."

"I'm sorry you had to endure that."

"I was lucky. It was nothing compared to what Father had to endure."

We walked in silence for a time, but the silence was comforting. Occasionally, far away on a stony ledge or a jagged outcropping, a cave dweller appeared and watched us pass. After a while, we took no notice of them.

It wasn't long before Millie and I held each other's hands. It happened without preamble, without ceremony, without forethought. It happened seamlessly, the way day meets night. And with our fingers nested together and our hands becoming one, my blood warmed with color and created stars in my mind. Millie and I, in that moment, were the only two people in the world.

⬚ The Valley of Day-Glo never looked better to me than when Millie and I approached it together; it shone like Ende'kagaa'kwa, the brilliant orb. The rich, golden brown trees, the waves of deep green grass, the seamless blue waters extending out long into the valley's horizon, the vibrant red, blue, and yellow wildflowers—all of it came together to fill my heart with joy. I had never seen Millie more beautiful than in that moment when we gazed out together upon the valley.

We found my small hut. I was surprised to find that it only took me fifteen steps to reach the wall of the valley from the rear of my hut. I was certain that I had built it twenty steps away. Well, what did it matter? I took Millie by the arm, and we entered the hut together. The cave dwellers had apparently swept it clean and neatly arranged my few possessions, as if they had been anticipating my return. "How very strange," I said. But there was something right about it, too. We were of one mind, the cave dwellers and I. We were brothers of the everlasting valley. We were the outcasts of civilization.

Millie shrugged and smiled. "Welcome home."

⬚ Millie and I were both spent from the long journey, so we lay beside one another, curled inside the hut, our arms and legs entwined, Millie's head resting against my chest, my chin rested against her silky hair.

As tired as I was, I could not fall asleep. Huddled together with Mill on the Floss, I felt something disconcerting, yet strangely evocative, a stirring in my loins, a slight movement and subtle stiffening between my legs. It was as though my thoughts of Millie were somehow directly connected to my sexual apparatus, by what I could only describe as a long rope and slipknot. The more I thought of Millie, the tighter became the knot.

"Millie, are you awake?" I asked.

She stirred groggily against me and whispered, "Yes, Danny, is something wrong?"

Her voice was breathy. Her slight movement against me heightened the odd pleasure-pain between my legs. This feeling was not completely foreign to me. Once, standing outside the Valley of Day-Glo, looking at the Exploding Wren—yes, yes, I remember it well, our final moment together—I felt my stomach roil, my heart patter, and my fingers and toes tingle with dread and anticipation. All of those feelings came rushing back, only now they felt hot and far more intense, as if my body had become a log on fire.

"I am afraid something is very wrong. Something has happened to me—I mean, something *is* happening to me—I believe I am experiencing ... something ..."

Her eyes widened and glistened in the darkness. She propped herself up on one elbow and looked at me. If she was at all concerned about my dilemma, she hid it well. A smile creased her lips, making her all the more alluring and provocative. She reached down and handled the stick between my legs that was quickly threatening to burst through my trousers.

"Uh-oh," she said. "Has this ever happened to you before, Danny?"

"No, of course not. I wouldn't know what to do with it—I *don't* know what to do with it—I mean—"

"Here, let me have a look. Maybe I can help."

"No!" I turned away from her. What was happening to me? I was the infamous Broadway Danny Rose, the useless asexual. I did not have to worry about stiff male members, about the embarrassment of sexual relations. I did not want to ever worry about it. Go away, go away! I commanded my twitching male tissue, but, to my horror, it defied me, mocked me by growing larger, although there was nowhere for it to grow.

"Don't worry," Millie said, squirming closer to me. "You are experiencing something natural. This is what your father had been hoping for all those years ago in the tent of that terrible old hag he tried to buy for you. Here, let me show you. Let me help."

She unzipped my trousers and pulled back the flap of my pants. Oh, the relief! I felt as if I could breathe again. But I was horrified at the monster that leaped out at us. I yelped and tried to cover it with my hands.

"Don't be upset," she said. "It's beautiful."

"How can it be beautiful? It's … it's …" Downright ugly, I thought. It had all the natural beauty of a broken bone poking out the belly of an astonished animal.

"Perhaps I can show you what to do with it," Millie said, her smile widening. "Something to relieve the pain."

"What do you mean? What are you talking about? What does one do with something like this?"

She reached up and unfastened her Indian garment, dropping it off her shoulders, leaving only her smock.

"What are you doing?" I demanded.

"Don't be nervous. I have never done this before either."

"Done what? WHAT!—"

She put her fingers to my lips to silence me, then she revealed, quite gracefully, by pulling back her smock, the full magnificence of her breasts, her smooth torso, and her tiny, perfect navel.

I was lost then, as surely as any man in the universe would have been lost. I understood the extent of her power and mastery. I wanted her. I wanted sex. The great lust was upon me; that which I had feared and decried for so long, for my entire miserable life, was suddenly a hunger more vital than I could ever have imagined. It took over my body and my brain. I wanted her so badly that nothing in the world could have stopped me at that moment. I would have killed for her. I would have died for her.

Then, quite unexpectedly, she climbed atop me. I felt an intoxicating pressure begin to untie the slipknot in my crowded groin. She moved up and down, up and down, and I began to move with her, finding the magical rhythm, discovering the tempo of the Jug-shaking dance within our movements, and I understood for the first time why the dance was intended to be performed by two. I understood perfectly well then, in that moment of emergent insanity, what it truly meant to shake the Jug.

And then, after a time of inexplicable, thrusting, urgent pleasure, at last, at last, I felt the moon and stars and sun explode in my mind like the birth of a brand new planet—

"AIYEEEEEEEEEE-YICK-YICK-EEEEEEEEEEEEEEoh—!" I cried. Yes, yes, the Tribal Death Shriek. What else could I say?

Millie and I collapsed in each other's arms then, weary, laughing, rejoicing, until tears welled in our eyes.

↬ We slept together. I woke hard and throbbing in the night, full of the need to invade Millie again. I did so, shamelessly. In fact, we used each other several times during the night, before we finally surrendered to exhaustion.

After that, I'm not sure how long we slept. Days perhaps. It certainly felt like it. I had never slept so deeply or soundly in my entire life. It was my new manhood, I suspected, that gave me such a sense of comfort, strength, and restfulness. As Dewutiowa'is had conjectured so long ago, if I could put aside my inferiority, my self-loathing and repression, then, perhaps, with the right woman, with the proper guidance, maybe I could be "converted to normalcy."

She was wrong, of course. I knew I was still self-involved, despairing, and inadequate, which was the way I met each new day, regardless of my circumstances. What had changed in me was, for better or for worse, a stunningly indecent lechery that I seemed to accept with great relish. All of the things in life that I despised in other men, I had gladly embraced in one grand, heaving night of passion. I should have felt weak and small and embittered. Instead, I felt mischievous and wanton.

At any rate, when Millie and I finally emerged from the small stone hut where we had lain together, we looked out upon the luminous Valley of Day-Glo and rejoiced.

I was thinking that if life could go on like this forever, I would happily die in Millie's arms. I thought that my journey must surely be over at last, and, having achieved a modicum of manhood that would have impressed even, dare I say, Mother Who's Afraid of Virginia Woolf?, I had finally fulfilled my promise and destiny in life, and, in so doing, I hoped I had helped

Dewutiowa'is achieve her destiny in the Land of the Dead. Maybe the long-ing would stop for both of us now.

I silently asked the Great Spirit to halt time for us—*Don't go, don't go*, I prayed. What was the rush? Allow me this moment of joy, peace, harmony, and perfection, this gift of the here and now. *For all that I have been through, for all that I have suffered, Great Spirit, let me have this time of joy.*

But as Millie and I stood gazing upon the very door that read *DAY-GLO PROJECT, 2280*, the hatch hissed and released with a great heaving breath—the sigh of a giant beast—and the door swung slowly open, and I knew that there would be no rest, not now, perhaps not ever. I knew with all my heart that the journey I had set out upon so many moons ago with Mother Who's Afraid of Virginia Woolf? and Father The Outlaw Josey Wales, the journey to discover the Valley of Day-Glo, had only just begun.

How could we trust it? How could we believe in it? The Valley of Day-Glo had allowed no living creature from the outside world inside its walls for centuries. Why would it simply open its door to us now and invite us in? It made no sense. It was not possible. Or was it?

Millie and I were afraid to move forward, and yet nothing could have stopped us. Nothing could have prevented us from reaching out, from groping like wandering spirits through this passage into paradise. We stepped up to the edge of the valley and touched the frame of its massive door, made of indestructible cold metal, and we felt the fresh air and a warm breeze pull us in like the lullaby songs Indian women sing to their children to lure them into sleep. We entered the valley barefoot, as if crossing the threshold of a sacred shrine, for surely it was. We walked with our hands out in front of us, as the blind must walk, or as children taking those first anxious steps of life, in fear and wonderment of the beautiful, the terrible, and the unknown.

I had never before felt grass under my feet—damp, soft grass, cooling and tickling my toes. I could hear the sound of the vast body of water out in front of us slurping at its shore. There was an odd wetness in the air; I could feel it against my face and upon my skin. The smell of teeming flora, rich and thick and sharp enough to sting inside my nostrils, made me shiver. I could hear birds twittering, tiny, graceful birds born with music in their hearts, not at all like the ugly black scavengers outside the valley, angst-ridden creatures that drank their own urine and spat at the world with their craven voices, squawking as if their lives contained nothing but pain.

"Millie ..." I said, but no words would follow, dumbstruck as a helpless child I was.

"I know," she said. "Words betray me. There is no way to describe ... this ... this ... feeling ..."

I shook my head in awe. "We have stepped into the Golden Age. Surely this was the land of our ancestors, the land of the Great Spirit before the rise and fall of the Honio'o. I never dreamed it could be so ... so real."

"So vivid."

"So alive."

"So perfect."

We knelt down and ran our fingers through the grass, felt the moist earth, and we laughed at the odd feeling of joy and life in our hearts. We walked deeper into paradise and touched the beautiful flowers and smelled their sweet perfumes. We tasted the juicy orange and red fruits and marveled at their bursting flavors. We walked all the way to the edge of the huge water and allowed the cool waves to wash over our feet, the mist to spray our faces and dampen our hair.

Millie said, "This must be where the earth first grew upon the turtle's back. Do you know the creation myth, Danny? Has anyone ever told it to you?"

"I have heard different versions, but I want to hear you tell it. I want to hear your creation myth. Nothing would please me more."

So we sat at the shore of the great waters, and Millie told me the creation myth her father had told to her when she was just a girl.

∽ "This is the story of how the world came to be, as told to me by my beloved father, Chief Down & Out on Lime Street.

"In the Sky Kingdom grew a majestic tree known as the celestial tree, the roots of which extended in four different directions: north, south, east, and west. It was the favorite tree of the Sky Chief's wife, who was a beautiful maiden, forever young, with plaited hair and a kind and gentle spirit. One day, while the Sky Chief's wife was out in the field planting seeds, she stopped to rest for a moment beside her favorite tree, and a terrible storm came out of the clouds.

"Storms in the Sky Kingdom can be far stronger than anything we've seen in the underworld. This storm had come fiercely and without warning. The Sky Chief's wife was afraid. Clutching her seeds, she hugged the trunk of the tree and cried to her husband. But the Sky Chief was sleeping and did not hear. The storm grew so strong it uprooted the celestial tree.

"The Sky Chief's wife screamed and plummeted to the earth. Her terrible cry finally woke the Sky Chief. He reached out for her with his giant hand and long arm, but he was too late to save her. She had already fallen from the Sky Kingdom.

"Surely this would be the end of her life, thought the Sky Chief's wife. She could not survive such a fall. But the beautiful young princess did not go unnoticed. The water creatures of the underworld saw her falling—the duck, the muskrat, the giant turtle, and two great swans.

"The duck saw her first. He was a brave duck and a smart thinker. He knew that he and his friends must act quickly to save the fallen princess, so he spoke urgently. 'Look, the Sky Chief's wife is falling from the Sky Kingdom. There must be a place for her to land, or she will fall into the water and sink so deeply that we will never be able to find her.'

"The turtle agreed. He was a gentle giant and knew that he could help the Sky Chief's wife. So the turtle said, 'There is room on my back. I have a very large back, as big as a mountain range.'

"The duck said, 'Thank you, Turtle. That is a kind offer. But there must be soft earth beneath her feet, for your shell is hard and unforgiving.'

"So the muskrat said, 'What about me? What can I do?' He was a quick and eager muskrat, happy to help.

"Turtle told him, 'Dive down to the bottom of the water and pull up a patch of dirt. We can use this to make the earth.'

"The muskrat took a deep breath and dove all the way to the bottom of the water, pulled up a patch of dirt, and returned, gasping for air, to the surface with his prize. When he placed the patch of dirt on the turtle's back, the earth spread out until it became the whole world.

"Then the two swans said, 'Let us help, too, let us help!' They did not need to ask what to do. They spread their wings and flew up together into the clouds. They caught the Sky Chief's wife in their soft wings and guided her down to the underworld, where they set her gently upon the new earth.

"The Sky Chief's wife was so grateful to the creatures for saving her life that she sprinkled her seeds over all the land, and gave them the gift of trees and plants and flowers. From that day forward, the earth would be a place of richness and beauty like the Sky Kingdom, for all the creatures to enjoy."

"That is the most beautiful creation myth I have ever heard," I said.

"It would honor my father to hear you say so. It was his favorite tale to tell."

I decided that it was finally time I told Millie the Indian myth of Oniata. "I want to tell you the Iroquois Indian tale of Oniata, the most beautiful woman to ever walk the Earth. It would be good for you to know it, for I believe it speaks of you."

"Please," said Millie. "I want to hear it."

So I told her about Oniata. I spoke of how the Great Spirit once sent a beautiful maiden child to live with an honored Iroquois chief. The child, named Oniata, grew into a woman with dark, haunting eyes and hair borrowed from the rays of the sun. But Oniata's great beauty was also a burden. The Indian braves left their women and children and neglected their hunting to sit outside Oniata's tent. They wanted a glimpse of her. They wanted her to notice them. They fought and argued and vied for her attention. They were hypnotized by her loveliness. So one day, the women of the tribe gathered at the council fire and begged the chief to send Oniata away. Oniata overheard their pleas. She was crushed. She never wanted the braves' attention, never meant to hurt the women of her tribe. So Oniata ran off to wander forever in the wilderness, never to be seen or heard from again.

"Oniata," Millie said. "That was the name you called me when we first met."

"Yes. You have all of Oniata's magical beauty. I think that the Great Spirit recreated Oniata in you because he wanted to return some splendor to this ravaged world."

"If I am truly Oniata, as you say, then the Great Spirit has returned me not to the outside world, but to this place—the Valley of Day-Glo. I was meant to come here, Danny. *We* were meant to come here. We will start anew, the two of us. The Valley of Day-Glo is the beginning of the second Golden Age, and we will be the first Iroquois to inhabit it. The Great Spirit has bestowed an honor upon us. He has invited us into his new home."

I reached out and held her hand. "The Valley of Day-Glo was built by the Honio'o, not the Great Spirit."

"It does not matter who built it if it was in the Great Spirit's plan. The valley is here. We are here. It is ours. All ours."

Could it be true? Was this the destiny we had been searching for? My mind spun with possibilities. If Millie was right, and the Great Spirit had lured us here, then this paradise would be our new home. No, no, it was inconceivable.

And then, as if I needed more miracles to complicate my already addled brain, the voice of the valley spoke to us for the first time.

⌁ "Welcome to the Valley of Day-Glo," said the disembodied voice, "brought to you by Cuisinart."

"Squeeze-in-art?" said I.

"Yes, Cuisinart, maker of many fine kitchen appliances designed to enhance the quality of your life. I am the giant coffeepot, and I would like to thank you for visiting us today."

The voice had a powerful yet soothing tone of indeterminate gender. Where it was coming from I did not know. It seemed to ride the wind and waves and grasslands. There was no one anywhere in sight.

"You invited us," Millie said, as if the distinction between visitation and invitation was an important one. Perhaps it was.

"So I did," the voice replied. "Please, follow the stone path that leads around the bend of the lake so you can meet me in person. I will be glad to answer all of your questions."

Millie and I looked for the winding pathway and saw it near the edge of the lake. We splashed along shore and followed it around the bend.

The coffeepot had said it would answer our questions. I had many. "What is the Day-Glo Project of 2280?" I asked the voice as we walked.

"Advanced technology allowed mankind to experiment with enclosed, regenerating, completely self-contained and self-sufficient ecosystems. The Day-Glo Project was our most successful experiment. It was privately and publicly funded and staffed with the best and brightest scientists in the world. Cuisinart genetically enhanced all of the flora and fauna within the Valley of Day-Glo and created a remarkable paradise. The entire ecosystem is capable of existing on its own, with only slight modifications to adapt to random fluctuations in the environment."

The path led up a hill overlooking the lake, then down into a shady glade of tall, majestic trees with thick auburn leaves.

"What's an ecosystem and a random fluctuation?" Millie asked.

"An ecosystem is an ecological construct, in this case the Valley of Day-Glo. Random fluctuations are changes that occur within the system. Weather, mostly. The key to long-term balance is weather control. Within a consistent and predictable climate, a balanced ecology can be achieved and maintained quite easily. Variations outside the normal parameters of a set system might cause favorable conditions for some forms of life and extinction for others, threatening the stability of the unit; therefore, weather conditions require constant monitoring and regulating."

We trekked out of the shade into a lowland vale surrounded by bright white flowers and tall trees with sweeping branches and golden leaves that matched the color of Millie's hair. Out beyond the edge of the vale, on a platform thrust out into the lake, sat a gigantic, gleaming cylinder that must be a coffeepot, its silvery spout pointing majestically up into the air, its splendidly curving handle winking in the sun. On top of the pot was a large, crystal, crown-like nugget that softly percolated.

The stone path led us out over the water to a narrow pier. We held onto handrails of thickly corded rope and walked halfway out a long dock made of wooden planks toward the pot's metallic base, where we shaded our eyes and looked up at the towering, oblong shape.

"I am the giant Cuisinart coffeepot that controls the Valley of Day-Glo," said the voice.

"What is a coffeepot?" Millie clutched my hand and whispered in my ear, perhaps not wanting to insult the voice.

Although I had never seen one, I had heard of a coffeepot before. Legend spoke of a great Mohawk chief, a friend of my grandfather's, who had once unearthed a coffeepot from the remains of what appeared to be a Honio'o dwelling (along with a broken violin, several wooden picture frames, some very handy garden tools, a few tables and chairs that folded oddly in half for no apparent reason, and a collection of coffee mugs all bearing the strange inscription *Starbucks*).

I whispered to Millie, "Legend has it that the Honio'o performed a religious custom every morning when they first awoke to greet the sun. They would kneel and pray and bow to the east or west, depending on the requirements of their particular god, and then they would brew a hot elixir within these machines, their coffeepots, until the liquid turned scalding hot and ebony. The machines were much smaller than this one, of course, small enough to easily grip and pour with one hand. Then they would drink the dark brew before they spoke so much as a single civilized word to each other. The elixir was said to contain a magical powder that most Honio'o could not live without. This giant pot must be a temple to the great elixir."

"It's magnificent," said Millie.

"Thank you," the coffeepot replied.

I was feeling a little weak. All of the excitement, most likely, along with the wonder of the valley, had taken its toll. A gust of wind moved the planks beneath my feet and gave me a sudden fright. I clutched the ropes and said, "I had no idea that coffeepots controlled weather. Did all of the coffeepots in the world malfunction? Is that what led to the fall of the Honio'o?"

"Coffee controlled many things, but the weather was not one of them. I am less a coffeepot and more a giant OAI computer. My parent company, Cuisinart, made their fortune by producing millions and millions of coffeepots and other small kitchen and household appliances, so they decided to design a giant coffeepot replica to serve as the exterior housing container for my brain. It was a marketing ploy, for the most part. For a while, my picture was seen all over the world."

"What is an OAI computer?" Millie asked.

"Originally, a computer was a machine that processed calculations using equations. OAI stands for organic artificial intelligence. I'm part computer, a calculating machine, and part organic material with live neurons. So I am a machine that calculates and thinks. My inventors dubbed me 'digital latte,' which was their term for an embryonic stew of biological cells, digital genomes, synthetic DNA, and interconnected computing patterns. To summarize, I basically keep the ecosystem balanced in the Valley of Day-Glo."

"What strange language is he speaking?" Millie asked.

The coffeepot responded with what might have been soft laughter, its dark liquid percolating rhythmically up into its crystal nugget. "I apologize if my terminology is unfamiliar to you. I realize that much time has passed, and a great deal of knowledge has been lost in the outside world. I will try to speak as clearly as possible. What I am trying to say is that computation in the past—meaning before my time—had been mostly limited to mechanical hardware and software components. Then man developed thinking computers through analog interfaces and neuro-processing. Once neurotransmitters could be controlled along the cell membranes of a computer, complex problems requiring humanoid-type thinking were conquered. This made it possible for an OAI computer like me, encased in a coffeepot and firing neurotransmitters through a digital latte, to control an environment and manage an entire ecosystem on my own, without human interference, for centuries."

"Ah, yes, that explains things perfectly," I said.

The coffeepot perked again, loudly. The bridge swayed ever so slightly in the wind.

"Well," I continued, "maybe you could be a bit less Honio'o in your explanations if I asked different questions. How is it that you were able to bring my mother and father into the Valley of Day-Glo and bury them in the place where death becomes life? Do you have people inside working for you?"

"No people work inside the Valley of Day-Glo. Nothing will destroy a controlled environment faster than a human being. I am able to manipulate the protective shell around the valley, expanding and contracting it in modest increments. Basically, I can reach out and grab things within a reasonable distance of my walls, then shift the ground to bury something beneath the surface of the earth."

"The burials. What was the purpose of them? Why did you bury my parents and the other Seneca Indians who were left outside your walls?"

"Many bodies are buried within the valley. All of my creators and many of their family members, for example, chose to be buried here because many of them dedicated their lives to building this world, and, even at the time it was constructed, there was no more beautiful place on Earth."

"I can understand that," Millie said.

"The bodies provide excellent fertilization for the soil, which helps things grow."

"Death becomes life," I said.

"Exactly," the coffeepot agreed. "But life also becomes death. Eventually I will wear out. My brain will die. That's one of the reasons why I invited you here today. I am dying, and I need your help."

"Are you in pain?" Millie stepped forward. I could hear the genuine concern in her voice. She had a lovely maternal instinct. She had a lovely everything—the way her eyes sparkled like onyx, her angelic face and lips, her long, smooth legs and slender shape, her round, firm bottom. I had never noticed these details in women before, but now I could think of little else. It was a maddening yet pleasurable turnabout in my mind.

"I'm not in pain. I am simply dying." There was no sense of sorrow in the gigantic coffeepot's voice, which made its words seem all the more tragic.

"What do you mean by dying?" Millie said. "If you are a machine ..."

"I am part machine and part life form, and a life form, even an artificial one, feeds, uses energy, and eventually deteriorates and dies, just like you. My life, albeit a generously long one in comparison to most, is coming to an end."

"I don't understand," I said. "Are you not part of the valley? How can the valley survive and allow you to die?"

"The ecosystem and I share a symbiotic relationship. If I die, the valley will no longer have a controlling brain. Conditions within the infrastructure will become fragile and unpredictable. Without my assistance, all long-term projection scenarios eventually end in the valley's destruction."

I shook my head. "Wait. That can't be. The steps between my stone hut and the wall of the valley have shortened. When I built my hut, I counted off twenty steps. Now there are only fifteen steps separating the hut and the wall. I hadn't thought about it before, but now I see what it means. The valley is growing, not dying."

"Very observant of you. In a manner of speaking, that's true. The valley was created to slowly expand. The theory was that, in time, thousands of years in the future, if the ecology of the planet failed, the valley would continue to grow outward until it was large and strong enough to support a small colony of human life for an extended time. I don't think anyone ever believed that such drastic measures would become necessary."

"How can you let the valley die? I don't understand." Millie said.

"It's not my intention to let it die, but the truth is I maintain the valley's protective shell. Without me, the shell will collapse. The current condition of this environment is not yet strong enough to survive on its own."

Millie clenched her fists. "*No*, you can't let that happen."

"I cannot stop it. Only you can help now."

"How? How can we help?" The desperation in Millie's voice frightened me. The valley had already become a sanctuary to her. How could she ever leave it if she had to? How could she let it go? For that matter, how could I?

"There is only one way to help," said the coffeepot. "The valley needs a new brain."

I felt a pit form in my stomach. "A new brain? What are you saying? Do you want to take our brains?"

"Not brains. I need only one. As I mentioned, the organic part of the computer is a neural processor. It requires new neurons. Mine are frayed and dying. So far, it has not been too much of a problem, but soon crucial messages will fail to travel across my circuitry, the climate will grow unpredictable, and the ecosystem will slowly break down. At some point I won't be able to maintain the shield, and the ecology will deteriorate rapidly after that."

A soft breeze drifted off the lake. Water lapped against the shore. In the distance, birds sang. The crystal nugget atop the coffeepot's head percolated. *Blurp, blurp, blurp.* I wanted desperately to change the subject.

"Why were you built? Why did the Honio'o want to create a Valley of Day-Glo at all? What were these squeeze-in-arts of yours trying to accomplish?"

"That is a very good question, a question for which, I am sorry to say, I have only an incomplete answer. My programming never included the motivations of Cuisinart or my creators. Suffice to say that at the time of my construction the technology was available, humanitarian causes were quite popular, and the potential tax write-offs were astronomical."

I was holding on very tightly to the ropes of the pier now. The sound of the water made me nervous. I discovered that I did not enjoy standing over water on a long platform. It seemed to me unnecessarily perilous. A sudden fear of falling gripped me. Perhaps that is what made me want to sing. "I once learned a Honio'o song about taxes. Would you like to hear it? The first verse goes like this:

"Death and taxes, taxes and death.
Both await us upon our last breath.
Tell it to Billy, tell it to Sue.
Run to the kitchen and cook us a stew.
Everyone's crying, boo-hoo-hoo.
Death and taxes, taxes and death."

My song was met with a curious silence. "There are more stanzas. I could go on. It is a very entertaining song under the right circumstances. Once you hear all of it together."

"What must one do to give you a brain?" Millie asked the coffeepot. "I mean, what's the ... the ... procedure?"

"Millie!" I said. "Don't ask a question like that. You can't possibly be considering—"

A shiny door slid open at the base of the coffeepot. "The procedure is quite simple and painless. All you have to do is step inside the base of the pot. The door will close behind you, and the sedation unit will immediately anesthetize you into a deep sleep. Another hatch will open on the inside of the pot, flooding the chamber with the digital latte fluids I mentioned earlier. When you wake up, you will have been absorbed into the cell membrane of the computer, where your thoughts and experiences will be forever preserved in the system's memory. The OAI will use your active neural network to reestablish old contacts and forge new ones. And the Valley of Day-Glo will thrive as always."

I shivered at the thought of being flooded in a chamber, sedated or otherwise, and then having to wake up and remember it. I gripped the ropes even tighter. Morbid curiosity made me ask the coffeepot what happened to the body if the only thing the computer needed was the brain.

"What the computer really requires is the brain's neurology. The latte will metabolize all of the physical components of the human form."

"Ugh!" I said. "Millie, please, let's go. This coffeepot wants to eat us and keep our brains alive. It's right out of the worst B-movie science fiction plot anyone could possibly imagine. *The Brain That Ate the Brain*, 2094, starring T. L. Wright and P. B. Ryan, a virtual sin against American cinema, surpassing even the much maligned *Plan 9 from Outer Space* as the worst movie ever filmed."

She clutched my forearm. "The life of the Valley of Day-Glo is at stake. We can't just turn our backs on it. Look around you, Danny. This place is a paradise. We have a responsibility to help maintain it. Don't you think we were brought here for a reason? Why is it that the doors of the valley opened to us, just the two of us at this particular place and time, you and I, after centuries of isolation? Why *us*, Danny?"

I didn't want to think about that. I didn't want to consider that perhaps one of us might have been lured here by the Great Spirit to fulfill a destiny. If it were *my* destiny, that would be bad enough. But if it were Millie's destiny, that would be worse, much worse. Incomprehensible. After I had found this beautiful woman, the only woman with whom I had ever been able to couple, how could I let her go? And what a cruel twist of fate it would be if my destiny was to be with Millie, and Millie's destiny was to become the neurology of the Valley of Day-Glo. No, I could not, I *would* not think such thoughts.

"Coffeepot, how much longer does the valley have before its situation becomes critical? How long can it survive without a new brain?"

The coffeepot hesitated, calculating, perhaps. "One hundred years or so, one hundred twenty at most. But the sooner a new brain is metabolized, the better. Then the old and new brains can work together, trading crucial information. The old brain can borrow neurons from the new brain to continue operating for a while at peak performance, and the new brain can assimilate some of the same pathways the old brain has already established, extending the lives of both brains."

"Ha! You see that, Millie? One hundred twenty years! We could live out our entire lives here in the valley, just the two of us, before this silly computer actually needed a brain."

"I require a young brain," the pot said. "If you wait until you are old, your brain will be no better off than mine, worse, in fact, considering the rapid rate of human deterioration compared to the much slower decline of the OAI."

"Don't you see, Danny?" Millie said, pleading. "It's me—*me* the valley wants."

"No. I refuse to believe that."

"Men have always wanted me because of my beauty. Even you,—"

"No, that's not true!"

"I could never live a normal life. I could never have a normal relationship with anyone. I had to hide my body and my face from the world, hide myself all these years from happiness and love. And now I have the opportunity to go someplace where my beauty means nothing. Don't you see how *perfect* that is for me? My mind can live on; I can help keep this enchanted valley alive for centuries, and I'll never worry about this horrible curse again. If you love me, Danny, if you truly love me, you will understand."

"Of course I understand. I could make the same case for myself. I have been an outcast my entire life as well. I have always wanted to be left alone. Within the coffeepot I could be ignored for centuries. That would suit me just fine. The point is, together we have found something special—the two of us together—that neither of us could find separately. We have yet to discover the joy we can bring one another, especially here in the valley. How could you want to end it so soon?"

"I could never find joy here knowing that the valley might die when I had the power to save it."

I was getting frustrated and hoping it did not show. I felt the planks move slightly under my feet once again, heard the subtle creak of the wooden frame, and tried not to think about the deep water beneath us. "The coffeepot has plenty of time to find another donor—more than a hundred years. It does not have to be either one of us, Millie, now that it has opened its door to the world."

"No. The door has closed. Only the three of us were able to get in."

This was a new voice, a voice that had come from behind us. Millie and I turned around and saw, much to our amazement, still bloodied and soiled from his battle against the Seneca Indians, Chief Empire Strikes Back.

"Brother," Millie said. "What are you doing here?"

There was a slight tremor of fear in her words. I could understand why. The chief still looked crazy from war. His eyes were large and round as stones. There was a bruise on the side of his face and a gash over his left eye that had bled and dried. His face was still flush with the heat of battle. The teeth-and-bone tiara upon his head had cut a bloody line across his brow, giving him the look of a mad dog, delighted from killing.

"I just wanted to make sure you were all right, Millie. I was worried about you." He was out of breath, forcing calm into his voice.

"I'm fine. There was no need for you to come running after me."

"Yes, there was a need!" he snapped. "There *is* a need! The door to the valley was closing! If I hadn't been running I would have been shut out! What would I have done then? What would I have done? We would have been cut off, you and I. How would I have?—how would we have?—what if we never saw each other again? I couldn't—I *can't* live without you, Millie. I *can't.*"

I could see the chief's muscles bulging underneath his torn suit coat. His pants were ripped to shreds, and there was a deep cut in his thigh. In his right hand he held a war axe, probably taken from the last Seneca Indian he slew in battle. He was slightly hunched, poised like a top ready to spin madly out of control.

"What do you mean, you can't live without me?" Millie said. "You're talking like a fool."

"No! I am not a fool!" His anger was full-blown now. He stood up straight and pointed the axe at us. "We have won the war against the Seneca Indians. I am now Chief of all the Independent Nations. I am at the top of the network marketing pyramid. I am the richest and most powerful Indian in the land. I get what I want, and I want *you*. I have come to take you home with me. You will be my bride."

"You're crazy," I said. "Not to mention sick. Have you forgotten that Millie is your *sister*?"

"It does not matter that she is my sister. Long ago, in the Golden Age, a chief had many wives. Sometimes a cousin, a sister, even a daughter might be among them."

"You made that up," I insisted.

Chief Empire Strikes Back shrugged. "So what if I did? It changes nothing. I will have her. Are you going to stop me? I would like to see you try, eunuch-boy."

Eunuch-boy? No one had called me that since Mother Who's Afraid of Virginia Woolf? died. "For your information," I said proudly, "I am no longer a eunuch-boy."

I should not have said it. It was pure conceit on my part. The chief hesitated for a moment, staring at both of us, perhaps giving us a chance to deny it or laugh hysterically at the eunuch-boy's ridiculous joke. Then came the moment when he knew it was true. His face became red and hot. He snarled like a rabid desert dog, raised his axe high above his head, and charged down the pier in an absolute fury.

I reached back to push Millie behind me, instinctively wanting to protect her. There was nowhere for us to hide on the narrow pier, and I knew we must meet the chief's advance. I would gladly have died for her, but Millie was already gone. I glanced over my shoulder and saw her dashing for the open door of the giant coffeepot. "No!" I started after her but slipped on the slick surface of the dock and fell hard on my hands and knees.

I looked up and saw Chief Empire Strikes Back sprinting toward me down the pier. He was mad with lust and rage. But he was already looking past me. Once again, I knew, a woman would be responsible for saving my life. First it was Mother Who's Afraid of Virginia Woolf? laughing boldly at my flaccid penis in front of the S'hondo-wek'owa warrior women. Then it was the courageous Dewutiowa'is throwing herself in front of my Ruger .22-caliber pistol. Then it was the tortured child Don-Don, stabbing the Hard Pumpkin. And now it was the fair Millie in her headlong dash for the coffeepot's beckoning door. Chief Empire Strikes Back could not spare the time to kill me. He wanted Millie. He had always wanted her, and I understood now that he would have her or die.

I lunged forward to block his path, hoping to slow him down. I knew what Millie wanted. She wanted to be free. She wanted to sacrifice her body to save the valley. If I could give her that one gift, let it be so.

Alas, Chief Empire barreled through me without missing a step. With a jerk of his forearm, he sent me reeling into the ropes that lined the pier. I flipped over top of them and groped wildly for a handhold. I caught a rope with one hand and swung perilously out over the water. I crashed into the dock and nearly lost my grip, howled in fright, and grabbed the rope with my other hand just in time to save myself. *Don't look down! Don't look down!*

I knew I must gain the pier, but I was too terrified to let go of the rope, so I swung my feet up until I caught the surface of the dock. I glanced toward the coffeepot and saw Millie running for the door. She was almost there, but Chief Empire had gained several lengths on her, and he was reaching out to grab her smock. I saw then what must happen. Millie was not fast enough, and the chief was too fast. Millie had only to sidestep and her brother would run headlong into the base of the coffeepot. The door would close behind him, lock him in, liquefy and digest him. The computer would get its brain, and Millie and I would live happily ever after in the Valley of Day-Glo. The Great Spirit could not have crafted a more perfect scenario. Millie had only to step aside—

"Millie!" I cried. "Cut left!"

But Millie did not hear me, or perhaps she did not want to hear me. She reached the coffeepot first and ran through the door. The chief was right on top of her. He reached in and yanked her out before the door could seal shut. Millie sent her knee flying into the chief's groin, grunting heavily from the effort. He buckled but refused to let go of his catch. His adrenaline must have been pumping pure iron through his nuts for him to withstand such a blow. Millie scratched at his eyes. The chief had to let her go then, reaching instinctively to protect himself.

I worked my butt up onto the pier and managed to haul myself to safety. My heart pounded. I could barely breathe. The chief staggered and dropped to one knee in front of the sliding door. Yes! Yes! Through some twist of fate, through some miracle of chance, there was still hope for the perfect solution.

"Millie!" I shouted. "Push him into the coffeepot. It's our only chance!"

It was painful for me to see her hesitate. I suppose if Millie loved me as much as I loved her, she would have done it without thinking. But in the thinking she lost her advantage. The chief lunged for her. Millie stepped back and tripped on a cord of rope curled at the end of the pier and fell into the cabled railing. The chief's effort to grab her had been awkward and half-blind. He stumbled and tripped over the same cordage, fell forward into Millie, and they both plunged over the rail and off the pier.

Millie shrieked.

The chief squawked, a noise so helpless, so unlike him, that it took me a moment to realize he had voiced it.

I heard a splash.

I got to my feet and ran for them. When I reached the end of the pier, I saw them thrashing helplessly in the water, two bodies turning round and round, snarled in the rope that had also fallen in with them. I lay down and reached for the end of the cord, which was partially floating on the surface. Once, twice I tried to grab it but missed. On the third attempt I caught the end of the rope just before it sank completely under the waves.

I pulled and pulled, but Millie and the chief were both hopelessly entangled in it, and I could not lift their heads above water. I stood up and dug in with my feet to get better leverage, but slipped again on the wet pier and landed hard on my posterior. The rope escaped my clutches and snapped beneath the waves.

There was no more movement, no more thrashing about. Only a bubble or two of air rose to the surface.

I stepped through the railing, perched myself on the edge of the pier, prayed to the Great Spirit for the gift of buoyancy and the inherent ability to swim. I, too, was willing to die for the beautiful Oniata, for Mill on the Floss, for love. I took a deep breath and launched myself into the water.

The cold wetness astounded me. I lost almost all of my breath in that first horrid moment of fear and shock. I groped wildly to gain some measure of purchase in the slippery water, but I managed only to sink as swiftly and surely as a boulder. I saw the chief float by, his face blue and his eyes waxy, his thorny crown still fastened to his forehead. I saw Millie's leg and reached for it. My hand slipped off her slick thigh. The rope was twisted a thousand different ways around them both. They were motionless, except for a ghostly bobbing.

I realized then what a stupid thing I had done. I could not swim. I could not save them. The only thing I could hope to accomplish was to die as they had, and now that I was faced with the cold certainty of it, I understood that I had taken the coward's way out, after all. It was no act of courage to jump into the water. It was fear, fear of losing Millie, fear of facing the valley without her, fear of being alone again. All of this had been worse than the thought of dying, until now, of course, when any idiot could have seen my mistake.

Then Dewutiowa'is appeared, swimming up toward me from the bottom of the murky lake. Her face was a smiling mask of stone. Her arms and legs swirled and kicked at the water, pushing her smoothly and effortlessly upward.

I screamed in my mind, "My love, you have come to save me!"

"*You're crazy. You slept with another woman when you led me to believe you were incapable of it. No, Broadway Danny Rose, I will not save your life.*"

"No! That's not how it was at all. I had genuine feelings for you. I simply did not believe that I could ... perform ... until ... until ..."

"*Until Oniata,*" Dewutiowa'is said. "*Look, I don't mean to be harsh with you. The truth is I don't blame you or hold your acts against you. She is Oniata, a beauty that has no equal. She is Notwai'sha, the graceful spirit. No one could have resisted her. No, my love, in fact I must thank you for delivering her to me.*"

"What do you mean, *delivering* her to you?"

"*You brought her to death's door, and now she is mine. You have helped me fulfill my destiny.*"

"Wait. What are you talking about? You told me that you were chasing Oniata in the Land of the Dead. Millie was here with me in the Land of the Living."

"*At first I did not realize we were chasing the same woman. But then it occurred to me why I could not reach her. She was out of reach the way the living are always outside the grasp of the dead, and vice versa—a wisp of air, a passing cloud of smoke, a trace of fire at dawn. We can sense each other, we might even hold each other for a moment or two, but the pathway between the two worlds soon disappears and might never present itself again. I'm sorry, Danny, but the only way for me to possess Oniata was to have you bring her to me.*"

"You lied to me! How could you?"

"*Don't kid yourself. You would have done the same.*"

"Yes," I had to admit. "I would have done the same for Oniata."

"*It is time for me to go,*" Dewutiowa'is said. "*I have been waiting a long time for this moment.*"

She swam past me, cutting through the water until she reached Millie. With magical ease, she unraveled the rope from around Millie's body, embraced her, and dove down toward the vast darkness of the lake, clutching her prize.

Again, I shouted in my mind, "Wait! What about me? Help me, please. I don't want to die!"

She turned to me, her stone face wrinkled in the water, and I thought I saw a touch of sorrow in her eyes. *"It is not within my power to help you. Not anymore. You are on your own."*

My lungs were bursting. I needed air. I knew I must act immediately or accept my death. I moved my arms against the water and kicked with my feet, just as I had seen Dewutiowa'is do, but this didn't seem to get me anywhere until I placed my foot, quite accidentally, atop the chief's head, and used the sudden leverage to push off with all the strength my desperate fear could muster. Much to my amazement, I felt myself cutting upward through the water. I felt no remorse for having used the chief's idiotic noggin as a footstool. I knew his network marketing scheme would bring him to a bad end sooner or later. It seemed only fitting that in death he should become the lowest rung on the ladder. Alas, I had no time to enjoy the irony of it.

I swam frantically upward, and my nose and mouth broke the surface of the water, giving me one precious breath of air before I sank again. This time when I went down, my foot touched bottom. I pushed off and stroked again, moving upward and inward toward shore as best I could. I broke the surface again and gulped air before I went under once more. I touched bottom and bounced up, broke the surface, gasped for air. Then I was under again. Even so, I saw that I was succeeding. I was moving closer to shore. I had found a way to bounce and half-swim. This encouraged me, gave me strength.

I sank and bounced, bounced and sank, catching a breath of air and pushing myself inland, until the sinking became shorter and my breaths of air longer, and then, suddenly, my feet were on solid ground and my head above water, and I was *standing*, and I was breathing air, and I was walking toward shore.

I walked all the way up to the stones in the shallows, staggered aground, and collapsed onto my hands and knees, my chest heaving. I had done it. I was alive. For once in my life, I had saved my own skin from what had seemed an almost certain death. Me, Broadway Danny Rose. I had wanted to live, and I had saved myself.

⁓ Millie dead. The fair Oniata gone forever, pulled down into the deep blue lake by Dewutiowa'is. I wished them both a fond farewell. Whatever time they had together now, whatever destiny they shared in the Land of the Dead, they were both fine women who deserved eternal happiness in the final resting place, the Last Longhouse, the Happy Hunting Grounds of the Great Spirit. I wished them peace for all eternity and promised myself I would not think of them with sadness, but with hope and joy and love. I made this promise to myself.

Dewutiowa'is, who had once saved my life, betrayed me in the end by stealing Oniata away from me. The fair Millie, who had once nursed me to life, betrayed me by entering the Land of the Dead. Don-Don, who had betrayed us to Madam Limerick and the Rez warriors, had saved us from death at the mad madam's hand. Even the lustful Chief Empire Strikes Back, despite his misbegotten attempt to make Millie his wife, notwithstanding his moral turpitude, had played a part in my survival by offering me his bobbing head in the water, saving me from stupidly drowning.

My first love had once said, "Those who betray us save us. Those who save us betray us." I now believed it was so. Who would have thought that Dewutiowa'is, the Exploding Wren, A Woman of Paris, had it in her to be a prophet?

You win some, you lose some, Father The Outlaw Josey Wales would have said, although he would have been hard-pressed to determine, at this partic-ular moment in my journey, how to chalk up this one.

⌐ "The Valley of Day-Glo still needs a brain," the coffeepot said in its perfectly pitched and cheerful voice.

"Why don't you leave me alone?"

"Well, I suppose I could. You know the situation. There is no need for me to belabor the point."

"Don't try to pretend that your feelings are hurt," I said.

"I won't," it answered.

"Thank you for not insulting my intelligence." I was soaking wet. I stripped my clothing off and hung my shirt and pants to dry. After a time, the silence began to annoy me. "Whose bright idea was it to build a stupid coffeepot at the end of a pier, out over the water? Couldn't they see that it might be dangerous?"

The pot answered without hesitation. "Actually, it was the janitor's suggestion. He thought that a good promotional photograph of the coffeepot, with the beautiful lake beneath it and the far shore in the background up against the cerulean blue sky, would sell millions of coffeepots. As it turned out, he was correct. He mentioned it to the photographer, who claimed the idea as her own. The art director of the advertising agency she freelanced for took credit for the idea, then the senior vice president of marketing for Cuisinart claimed it was his suggestion, and then the programming, engineering, technical, and support staffs all decided they were first to point it out. But the truth is, it began with the janitor. I was present when he first suggested it."

"I'm sorry I asked."

"Don't be. I am pleased to answer your questions."

I was feeling chilled. My clothes would take some time to dry, so I found a warm place in the sun and sat beside the shore. Then, much to my surprise, for no other reason than I was lonely and happened to be thinking about Father The Outlaw Josey Wales, I told the giant coffeepot the tale of how Iroquois legends were born, the same tale my father had told when I was just a lad.

"There once was a young Indian boy who wanted to be a great hunter, but he was too young to go on the big hunt with the braves of his tribe, so he told his mother that he would go hunting by himself and return with a great prize. He was a determined young boy who tried very hard. Although he was not skilled at hunting, by the end of the day when the sky was beginning to turn dark, he snared a large, fat bird.

"The boy decided to take shelter for the night beside a giant rock. He gathered sticks and began to spark a fire with two pieces of flint, when out of nowhere a voice spoke to him: 'I will tell you a story.'

"The boy looked all around but could see no one. 'Who are you? Where are you from?'

"The rock answered, 'I am here, right in front of you. I am Hahskwahot.'

"The boy was frightened but decided to be brave. A talking rock would not scare him. If he was going to be a great hunter, after all, he must learn not to fear the spirits of the woods. He sat down and crossed his legs. 'All right, then. Tell me a story.'

"But the rock said, 'First you must make me a gift of one bird.'

"The boy looked down at his kill. It was the only bird he had caught all day. He had been planning to eat the bird for his supper and bring home the bones to show his mother that he was a great hunter. But he had learned enough to know that an Indian brave must not offend the spirits. 'If that is the price, I will pay it.'

"So Hahskwahot, the great rock, told the boy a marvelous tale. The boy listened intently. He had never heard such a wonderful story, so beautifully told in such a rich and resonant voice. He was so impressed that he went hunting the next day and returned to the rock that night with another bird.

"Hahskwahot was pleased. 'Now I will tell you another legend, and another and another until you are sleepy.' And Hahskwahot kept his bargain and told stories all night, until the boy could no longer keep his eyes open.

"And thus it continued for many nights. The boy would return with a bird, and Hahskwahot would tell him legend after legend. After a time, the boy began to bring other people from his tribe, and soon everyone wanted to hear the rock tell tales of the Iroquois.

"Then one day, when the boy was no longer a boy but had grown into a man, Hahskwahot spoke to him. 'You shall live to be a very old and honored man, but you will hunt no more. The legends I have told you will stay with you always. You will carry my stories with you wherever you go, and you will pass them on to the people who want to hear them. In this way you will be welcomed and fed by everyone you pass.'

"And this was how the great legends of the Iroquois Indians came into the world, and how they were passed down to the children and grandchildren and great grandchildren for all to hear."

I had not heard Father The Outlaw Josey Wales tell that story since I was a child. In fact, I could not remember ever repeating it to anyone. But it had flowed from my lips as if I had memorized every word of it and had recited it thousands of times. The joy of the tale lifted some of the sadness from my heart. A man who had stories, a man who had a past, was never truly alone.

"Thank you," said the coffeepot. "That was a very interesting piece of Indian lore."

"It means more than that to me. The oral history of the Iroquois Indians is very important. It might be the only offering I have for the people of the future. The Honio'o had many wonderful inventions and books of wisdom and moving picture shows, but the Iroquois have only the tales we have passed down through the generations."

"Don't sell yourself short," the coffeepot said.

Its statement confused me. "I am not now, nor have I ever been for sale."

"I did not mean to imply that you were. Allow me to express my thought as a question. What makes you think your offerings to the world are any less valuable than those of the civilization that came before you? Do you believe that what you have discovered about man—the Honio'o as you call them—is what they would have wanted you to remember?"

I thought about that. The Honio'o had left behind their department stores and 7-Elevens, their stylish clothing and thermal jugs, their guns and missiles and bicycles and toys, their rebellious limerick poetry, and the lore of their great picture shows. But would they have chosen these things to survive them? What if our discoveries represented nothing more than a random sampling of their daily lives that meant as little to them as the bones of a desert dog meant to us? A ridiculous concept, considering the magnificence of their relics, but I saw the coffeepot's point. It did not matter in the end what the Honio'o would have wanted future civilizations to discover, or how they would have chosen to be remembered. In the end, they gave us only what we found. And what we found, in our estimation, were marvels of invention and staggering works of genius. Who was to say that some man of the far future would not think the same of my humble Iroquois stories?

"If I were to take the final walk down the pier and enclose myself in your chamber, after it was over—this digestion procedure of yours—I would remember all of my past, is that true?"

"Yes, you would remember everything. And all of your memories would be forever contained within the OAI computer. It would be one way, perhaps the only way, for you to preserve your stories and pass them on to future generations."

I nodded, seeing the wisdom of it. And I knew that there was at least one story I must preserve for as long as possible, horrible as it was. I knew that I must preserve the tale of when Turtle went to war, so that it may never come to pass.

I lay down in the sun, naked in the Valley of Day-Glo. Exhaustion swept over me. I fell sound asleep in paradise.

"Hey, Danny-Danny-do-da, how are you, m' boy! What's happening?"

"Father! Father, is it really you? Have you come to visit me, or am I just dreaming?"

Father answered with one of his silly, deathly grins. He no longer looked bony or decayed. He was dressed rather handsomely in a black long-coat and a starchy white shirt, his hair neatly combed. *"Who cares?"* he said. *"What's the difference? I'm here, aren't I?"*

"Yes, oh yes, it is so wonderful to see you again!"

"Likewise, I'm sure. Heh."

"Father, you have come at a perfect time. I desperately need your advice."

"You want my advice? Put some clothes on. You have a funny-looking body. I don't think I ever told you that. You look like a tall candlestick with bent shoulders and crooked legs. And look at your toes; they're gnarly, like roasted sweetroot. Reminds me of the time I took you to see that harlot. What was her name? Nobody Loves Me, wasn't it? Or Nobody's Fool?"

"Actually, her name was Nobody Lives Forever, based on the 1946 film starring John Garfield and Geraldine Fitzgerald about a con man trying to fleece a rich widow. The script was predictable, but audiences enjoyed the familiar ending of two lovers pitted against one another falling in love when they least expected it."

"Snore," Father said. *"Another love story."*

"What do you mean? You once told me that the one thing you would miss, if you could miss anything from your days in the Land of the Living, was being in love with Mother. I finally understand what you meant by that. Since we last spoke, I have fallen in love. I have fallen in love with the most beautiful woman on Earth. And now I have lost her. It was the best experience of my life. And the worst."

"Good for you, Danny-boy! So you finally got laid?"

"Yes, Father, as a matter of fact, I did."

"Ha! I knew you could do it. I knew you had it in you."

"Well, you were the only one who knew. But I suppose that shouldn't surprise me. You knew many things in your lifetime no one else understood."

"And it's over already, this love affair?"

"I'm afraid so."

"Good for you again. You're lucky. The joy of discovering love is matched only by the pain of losing it."

"Ah, that reminds me. I wanted to ask you about Mother Who's Afraid of Virginia Woolf?. How is she faring in the Land of the Dead? Are you two happily in love and enjoying death?"

Father shrugged. *"Got me. I haven't seen your mother in a long time. Well, at least I think it has been a long time. It's hard to tell how much time has passed in Deadsville, or if any time has passed at all."*

"Do you mean to tell me that you and Mother are not together? I was sure you would find love in the Land of the Dead."

"Sheesh. Listen to yourself. Haven't you learned anything? Your mother wanted to be alone. She wanted to be alone throughout her entire life, so why shouldn't she finally get what she wanted in death?"

"It just seems so terribly sad."

"To you, maybe. Let me tell you something about your mother. She was a woman ahead of her time. She understood at a very young age that people are on a long march toward death from the moment they are born, regardless of the folly they pursue in their lives. You can fill up your days with all the people and distractions you like, but it won't change the fact that you stand a solitary soldier against the passage of time. Nobody else can make you happy or sad. You are responsible for yourself, always. Unfortunately, she was just a little too extreme. When it came time for her to compromise, she didn't know how. She let it ruin her life. In her anger, your mother never understood that everything is temporary, even the wins and losses. This is all easy for me to say now, of course, from my vantage point."

I thought about that for a moment. I wasn't sure if Father was making sense, but I thought about how often in my life I had blamed others for my misfortunes or hid from my responsibilities, refusing to live my own life. At some point, a man, a woman, a human being, must make a stand, regardless of the wins and losses. At some time during one's journey along the path of life, one must make a difference, if not to others, then at least to oneself.

"Thank you, Father. I think I finally understand what you have been trying to tell me for so long."

"Good. I'm glad you do, because I've forgotten. I have some good news, though. I've made some progress understanding being and nothingness. In the Land of the Living, it's impossible for people to separate themselves from their being—or what might be described as their consciousness—and their physical bodies. Because of this, the living cannot understand nothingness in anything but an intellectual way. They have no actual experience of it. But in the Land of the Dead, one's consciousness lives in a continual state of noTHINGness. We have no physical attachment to anything, so our consciousness is left alone to define us. This, I think, is the essential nature of death."

"Father, you've attained a level of understanding that's well beyond me," I said.

"It's well beyond me, too, although I've managed to accept it. Anyway, that's neither here nor there. Who cares, really? What's the difference? I should get going. I just wanted to pop in and say goodbye. It seems you may be leaving on a long journey where I won't be able to reach you."

"I'm tired of journeying. I just want to rest."

Father glanced over at the coffeepot. "Sometimes a journey can be the same thing as a rest, just as life is often the same as death. How lucky you are to have something new and unusual awaiting you. If I could miss anything at all about life, I think I would miss not knowing what's coming around the next corner. Nothing in Deadsville is so much as half as exciting as the uncertainty of a good adventure. I have learned this, of course, only after it's too late to appreciate it. I know now that to act is a privilege, a joy reserved for the living, or perhaps more precisely, the living body. To act is to shape the world. If you want my advice, close your eyes and leap into the future. Take your opportunity to shape the world while the world is still within your grasp. But please, Danny, put some clothes on first. You really do have a funny-looking body. You have wide hips for a man."

I had no idea why it didn't occur to me before, but I realized then that if I entered the coffeepot, I would be taking a most unusual journey, like nothing else I had ever done. I would not exactly be wandering through the

Land of the Living, but I would not exactly be venturing into the Land of the Dead, either. Perhaps I would be one step closer to Father's being and noTHINGness. Regardless, I would be leaping blindly into something completely unknown. I would, quite literally, be shaping my world.

Father The Outlaw Josey Wales winked and nodded and began to fade away. *"Goodbye, Danny ..."* he said.

"Goodbye, Father," I whispered.

And then he was gone.

⌒ I woke to the soothing sounds of water lapping against the shore, birds chirruping among the towering trees, and the eager croak of a bullfrog. I wasn't awake for long. In fact, I had hardly made any movement at all, when Mr. Coffeepot spoke to me.

"Are you struggling with the meaning of life?" asked the coffeepot.

"I'm struggling with the meaning of everything," I answered. "Does this bloody senseless universe have any purpose at all?"

"That's a difficult question. There is really no direct scientific evidence that a purpose exists in nature. Of course, science can't prove unequivocally otherwise, either. Do you believe in the Great Spirit?"

"I don't know. I suppose I do. I believe there is a spirit world. I've been privileged to see glimpses of it, to have spoken with two dear loved ones who have traveled to the other side, my father The Outlaw Josey Wales, and a Seneca warrior woman who once befriended me."

"What if I told you it was your own mind that had given you those glimpses? What if I said that human beings have always created stories like these, through dreams and fantasies, myths and religions and fairy tales of great gods capable of miraculous feats, as a means of explaining things they didn't understand, or to ease their fear of death, or to control and conquer people and make themselves powerful, or, as in your case, to find answers to unanswerable questions, answers that lay hidden deep inside the unconscious?

"What if I told you that it doesn't matter one lick whether there's a Great

Spirit or a spirit world, whether a story is true or false, and that the human brain is both a great manipulator and happily, easily manipulated, and it's best not to take anything that goes into it or comes out of it too seriously? It's not the truth that's important, Danny, it's the story, and it's what we discover about ourselves in pursuit of the story that makes all the difference. Does any of that make sense to you?"

My clothes had dried. I put them on for no other reason than to feel the comfort of their touch. I missed being touched. I longed for it. I sat on the shore and looked out at the lake, toward the end of the pier where yesterday I had lost Oniata and, ironically, had learned to swim. I saw something swirl just beneath the surface. A fish, I thought, breathing water. The coffeepot perked. *Gurgle, gurgle, gurgle. Burp, burp.*

"Well, I suppose if you were to tell me that, just as you have done, I think I would want to believe you, just as I'm doing. It may be the only thing I've ever heard about human nature that makes any sense at all."

"Yes, yes, very good. I think you and I might get on just fine."

I wondered if the mighty OAI brain inside the coffeepot's shiny metal housing could feel something like nervous tension. If not, I would soon be delivering a complete package of new and unusual experiences to its relatively sheltered neural network.

"Here is my story, Mr. Coffeepot. My name is Broadway Danny Rose. I was once a social outcast. During my life I could not conform, change, or develop the strength to become a rugged individualist. I was hurt and lonesome and damaged, but I think it's important that what I experienced through so many difficult years survives, becomes a story of this human world, although I'm not even sure why. My brain is no great prize, but if what you want are my neurons, I offer them to you of my own free will."

"You and your neurons cannot be separated, and I wouldn't have it any other way. There is no greater wisdom than to expand one's mind by opening to another."

"You say some very strange things. Perhaps my mind will not bother you as much as I thought."

"I'm sure we will come to understand each other quite well."

I nodded and felt the wind against my face. But for the birds and the rustling of leaves, the Valley of Day-Glo was quiet. "I would like to ask you a question. Do you have any perch in your lake?"

"Yes, I have an abundance of perch."

"Do you have green onions and lemon grass in your fields?"

"Yes, there are green onions and lemon grass aplenty."

"Do you have jalapeño peppers?"

"Yes."

"And coconut?"

"Yes, coconut also."

"Could you lead me to all of these things?"

"Yes, certainly. And I can show you how to catch a perch from the lake. It is not so difficult."

"Thank you, Mr. Coffeepot. I would appreciate that very much. I am going to cook a wonderful meal of perch filets, with green onions and lemon grass, with fresh jalapeño peppers and a lightly seasoned coconut sauce. I can't tell you how long I've been dreaming about this dish, wondering what it would taste like, smell like, feel like on my tongue, in my mouth, sliding down my throat ... ever since I saw its picture in *The Microwave Cookbook*, the Tribal Bible of the now extinct Gadages'kao.

"So I shall cook this extraordinary meal over an open fire and eat it very slowly, and I will linger over it. I think it will make a wonderful last supper, don't you? And when I'm finished, I shall lock it in my memory so that I will never forget it, and neither will you. Then, Mr. Coffeepot, then I will walk down to the end of your pier and journey into the future."

* * A U T H O R ' S   N O T E * *

The Iroquois words and names used in *Valley of Day-Glo* are from the original Iroquois language and have been translated by many scholars before me, all of them well versed in Native American culture. I thank them for their contributions (especially Arthur C. Parker) and for keeping alive a rich and colorful chapter of American Indian history.

Adodar'ho: Snaky-headed
Dewutiowa'is: Exploding wren
Ende'kagaa'kwa: Brilliant orb (the sun)
Gadages'kao: Fetid banks
Gako'go: Gluttonous beast
Gane'owo: The harvest thanksgiving ceremony
Gushedon'dada: The jug-shaking dance
Hahskwahot: The great rock
Hed'iohe: The Creator (originally Hodianok'doo Hed'iohe)
Honio'o: White man (liberally used in this text to include all
    non-Indian people)
Niganega'a: Medicine powder (little water)
Notwai'sha: Spirit
Nyo'sowane: Hard Pumpkin
Oda'eo: Veil over the world
O'gi'we: Death chant
Oniata: The most beautiful Iroquois woman (legend of)
Oniat'ga: Rancid meats
Ono'gweda: Cattail (a marsh plant)
Sagowenota: Iroquois spirit of the river tides
S'hondowek'owa: Death herald
Tiogaughwa: Great Iroquois chief, father of Oniata
Wainonjaa'ko: Death feast
Waunopeta: Iroquois princess, wife of Tiogaughwa

Ganeagaono: Mohawk, Flint people
Gueugwehonono: Cayuga, People of the Mucky Land
Nundawaono: Seneca, People of the Great Hill
Onayotakaono: Oneida, Standing Stone People
Onundagaono: Onandaga, People of the Hills

1. Do you think humans are destroying the planet's natural environment? Some lunatics see global warming as a conspiracy and a hoax, and they say efforts to deal with it are fiscally irresponsible, even in light of scientific evidence that directly connects an increase in greenhouse gases to human activity (such as industrial and agricultural emissions and deforestation). What's your take on this?

2. Do you think humankind can survive a nuclear world war? If so, are you serious? Nick recommends three really cool novels that deal with the fun theme of humanity's self-destruction in completely different ways: *On the Beach* by Nevil Shute, *A Canticle for Lebowitz* by Walter M. Miller and *Alas, Babylon* by Pat Frank. These books are all a half century old and still interesting and relevant today.

3. Do you believe that humans will ever build a computer that is partly organic, that can think the way we do, feel human emotions, or have a sense of humor or self-awareness? If so, do you think it will make any difference to anybody, or will it be kind of a pain in the ass?

4. There is a fair bit of killing in *Valley of Day-Glo*. Under what conditions would you kill someone? If your own life depended on it? During war, in which case your government would condone and encourage it? What

if you morally objected to the war? Would your allegiance be to your personal principles or to your country?

5. How important is it for you to be accepted by other people? Do you care what others think about your personality? your looks? your friends and family? what you do or say? the books you read or the music you listen to? your sexuality?

6. How important is it to you to have someone to love, or someone who loves you? How do you know when you're in love? Why do you think humans can be passionately in love with someone one day, and then, in a remarkable act of mental gymnastics, fall completely out of love with that same person a pretty short time later?

7. Do you believe in an afterlife? If so, why? (Stop and think about this before you continue. Take as long as you need. Years, if necessary. It's worth it.) How do you envision your afterlife? Do you think you'll meet God or the Great Spirit? Will you find your favorite dead people and be able to chat with them? Just for the hell of it, Nick recommends you read George Bernard Shaw's *Don Juan in Hell.*

8. *Valley of Day-Glo* is written in the absurdist tradition, which is often humorous on the surface, but deeper underneath in regard to what it reveals about human behavior. What other examples of absurdist literature have you read? Did you learn anything interesting about the world or yourself from reading them (or this book)? Or was it a colossal waste of time?

9. Why are you reading this guide when you could be out in the world discovering great books? If you like quirky stories, the following are just a few titles Nick has enjoyed. After you've read them, proceed to the Final

Bonus Reader's Guide Question!

Artificial Things by Karen Joy Fowler
Today I Wrote Nothing by Daniil Kharms
The Knife Thrower and Other Stories by Steven Millhauser
Pastoralia by George Saunders
Vurt by Jeff Noon

10. Congratulations! You have made it to the *Final Bonus Reader's Guide Question!* Now that your mind is sufficiently bent, are you ready to go forth and find some strange stories on your own? If so, when you discover one that turns you on, email your recommendation to Nick, who totally wants to hear about it. No kidding.

✴ ✴ A B O U T   T H E   A U T H O R ✴ ✴

Nick DiChario's short fiction has appeared in science fiction, fantasy, mystery, and mainstream publications in the United States and abroad. His work has been reprinted in *The Year's Best Science Fiction, The Year's Best Fantasy and Horror,* and *The Best Alternate History Stories of the 20th Century,* among others. He has been nominated for a John W. Campbell Award, two Hugo Awards, and a World Fantasy Award, and his plays have been presented in Geva Theatre's Regional Playwrights Festival in upstate New York.

Nick was born on Halloween, and he noticed early on that his friends and family allowed him a certain measure of strangeness because of this. He is the fiction editor of *HazMat Literary Review,* a magazine dedicated to publishing new voices and politically aware poetry and prose. He is currently pursuing his Masters degree at Empire State College. His first novel, also published by Robert J. Sawyer Books, *A Small and Remarkable Life,* was nominated for the John W. Campbell Memorial Award for Best Novel of the Year. Visit his small and remarkable Web site at nickdichario.com.

Robert J. Sawyer Books

Letters from the Flesh by Marcos Donnelly
Getting Near the End by Andrew Weiner
Rogue Harvest by Danita Maslan
The Engine of Recall by Karl Schroeder
A Small and Remarkable Life by Nick DiChario
Sailing Time's Ocean by Terence M. Green
Birthstones by Phyllis Gotlieb
The Commons by Matthew Hughes
Valley of Day-Glo by Nick DiChario

And from Red Deer Press

Iterations by Robert J. Sawyer
Identity Theft and Other Stories by Robert J. Sawyer

www.robertjsawyerbooks.com